"It is my ho[...]
nation can work through
this."

Trofimov was somber. "But I will not lie to you. It
will be difficult. We will have to make some hard
decisions about our standing in the world. We will
have to come to terms with the barbarism that
lurks, even now, within our armed forces. This
will not sit well with many of us, but I know we
are up to the challenge. For TBT News, this is Yuri
Trofimov."

Schrader switched off the miniset in disgust. "Can
you believe that?"

"What happened?" Bolan asked.

"They're reporting that a bunch of our guys attacked
a village in Afghanistan," Schrader said, "totally
unprovoked. Burned the place to the ground. Shot
women and children, and the news report says TBT
has a videotape with our guys doing it and laughing
about it."

Bolan's jaw clenched. Things were getting ugly.
And they were about to get uglier.

Don Pendleton's **Mack**
Bolan.
Sabotage

PAPL
DISCARDED

A GOLD EAGLE BOOK FROM
WORLDWIDE.

TORONTO • NEW YORK • LONDON
AMSTERDAM • PARIS • SYDNEY • HAMBURG
STOCKHOLM • ATHENS • TOKYO • MILAN
MADRID • WARSAW • BUDAPEST • AUCKLAND

First edition April 2010

ISBN-13: 978-0-373-61536-0

Special thanks and acknowledgment to
Phil Elmore for his contribution to this work.

SABOTAGE

Printed in U.S.A.

If you know the enemy and know yourself you need not fear the results of a hundred battles.
—Sun Tzu

The enemy doesn't play by the rules. He will ruthlessly commit murder and a hundred other crimes. The enemy won't stop, doesn't feel pity and never feels shame. The enemy has to be engaged, and overwhelmed with superior force. That's where I come in. That's what I do.
—Mack Bolan

CHAPTER ONE

The graveside service was drawing to a close. Family members paid their respects in turns, filing past the casket as it sat poised on its winch straps. Even for a funeral, the mood was grim; the body language of the mourners was tense, brittle with anticipation. That much was obvious as Mack Bolan, the man known to some as the Executioner, watched through a pair of compact Zeiss binoculars. He knelt on a hill in an older part of the cemetery, surrounded by grave markers that were, in some cases, almost a century old. Partially hidden behind a gnarled weeping willow that stood, incongruously, among the oldest of the tombstones, Bolan monitored the narrow, paved access road leading through the cemetery and past the temporary awning sheltering the mourners below.

The soldier checked his watch. If intel from Brognola and Stony Man Farm panned out, it could happen any minute now.

He didn't need to check the weapons he carried; they were as much part of him as his hands, after so many missions. The custom-tuned and suppressed

Beretta 93-R pistol was holstered in its customary place under his left arm. The massive .44 Magnum Desert Eagle rode in a holster on his right hip. Across his chest, he wore an olive-drab canvas war bag on its shoulder strap, over the close-fitting combat blacksuit. His pants were tucked into well-worn combat boots. His battle gear, including a Boker Applegate combat dagger clipped in a Kydex sheath in the appendix position, was concealed under his black M-65 field jacket. On the ground near his right knee, a Pelican case waited, the customized Remington 700 rifle inside another work of art by Stony Man Farm's armorer.

Mack Bolan knelt, watched and waited, a black-clad and silent wraith watching over the final resting place of so many Americans.

The Executioner reflected upon what had brought him to this place. The scrambled phone call from Brognola had left a taste like ashes in his mouth.

"Someone," the man from Justice had said, calling from his office in Washington, "is killing our soldiers."

"I'm listening."

"We thought, at first, that it was random," Brognola went on. "Murders occur, of course. It stands to reason that some of them would affect returning servicemen and -women. But Aaron takes a special interest in veterans, especially wounded vets, and he started flagging the news reports in a database in the Farm's computers."

"Understood." Bolan nodded, unseen by the big Fed on the other end. "Aaron" was Aaron "the Bear" Kurtzman, head of the Farm's cybernetics team and a wizard with computers of all types. If it existed in the ether, if it could be located within a network somewhere on the planet, Kurtzman could find it. The computer expert was confined to a wheelchair, the result of an ill-fated attack on the Farm some years before.

"What began to emerge," Brognola said, "was a disturbing pattern. Aaron's computers pulled up report after report of murders across the country—involving a returning veteran of combat in Iraq or Afghanistan. Six men, three women. In two of these cases, the reports included similar crime-scene evidence, including cryptic notes about 'peace' and 'love' and 'ending barbarous imperialism.' When we dug further, we found that it wasn't just those two. These notes were found at all nine crime scenes."

"So you've found a serial killer, or killers, who target war vets."

"No," Brognola said. "That's just it. It's meant to look like that, but Aaron delved deeper." He paused. When he continued, his voice was tight with anger. "Each of the funerals for the murdered men and women were…protested."

"Protested?" Bolan asked. "What the hell for?"

"It's becoming increasingly common," Brognola said. "There have been a few different groups, mostly crackpots and malcontents, trying to turn funerals for our service people into media circuses. The reasoning behind it never makes much sense. And of course these bastards don't care how much pain they cause the families, who are already suffering. But this is different."

"Different how?" Bolan asked.

"Each of the funerals connected to this 'serial killer' was protested by the same group, an outfit called Peace At Any Cost. The PAAC organization appeared out of nowhere last year and started staging major publicity stunts during high-profile political events, public appearances by celebrities, even other news reports. Six months ago there was a big media feeding frenzy at the home of a mother in Florida believed to have killed her toddler. When the body was found buried behind the mother's apartment building, the reporters were ten feet thick. Sign-wavers from PAAC showed up and turned it into a referendum on the war in Iraq, or tried to. It was a mess."

"So PAAC specializes in veterans' funerals for the publicity."

"So it would seem," Brognola said, "but peel away that layer and there's more rot underneath. Aaron went after PAAC in a big way, once he made the connection. He found a 'secure' bulletin board where PAAC members keep in touch with one another and coordinate their protests. I'm sure they believe it's secret, but nothing stays hidden on the Net for long once Aaron starts digging. He's been keeping them under observation ever since, and cross-referencing posts to their board with what we know of the murders and protests so far."

"And?"

"In most cases," Brognola explained, "there's at least a slight delay between when the murders hit the media and when PAAC found out about them and made plans to protest the funerals. But twice, they screwed up. In two of those cases, PAAC referenced the murders before they hit the news."

"But that could be as simple as a source within the police. Or the media. Or even the coroner's office."

"True," Brognola said. "Any of that is possible. Except in the case of a single post about the murder of Hospital Corpsman Third Class Charles Stevens, recently returned from Afghanistan. The post was made almost an hour before the coroner's office estimates Stevens was shot in the driveway of his home."

Bolan frowned. "So PAAC is involved in the murders themselves."

"Them, and whomever's behind them," Brognola said. "It's expensive to be as high profile as PAAC has become. Yes, controversy plays a role in that, but they also do a lot of advertising. Full-page ads in national papers, billboard campaigns, that kind of thing. The money has to come from somewhere, and a group this young couldn't have pockets that deep. Aaron kept at it and followed the cybermoney trails back to the well. It's a shell game of holding companies, fictional identities and supposedly anonymous donors acting in concert, but the money all tracks back to the same place."

"Who?"

"His name is Yuri Trofimov," Brognola said. "Naturalized citizen of the United States, as of almost ten years back. He was born in Russia and is now a considerably rich man."

"I've heard that name before," Bolan said.

"Yes, you have," Brognola said. "That's because Trofimov owns the Trofimov Business Trust. It's a major conglomerate that first got big manufacturing and importing cheap goods from its factories in China and Russia for consumption here in the United States. Consumer electronics, for the most part—you can't walk into a big-box store in the U.S. without seeing TBT's imports on the shelves—but also automotive parts. Trofimov owns a considerable share of Kirillov Motors, which as of last year's sales figures is the latest thing in low-priced, high-volume compact cars. Kirillov also manufactures, busily and discreetly, subcontracted parts for the aerospace industry, including some contracts for the DOD. Before it started making cars, Kirillov built parts for Russian MiGs, among other things."

"That's not where I've heard of him."

"No," Brognola said. "Trofimov is also the public face of TBT News, the twenty-four-hour cable news channel he started three years ago. In that time, it has become one of the most watched of the networks in a very competitive, cutthroat industry."

"Let me guess," Bolan said. "Their success is due at least partly to their sensationalist reporting philosophy."

"Exactly right," Brognola said. "Trofimov's network was nicknamed the 'Terrorist Broadcast Team' by a popular radio talk-show hawk. That's because TBT's stock in trade is negative stories about the United States military and United States military personnel. Every alleged atrocity, no matter how speculative, leads their newscasts. Every negative spin they can put on military expenditures, supposedly botched military operations, and everything else to do with American war and anti-terror efforts abroad, they use. There have been low rumblings of congressional inquiry and even a few murmurs in the halls of power that use the word 'sedition,' but the fact is, there's nothing that can be pinned on TBT News. Once or twice their sources have been called into question, and at least once an Iraqi war veteran has filed a civil lawsuit alleging defamation and outright fabrication of the atrocities described, but nobody's been able to prove anything. The simple fact is that TBT News is the worst thing to happen to military public relations since the controversy over Vietnam."

"All right," Bolan had said, his jaw clenching. "I'm in."

"I thought you would be," Brognola said. "Aaron's team gave Trofimov's computers a cavity search. There was a lot of security, as you can well imagine. They were, however, able to dig up an interesting set of cross-referenced and suspicious facts. Specifically, Trofimov's company owns a few other companies that in turn own a very peculiar list of business interests. These interests don't seem to actually do anything that we can determine, but they exist, they remain on the books and, more important, they consume a lot of cash. We know that Trofimov is secretly funding PAAC, and they've got blood on their hands, no doubt. But that's clearly not all, and until we know what's going on, we won't move directly on PAAC's members. Plus, Trofimov is slippery. We can't trust the legal system to deal with him if Justice sets something in motion against PAAC."

"Which is where I come in."

"Yes," Brognola said. "I'll have the Farm transmit to you the briefing Barb's put together with Aaron's data. You'll have a prioritized list of TBT's suspect businesses and holding companies, with addresses and intelligence rundowns. We'll also establish for you a running link to the PAAC discussion board, so you can monitor what they're doing. But, Striker," Brognola said, using Bolan's code name, "there's one more thing."

"It gets even better?" Bolan said flatly.

"Did you hear of the shooting last week at a church outside Denver?"

"I did. Two people were wounded. They said it was a random crazy with an ax to grind, a former church member."

"That was all a cover-up," Brognola said, "to prevent a panic. I don't necessarily agree with the tactics used, but it was Homeland Security's call, and they stepped in before another agency could lay claim. The church service was a memorial for Sergeant Kevin Wyle, recently returned from Afghanistan. He was shot in his home by someone aiming through the bay window of his living room. The official story bears no resemblance to the actual details, and with all the people in attendance the facts are already starting to leak. Wyle's service was disrupted by three young men wearing ski masks, who fired on the attendees with shotguns. They fled as fast as they came. The local police have no suspects."

"Amateur hour," Bolan concluded. "You think PAAC is working its way up from protests to terrorism?"

"Possibly," Brognola said. "DHS is trying desperately to keep that from public knowledge, as I said, to prevent a panic. They've gotten the buy-in of most of the other federal agencies that might take an interest, including elements within Justice. While they may not be able to make it work, I see their point. Tempers are already flaring over the protests of military funerals. Can you imagine what could happen if those who are already hurting are looking over their shoulders for murderers? We could see the protesters getting shot."

"If PAAC is in on the murders in the first place," Bolan said, "that would be simple self-defense."

"I wouldn't disagree," Brognola admitted, "but you know as well as I do that innocents will get caught in the cross fire."

"I know," Bolan said. "We can't let that happen. And there's a good chance that PAAC's rank-and-file membership don't know about the killings. It may not be the case that the whole group is dirty."

"I'm going to send you the time and location of the next PAAC protest," Brognola said, "with dossiers on the group's leaders as we understand them to be."

"It's a confirmed, planned protest?" Bolan asked.

"Yes," Brognola said. "But I'm not sure what you'll find, exactly. Sergeant Wyle's service was discussed on the PAAC board, but the group leadership nixed the appearance, citing schedule conflicts. That's a little too convenient for my tastes. Whether elements within PAAC are planning similar treatment with their fellow protesters in evidence, we don't know. It's possible, but nothing explicitly illegal has been discussed on the board."

"I'll need something fast," Bolan had said. "Something that can get me across the country and maybe even out of it."

"It's already covered," Brognola confirmed. "I'm sending the data to your secure satellite phone now."

"All right, Hal," Bolan said. "I'm on it."

"And, Striker?"

"Yeah?"

"Take them down. I want these people, and so does the Man."

"So do I, Hal," Bolan said. He closed the connection.

The conversation, still fresh in Bolan's mind, had taken place several hours ago. The cemetery in which Mack Bolan now stood was a short drive outside of Green Bay, Wisconsin, where Stony Man pilot Jack Grimaldi waited at the Austin Straubel International Airport. Grimaldi would even now be crawling over every inch of the C-37A that was Bolan's transportation for the duration of his mission.

The Stony Man pilot had traded up; he and Bolan had hopped an available USAF C-21A Learjet to Straubel while local federal assets had the longer-range C-37A prepared and positioned for their use. The modified Gulfstream V was a twin-engine, turbofan aircraft with an intercontinental range of 6,300 miles. This particular jet had been outfitted by a black-ops shop affiliated with the Farm. All in all, Bolan was traveling in style. Except for the new jet's speed and range, however, these details were irrelevant in Bolan's mind. He had work to do. He refocused his Zeiss binoculars, taking a more critical look at the scene below.

Then he heard the motorcycles.

The soldier zoomed in on the reactions of the mourners below. The set of their bodies, the way they stood or moved, indicated surprise—and relief. The loud roar of two-dozen motorcycles rolling up the access road drowned out all other sound. As Bolan watched, the men on the motorcycles brought their machines neatly into line and killed the engines. After they dismounted, they conferred briefly, and the largest of the bikers walked forward to speak with someone from the funeral party. From the man's dress and bearing, not to mention the large zippered portfolio he carried under his arm, Bolan thought he might be the funeral director.

Brognola hadn't mentioned these guys on the phone, but the data files that were part of Bolan's briefing had included their write-ups. The men on the motorcycles were the Patriotism Riders, a group of citizen bikers, many of them also military veterans, who rode to military funerals to protect the families from protesters. They were nonviolent and apolitical, for the most part; they sought only to put themselves between the families and the protests to protect the relatives of dead service people. Someone within the Patriotism Riders' network had alerted them to this service at the last minute, apparently. Bolan admired their dedication and the service they provided.

As Bolan watched, the Riders took up their position on the access road, linking arms and forming a human chain across the pavement. They stood, quiet and watching, their eyes scanning the access road, their heads slightly bowed out of respect for the mourners.

They didn't wait long.

The funeral director and the representative from the Patriotism Riders finished whatever hushed conversation they were having. The Rider joined his fellows on the access road, while the director hurried back to the graveside. As if on this signal—Bolan realized as his brain processed what his eyes took in through the binoculars that there had to be some unseen coordination by scouts or observers hidden from view—a cargo van roared up the access road.

The van was moving too fast to be harmless. The Patriotism Riders scattered as the old Ford barreled through their ranks, narrowly missing the men closest to the center of the road.

Battle was joined.

The Remington 700 came up in Bolan's hands as the van below lurched to a stop on whining, squealing brakes. As the van's side door was shoved aside, the Executioner was already acquiring the first target through the Leupold telescopic sight.

The group that piled out of the van was a mixed half dozen—four men, two women. They ranged in age from perhaps early twenties to maybe middle thirties, wearing a mixture of grunge and protest chic. Each one carried a hand-lettered cardboard sign attached to a wooden handle.

Through the Leupold scope, Bolan could see that each also carried a gun.

Whether to make some political point or as a means of distracting their victims before they struck, the "protesters" were waving their signs with one hand while holding handguns behind their backs. Bolan, from his vantage, could see that clearly; the Protest Riders and the mourners beyond them couldn't. The first of the protesters started to bring his weapon up from behind his leg.

Bolan took a breath, let out half of it and allowed the rifle to fire itself as his trigger finger applied pressure. The first 146-grain, 7.62 mm M-80 NATO specification bullet screamed toward its target. The metal-jacketed slug struck the would-be shooter before he could utter a sound, the fist of an avenging god smiting him from on high.

The gunner was dead before he hit the pavement.

For a fraction of a heartbeat, nothing moved. From mourners to Riders to the attackers themselves, each man and woman present struggled to process the sudden death that had appeared, unbidden and unforeseen, in their midst.

Then someone among the funeral-goers screamed and hell was unleashed.

Bolan was working the bolt of the Remington before the dead man completed his fall. He had lined up the next of the armed protesters as the mourner's scream reached his ears, and he was pulling his rifle's trigger before the next shooter in line could bring his handgun to bear on the nearest potential victim. For a second time, thunder pealed, and a second man fell dead before he knew the end had come.

One of the protesters, near the rear of the suddenly dwindling group, started to fire blindly. He emptied the .45 pistol in his fist—straight into the backs of the two women in front of him, cutting them down in his haste to react to the threat he couldn't find. Bolan calmly worked the Remington's bolt, tracked the shooter and put a bullet through his brain.

The Patriotism Riders had recovered quickly from their initial shock, surging toward the attacker. Several of them tackled the last of the men, burying him in a crush of bodies. Bolan caught this but ignored it; there was one other variable still unaccounted for.

The van's engine roared to life and the vehicle started backing down the access road.

That would be the Ford's driver, whom Bolan knew had never left the van. It was a tricky shot, through the windshield of the moving van, but there was no more experienced a sniper than Mack Bolan. He made the shot easily. Beyond the suddenly spiderwebbed windshield, the driver slumped over the steering wheel. The van slowed to crawl, and then came to rest half on and half off the access road.

Bolan ejected the empty brass from the Remington and placed the rifle on its hard case. Drawing the Beretta 93-R and flicking the selector switch to 3-round burst, he surveyed the killing ground below him as he stalked toward the aftermath of his deadly handiwork. The Riders were dragging the subdued, disarmed survivor out of the road. Several had spotted Bolan and were pointing at him. A couple looked ready to charge him, and Bolan mentally lauded them for that; they were taking no chances, and Bolan was an armed, unknown man who could be foe as easily as he could be friend.

"Cooper," he said as he neared them. "Justice Department."

"Justice?" One of the Riders shook his head. "Man, you ain't kidding."

Bolan nodded grimly. Justice, it was.

This was only the beginning.

CHAPTER TWO

Bolan stood, leaning against the nearest of the police cruisers, as local law enforcement prowled the area. Already the crime scene was being meticulously photographed, tagged and logged, while uniformed officers and a couple of plainclothes personnel circulated among the Patriotism Riders. The mourners had been questioned first, their statements taken quickly. Most of them had left. Bolan sympathized with them. Most wouldn't be able to imagine the emotions that the family and friends of the dead serviceman had to be experiencing, with a tragedy in the family burned so raw by fresh, seemingly random terror and gunfire. The Executioner, on the other hand, had seen more than his fair share of death, tragedy and inhumanity. He understood. He also felt a grim satisfaction at being able to stop these killers before they could take more innocent lives, before they could pervert this graveside service into the type of obscene political statement their kind craved.

The local law enforcement had, as usual, been extremely suspicious. Bolan had given them his "Matthew Cooper" identification and the Justice Department credentials Brognola's people had issued to that alias. It had still taken a few phone calls, one of them eventually fielded by the big Fed himself, before the police were satisfied. They had grudgingly accepted Bolan's presence after that, and even done a pretty good job of pointedly ignoring him. The soldier could understand some of the territoriality that came with the job, and he knew only too well that his violent intervention wasn't something that good cops just dismissed easily.

To those police and any other observer, Mack Bolan was simply waiting around. There was no good reason, in the minds of the police, for this mysterious federal agent not to leave the scene. Bolan imagined they thought he, too, was being territorial, perhaps not trusting the local boys to do a thorough job with the crime scene. The truth was something far different, of course. Bolan was playing a hunch, one spurred by long experience and countless battlefield scenarios.

Something wasn't quite right, and he could feel it.

There was a loose end somewhere; Bolan was sure of it. As he stood, seemingly observing the police as they took the Riders' statements, he was surreptitiously scanning the perimeter of the cemetery. The spotter, if indeed there had been one working with the shooters in the van, was bound to be somewhere along that perimeter somewhere, offering him a view similar to the one Bolan had enjoyed from his sniper's vantage. Unless the man—or woman—had the sense to flee immediately when the action went down, he or she was still up there. Bolan had been watching. That feeling that he, in turn, was being watched was something he couldn't shake. He had been under fire enough times to know to trust his gut. His finely honed combat instincts were screaming at him. He was listening.

A knot of the Riders no longer speaking with the police had drifted toward Bolan. They were a fairly typical bunch, at first glance—mostly large men in leather jackets, boots and jeans, with a sprinkling of other accessories and licensed motorcycle brand accoutrements. There were a few tattoos in evidence. They looked like bikers, but without the hard edge that Bolan had seen in so many outlaw clubs. These were simply citizens who rode motorcycles, first and foremost, and in this case for a good cause.

The nearest man, who sported a blond crew cut and wore a pair of sunglasses on a cord around his neck, shuffled closer to Bolan and cleared his throat. This was the man Bolan had seen talking to the funeral director.

"Excuse me, sir?" the man asked.

"Yes?"

"Mitch Schrader, sir," the biker said, extending his hand. Bolan shook it; Schrader's grip was firm, but not aggressive. "With the Patriotism Riders."

"So I gathered." Bolan nodded. "Matthew Cooper."

"So you said." Schrader grinned. "You really with the Justice Department? You're not FBI, or something?" Schrader asked.

"I really am," Bolan said. In a certain sense, it was true. The soldier worked for nothing more than unbridled justice, justice in its purest and most righteous form.

"I wanted to thank you," Schrader said. "The boys and I, we, well, we wondered if maybe something like this might happen."

"What do you mean?" Bolan asked.

"Well—" Schrader shrugged "—the protests, they're bad enough. We've been fighting that for a while. But we figured it was only a matter of time before they stopped being 'peaceful,' you know? It wouldn't be the first time."

"I'm not aware of any violence at the funerals of military personnel," Bolan said warily.

"'Course not." Schrader grinned. "You'd have to say that, wouldn't you? But come on, Cooper, you and I both know that's probably not true. You hear things. Most of the guys are vets themselves. We stay in touch. We network. That's how we know what the buzz is, where to ride, what services to protect. Makes me sick." Schrader turned and jerked his chin toward the bodies of the attackers. "They aren't all like them, I suppose. Not all terrorists or murderers or whatever. But the ones who march and chant, they're just as bad, aren't they? Pissing on the graves of war dead. Upsetting the families. Turning the deaths of brave men into a political statement."

"And women," one of the other Riders put in.

"And women," Schrader stated, grinning. "That's Ben. He's our resident equal rights activist."

"Up yours," Ben snarled.

"Anyway," Schrader said, his smile fading, "I mean it, man. You didn't just save them—" he motioned toward the few mourners still present, who were speaking with the funeral director beyond the circle of bustling police "—you saved all of us. We'd have been the first to catch one. I thought maybe, well, it's hard to explain. But I knew coming here might be bad for us. We couldn't stay away, though, not thinking there was a protest going down."

"How did you find out about that?" Bolan asked.

"I got a phone call, man." Schrader shrugged. "Last minute. Don't know the guy. He said just that he was a fellow American, and that he knew the service today was going on, and that there was supposed to be a big peace protest here. Said he figured that would be of interest to me, and yeah, it was. It's what we do. We stand up for people who can't do it themselves, you know? People who've already given everything there is to give. You can dig that, right?"

"I can." Bolan nodded. Indeed, he could.

"We network," Schrader said, indicating his fellow Riders. "There are other chapters of Riders in this part of the country, and a few other groups that go by different names, folks who do the same thing we do. We stay in touch and we tip each other off when a ride comes up, especially if we think one of those protest groups, especially the crazier ones you see on the news, is aware of the service and looking to march on it. We were, all of us, on CNN just last month. But I'm telling you, Cooper, this is the first time I've ever gotten an anonymous phone call like that. I'm thinking now it was some kind of setup."

"You could be right," Bolan acknowledged. He took a small notebook from inside one of the pockets of his blacksuit. Using the metal pen clipped to it, he wrote down a phone number. The number would route a call through several satellite cutouts and eventually to Bolan's secure satellite phone, while flagging the call as an unsecured transmission from a potentially unknown third party. No amount of tech-tracing would produce any intelligence on Bolan's phone or the soldier's whereabouts, but to the caller it would still appear to be a direct line. Bolan tore out the slip of paper and handed it to Schrader.

"If you hear anything more," Bolan said, "anything through your contacts or those in your organization, call me. I'm interested in anything you hear about protests, or if you anyone calls you."

"Here," Schrader said, pulling out his cell phone and flipping it open. "I have the number on my phone from this morning, the number this Deep Throat or whatever called me from." He recited it, and Bolan copied it down.

"That may help."

"You're wondering who's got it in for our boys, aren't you?" Schrader asked quietly, looking shrewd.

"Justice," Bolan said simply. "I'm just looking for justice."

"I heard that."

Bolan excused himself and moved to the corpses of the shooters. He had already taken photos of each of them and sent them via secure upload to the Farm for analysis. The locals hadn't liked that much, from their body language, but they hadn't tried to stop him and they hadn't asked any questions. Bolan had left the scene undisturbed while they were tagging and cataloging, but they were finished now. He knelt and carefully started searching the closest corpse.

"You won't find much, sir," one of the uniformed officers said. He nodded at Bolan and help up a plastic evidence bag. "I personally checked their pockets and the lining of their clothes. No IDs."

"Thank you," Bolan said. "Officer…?"

"Copeland, sir," the cop said.

"Anything of consequence there?" Bolan nodded at the evidence bag.

"No." The officer shook his head. "A few personal effects. Combs, pocketknives. A pair of wristwatches, domestic and unremarkable. Nothing, really. No car keys, no money, no matchbooks or scraps of paper. They more or less emptied their pockets beforehand, I guess."

"What about him?" Bolan pointed to the driver, dead behind the wheel of the van. "And the vehicle."

"We're checking the vehicle identification number now." Officer Copeland shook his head. "The plates came back already. They were stolen off a Toyota pickup twenty-five miles from here. I can tell you that van will come back as stolen. See that shattered side window up front, the little access window? That's how they get in to hot-wire it. Sure sign the thing is hot. They must have grabbed it and then switched plates. It would have been enough cover in transit from wherever they got it, to here."

Bolan nodded. He liked this Copeland. He was young but knew his business, and wasn't afraid to share information with another department—in this case, one he had to know was decidedly above his pay grade.

"Nothing on the driver, either."

Bolan looked over the dead men and women once more. That was strange. Amateurs were rarely so thorough, and these sign-waving shooters had hardly been professionals. They'd been sloppy, careless and, in the case of the one man who'd taken down two of his partners, dangerous to one another as much as to their targets. That didn't make a lot of sense...unless these were the types of politically motivated pawns some greater interest, such as Trofimov, was controlling from higher up. That scenario made more sense. But if that was the case, then there definitely was likely to be someone—

"Agent Cooper?" Officer Copeland broke into Bolan's reverie. "Uh, sir, is he one of yours?"

Bolan saw the man just as the uniformed cop pointed him out. The figure, dressed in a dark hooded sweatshirt and slacks, had taken off at a dead run from the very edge of the cemetery, headed away from the graves.

Bolan broke away and sprinted.

He raced through the maze of tombstones, dodging this way and that. The runner looked back, saw him and produced a handgun of some kind. He loosed a round, but it went wide, ricocheting off one of the marble memorials. Then they were both free of the cemetery proper, the running man cutting across a two-lane road that backed the rear of the graveyard. A Honda narrowly missed the man, the driver honking in outrage.

Bolan yanked the Beretta 93-R from his shoulder holster, risking a glance left and right before rocketing over the road. His combat boots chewed up asphalt and the muddy grass of the field beyond in long, rapid strides. The distance closed; there was a small copse of trees some yards beyond, but no real cover for the fleeing man to seek. He snapped another shot in Bolan's direction. The bullet never came anywhere near the sprinting soldier.

Mack Bolan was a crack shot, a trained sniper and marksman of decades' experience. Even he, however, wouldn't risk a shot on a running man he wished to keep alive for questioning. Instead, he poured on the speed, judged the distance and then launched himself in a flying tackle. He took the smaller man around the knees and rolled through the muddy earth. He came up standing above the runner, who looked up from his back. The Beretta 93-R was trained on the smaller man's face. His hood had come off to reveal that he was Asian, maybe midtwenties.

"Don't move," Bolan ordered.

The Asian was lightning fast. His body torqued and his foot came up like a rattlesnake, snapping a vicious blow into Bolan's wrist. The Executioner lost the Beretta and took a step backward. The Asian leaped up and was at him, raining a flurry of brutal, acrobatic kicks. Bolan felt the wind being pressed from his rib cage. He reeled, clawing for the Desert Eagle still in its sheath, protecting his head with his left forearm as kick after vicious kick hammered away at him.

He ended up on his back, pulling the Desert Eagle free as the Asian man dropped a knee onto his chest. Firing from retention with the massive weapon pressed against his body, Bolan put a single .44 Magnum round through the little man's midsection. He yelped in surprise, rolling over and off Bolan, scrambling to his feet once more and taking a few shaky steps away from the soldier.

"Stop!" Bolan ordered, surging to his feet and leveling the hand cannon. The Asian man seemed not to hear him. He took another drunken step, lost his footing and collapsed on suddenly rubbery knees. His legs were folded beneath him as he stared at the sky and took a last, ragged breath, his eyes wide.

The death rattle was unmistakable.

Bolan checked the body carefully. There was little chance a man could fake that sound; the Executioner had heard it often enough for real. Satisfied that the man wouldn't be going anywhere ever again, Bolan searched the grass for his Beretta and surveyed his surroundings.

Silence.

The empty field bordered several properties, a couple of them residential. The nearest buildings were quite some distance away. No one had heard the gunfire, or no one thought to check it. Either way, Bolan was alone with the dead man.

He'd hoped to question the Asian, but as viciously as he'd fought, it was unlikely he'd have been very talkative. Bolan knew the type. This man was a fighter. He'd have gone down struggling.

Bolan holstered the Desert Eagle and retrieved the Beretta. He ejected its magazine, catching it in his free hand, then racked the slide and caught the ejected round in his cupped hand. He inspected the barrel of the machine pistol, peering through the open slide up the spout, making sure there was no mud or other foreign matter obstructing the weapon. Then he loaded the loose round back in the 20-round magazine.

"Agent Cooper!" Bolan turned at the sound of his cover name.

"Are you all right?" Officer Copeland asked, breathing hard as he ran to catch up.

"Fine," Bolan said. He gestured to the dead man. "I can't say the same for him."

"You got him," Copeland said. Bolan made no response as none was required.

Bolan checked the body. The man's gun, a Glock 19, was on the ground nearby. Copeland retrieved the weapon, checked it, then unloaded it. Bolan nodded his approval. The dead man had nothing on him except a spare magazine for the Glock, a compact pair of binoculars and a short-range two-way radio, the sort of device hunters and other sportsmen used to coordinate groups of people in the field.

"Did you find one of these?" Bolan held up the bright yellow, rubberized radio. "In the van, or on any of the bodies?"

"Yes, actually," Copeland confirmed. "It was in the van, in the back with a bunch of junk."

"Junk?"

"An old dog blanket, a few cardboard boxes full of mostly trash." Copeland shrugged. "The sort of thing that collects in the back of a van. It was rolling around loose back there. We thought it was just part of the debris, along for the ride after the vehicle was stolen."

"Not an unreasonable conclusion," Bolan said, nodding. "But this—" he wagged the radio at Copeland "—changes everything."

"Who was he?"

"My guess," Bolan said, "is that this man was a spotter. He was watching the service and called in the gunners in the van for maximum effect."

"Copeland," a distorted voice said from Copeland's belt. "Copeland, come in." The officer unclipped the walkie-talkie from his duty belt.

"Copeland here," he said.

"We've found something. That federal hotshot will want to see it."

"That federal hotshot is right here." Copeland grinned at the Executioner. "What have you got?"

"We found a video camera on one of the gravestones," the voice came back. "It was still running."

"Set to record what?" Copeland asked.

"It was pointing at the grave site."

Copeland looked at Bolan.

"Publicity," Bolan said. "Had this gone off as planned, they would have killed everybody down there, collected their video and left. Chances are the camera was left by this one." He jerked his chin toward the dead Asian. "He must have decided getting clear was more important than working his way back around to retrieve the camera."

"So if the shooting had worked—"

"If it had worked," Bolan said grimly, "the video of those people dying would have been all over the Internet by the weekend. Count on it."

"Bastards," Copeland muttered.

"And then some," Bolan agreed.

The soldier crouched over the dead Asian, once more

taking out his secure satellite phone and taking a digital picture. He paused to transmit it to the Farm. No instructions were needed. Aaron Kurtzman and his team of cyber wizards would know that any corpse shot Bolan sent was a request for identification and intel. He did, however, take a moment to text message Kurtzman with the phone number he'd gotten from Mitch Schrader. It was unlikely the number would prove to be useful, but one never knew. So far Bolan's enemies had been a curious mixture of sloppy and professional. Someone, somewhere, might have been careless and used a number that was traceable in some way.

Bolan and Copeland made the long walk back to the cemetery. The soldier's own vehicle, a rental SUV, was parked on the opposite end of the access road leading out the front of the property. He would need to collect his gear and get back to the airport, where Grimaldi and the jet would be ready to go. While the Farm checked on the intelligence Bolan had gathered so far, the Executioner would travel to the nearest Trofimov facility from his target list. There was no telling what he'd find, but it was his experience that if he made enough forays into enemy territory, sooner or later he'd find something or someone would take a shot at him. That would be the only break he'd need.

Once the Executioner was certain how far deep the rot went, he was going to slash and burn it out of the nation's heartland.

The Patriotism Riders remained on the scene, though the police were getting ready to pack up. The police changed their minds about that quickly when Copeland informed them that there was yet another body to account for. As they scrambled, a few of them shooting suspicious looks Bolan's way, the soldier went to the group of Riders to see what held their attention so firmly.

"I don't believe it," Mitch Schrader was saying. This was met by a chorus of agreement from the others, who sounded angry. Bolan looked over the shoulder of the nearest Rider, who noticed him and moved out of the way. Sitting on one of the motorcycles, another of the Riders had a small portable television, apparently something he carried in his saddlebags. The little device showed a newscast with the TBT logo in the corner. *Trofimov's cable news network,* Bolan thought.

"You're not going to like this," the man on the motorcycle said, looking up at Bolan. "You were military, right? You got the look."

Bolan had nothing to say to that. He focused on the little television.

"We were getting ready to roll out," Schrader explained, "when Norm thought to check the news, see if anybody'd gotten wind of all this." He gestured around him. "I figured, no way, there aren't any news cameras here, you know?"

"The locals are probably running interference," Bolan said. "It wouldn't surprise me if there's a marked car parked at the entrance to this property, keeping the reporters out."

"Figured as much," Schrader said. "Anyway, Norm turns on the TV, and this is what we got." He pointed to the television.

"…promising a full investigation at the highest levels of government and the military command in Afghanistan," the young female news anchor was saying. "We at TBT are proud to bring you the following commentary from our president and CEO, Yuri Trofimov."

The scene cut to the interior of a sumptuously appointed office. Behind a gleaming desk, Yuri Trofimov—text near the bottom of the screen identified him as such—looked out at the screen, his features grim. When he spoke, he had a slight accent, but this coupled with his expensive suit and his aristocratic manner gave him the aura of a foreign diplomat. He exuded confidence, competence and, above all, a barely suppressed righteous indignation. Bolan took one look at the man and knew he was dealing with a master manipulator. It oozed from every pore, from the man's slicked, perfectly coiffed hair to the rings that glittered on his fingers as he clasped his hands on the desktop.

"We at TBT are deeply saddened to bring you this news," Trofimov said. "But as always, we are committed to nothing so much as the truth, and to the unflinching reporting of that truth, no matter how graphic or unpleasant. I think I speak for many when I say, as proud as I am of my adopted country, that this is a dark day for the United States, and a day when I am ashamed to call myself an American."

"Shut the hell up, you scumbag!" Norm interjected. Schrader shushed him, gesturing to the screen.

"It is my hope that we, as a nation, can eventually work through this," Trofimov said soberly, "but I will not lie to you. It will be difficult. We will have to make some hard admissions about our standing in the world. We will have to come to terms with the barbarism that lurks, even now, within our armed forces. This will not sit well with many of us, but I know that we are up to the challenge. For TBT News, I am Yuri Trofimov, and I thank you for trusting us."

Norm switched the set off in disgust. He looked ready to throw the little device.

"Can you beat that?" Schrader said. "I just...I just don't know."

"What happened?" Bolan asked.

"They're reporting that a bunch of our guys attacked a village in Afghanistan," Schrader said. "Totally unprovoked, they claimed. Burned the place to the ground, shot twenty, maybe thirty women and children. And Trofimov's news says they have videotape of our guys doing it…and laughing about it."

Bolan's jaw clenched. Things were getting ugly.

They were going to get uglier.

CHAPTER THREE

"Word's in from the Farm, Sarge," Grimaldi said from the cockpit, his voice carrying over the jet's intercom. "You've got another rental truck waiting for you at the field, and the care package you requested will be inside. The GPS unit in the truck should get you to the target location without any trouble."

"Thanks, Jack," Bolan said. He had finished cleaning the Remington and was replacing it in its Pelican case.

"I'll stay with the jet once we land, and I'll be ready to get us in the air again as soon as you're done in Cedar Rapids. We'll make good time to Kansas City after that. Barb confirms that your 'driver' should be waiting for you when we hit the tarmac again."

"Copy that," Bolan acknowledged.

His "driver" was, in fact, a government agent. As he always did, he had his reservations about the arrangement, but Stony Man Farm's mission controller, Barbara Price, had done her homework. When she had contacted Bolan on his secure satellite phone minutes after the soldier boarded the new jet, she had wasted no time in breaking the news to him.

"The FBI," she said, "wants in."

"I'm listening," Bolan had said simply.

"Kwok Jin," the Farm's honey-blond mission controller had stated. "That's the identification that came back on your dead man, the Asian you said gave you such a hard time. I'm transmitting to you the files on the other shooters, too, but except for Kwok they're amateur talent. Rabble-rousers with ties to known political agitator groups. Two were former members of PAAC and supposedly expelled, presumably because they were more radical than the group could tolerate. That alone says something. A couple have rap sheets, but nothing too serious. Some of the records go back quite a ways, and in one case it was a sealed juvenile case."

"So in other words, they're nobody. But someone put guns in their hands and sent them to kill innocent people. And somebody coordinated them and planned the operation for them."

"That somebody was likely Kwok or, more probably, the organization that employed him," Price confirmed. "Kwok Jin. North Korean, formerly with the country's military. Fled the country and went freelance about ten years ago, in the company of a brother, Sun. Both of them sold the only skills they had on the open market. They've been mercenaries for the past decade, most of those ten years in association with one Gareth Twain."

"I know that name," Bolan had said.

"For good reason," Price said. "Twain was one of the most murderous terrorists ever to work with the Irish Republican Army. He was so bloodthirsty, in fact, that the IRA expelled him. That was a good fifteen years ago. He's been an international mercenary ever since, notable for the fact that he has absolutely no loyalties to any entity, governmental or personal. He'll kill anyone for the right price, and no body count is too high."

"Why hasn't the Farm targeted Twain before?"

"He's always stayed one step ahead of us," Price said. "Always on the move, and always in corners of the world where the most conflict was to be had. He's a brutal operator, and his organization is extensive, but he's managed to blend into the background noise of the various wars being waged in the Third World and elsewhere. He really gets around, too. He's done stints all over Africa and South America. In Gaza, while reportedly working for Hamas and the PLO, his people blew up a freighter bound for Semarang last year. He's been implicated three times in acts of domestic terrorism in the United States, including an aborted bombing of a federal facility in Virginia, sponsored by a homegrown 'patriot' group, and he's wanted for the murder of an Interpol agent in Paris last year."

"That's quite a résumé."

"It's the Virginia bombing that put him on the Bureau's radar," Price reported. "Their Omnivore computer processing programs, which of course Aaron has fully infiltrated, are set to flag any mention of Twain or his known associates in any law-enforcement database, including Interpol and a dozen others. We ran Kwok's identification and it generated a flag. The Bureau contacted Justice, wanting to know what we knew, and Hal ran some interference for us. He pulled a few strings and called in a few favors. Someone on the Bureau's end did the same. Ultimately it was decided that an agent be assigned to what Hal is characterizing as a 'domestic investigation' on the part of Justice and its assets. Hal, in the spirit of cooperation and goodwill among government agencies, of course agreed."

"In other words, they'll raise a stink if we don't let them in the door."

"Exactly," Price said. "And as sensitive as this could be, considering Trofimov's access to the media and the harm being done to the nation's military interests, our friend in Wonderland has decided it's best if we go along to get along."

"That's a dangerous game," Bolan said. "I'm not going to scale back my mission to accommodate the sensibilities of a by-the-book FBI agent."

"There's where we catch a break," Price had told him. "I'm transmitting the file to you now. Jennifer Delaney, thirty-four. Been with the Bureau for the past ten years. A decorated agent, but also one who's been disciplined more than once. You can read the details yourself, but I'll sum it up for you—she has a recurring problem with authority and no compunctions about bending the rules to get things done."

"But she's still with the Bureau, which doesn't tolerate loose cannons."

"True," Price said. "Which means she's a very good agent, for all her willingness to be pragmatic in the field."

"I can live with that," Bolan said.

"We don't know who talked to whom in the Bureau, but Delaney has a personal stake in Twain and has been pursuing him since the incident in Virginia. Her partner, a Paul Sander, was the lead on the investigation that eventually saw Twain and his outfit popped before they could plant their explosives. A couple of them went down, but Twain and his key people got away. Twain shot both Sander and Delaney in making his escape. Sander died."

"So she's looking for payback," Bolan said. "Can I trust her?"

"She wants Twain," Price said. "Wouldn't you? But there's no indication it has interfered with her work. There have been no disciplinary actions in her file since then, either, if it makes a difference to you."

"I can understand." The file was coming through on his phone. The digital photograph of Delaney showed an attractive red-haired woman with high cheekbones and green eyes. She had a small scar on her chin. According to the statistics appended to the file, she was five foot nine, with an athletic build. She'd twice won commendations for bravery in service to the Bureau. Bolan skipped the disciplinary flags; he wasn't interested in the second-guessing of bureaucrats, who were only too happy to criticize after the fact the split-second, life-and-death decisions men and women of action were forced to make in the field.

"Delaney is en route and will meet you in—" Price paused to check something "—Kansas City. Jack tells me you'll reach Eastern Iowa Airport momentarily, and that you plan to hit the facility in Kansas City after that?"

"That's the plan," Bolan said. "It's the next logical location, geographically, on the priority list. Until something breaks free, I intend to keep the pressure on, keep blitzing Trofimov's assets until he screams. I can't verify the timing, though."

"It shouldn't matter," Price said. "By the time you're done in Iowa and moving to Kansas Delaney should get there not too much before you do."

"We'll make sure not to miss her. How much can I tell her?"

"While her interest is primarily Twain, the folks at the Bureau aren't stupid," Price said. "Hal chose to share some off-the-record intel with them. She's going to be at least vaguely aware of the Trofimov connection.

Officially, there's no FBI interest in Trofimov, but unofficially you can bet they're every bit as concerned about murderous, possibly even seditious actions taken by an American citizen to undermine the United States military. You know how much they have to dance around these days, pretending not to peer too closely into the lives of private citizens. There's just been too much public outcry over things like the domestic wiretapping program, civil rights violations by Homeland Security, that sort of thing. The Bureau wants to know what Trofimov is up to as badly as we do, but they can't admit it right now."

"Meaning they'll be happy to take the credit once I've found all the loose ends and burned them down," Bolan said.

"Possibly," Price admitted. "Hal will be only too happy to let them, too, given how the Sensitive Operations Group's cover has to be kept out of the public eye. We can operate, at least partly, under the aegis of FBI ownership of this thing, if it plays out well."

"It's going to get ugly enough behind the scenes, once the body count grows. I assume Hal has worked the phones and okayed my involvement."

"As usual," Price said.

"All right, then," Bolan said. "This Delaney can ride along. Make no mistake, though, Barb. I'm not going to let her get in my way. My priority is Trofimov and whatever programs he's running to kill Americans and interfere with the military."

"Understood," Price said. "I doubt that will be a problem. You have goals in common. The implication here is, of course, that Twain and his people are working with Trofimov, and probably have been for some time."

"Yes," Bolan had agreed. "The activists, the amateurs

with the guns, were obviously being run by someone else, and that someone in this case was apparently Kwok and whoever he works for. If Kwok is known to work for Gareth Twain, we likely have a winner. Twain is just the sort of gun for hire that someone like Trofimov would use. Given Twain's history, and Trofimov's deep pockets, it's likely Trofimov is using Twain and his organization extensively."

"Taking out Gareth Twain would do a lot of people a lot of good."

"Don't worry, Barb," Bolan said. "I won't leave anyone out. Anybody connected to Trofimov, everyone involved in the killings of U.S. service people and in Trofimov's antimilitary operations, is going to answer for their crimes. What have you heard about this video-taped massacre TBT is shouting about?"

"Nothing beyond the reports so far," Price replied. "We're checking. So far our contacts within the armed forces are drawing blanks. The Pentagon is stonewalling, saying only that it will conduct a full investigation."

"Which means they have no idea what's going on."

"Exactly," Price said. "That's the response they give when they're caught flat-footed. So far, we have no confirmation of the incident itself, or even of the identities of the soldiers supposedly involved. The quality of the tape is poor. It's going to be hard to get facial recognition, and the names on the soldiers' uniforms are too blurry to be readable. Bear did uncover some data traffic indicating the Pentagon is trying to run some enhancement on the tapes, to get to the bottom of just who is doing what to whom. Nothing so far."

"How bad is it?"

"Really bad, Striker," Price said. "The foreign press is screaming bloody murder. Our own people are just as loud. The massacre is the talk of every cable news show, radio program and major network broadcast. It's on every channel and it's twenty-four hours a day."

Bolan said nothing; his fists clenched in anger as he considered the implications. "All right. Let me know if anything changes."

"Understood. Everything's uploaded. You have all the data now," Price said. Bolan checked his phone and confirmed that. "We're still working on the phone number you gave us. It has several layers of redundant encryption protecting it. Bear has Akira running a back-end trace to try to find it through the network in which it's hidden."

"Understood," Bolan repeated. Price was referring to Akira Tokaido, one of the Farm's computer geniuses. "The fact that someone wanted the Patriotism Riders there, just to make sure they were killed with the others, is significant. It makes the whole thing that much bolder a statement, that much more horrible. It says a lot about the people we're dealing with."

"We're on it," Price said.

"Let me know if you find anything. I'll see you when I see you."

"Striker?" Price had asked.

"Yeah, Barb?"

"Be careful."

"I will."

The soldier had busied himself with cleaning his weapons, making sure to disassemble the Beretta and give it a thorough once-over. The usually gregarious Grimaldi was quiet, for the most part, content to let Bolan work through the operation in his mind.

Bolan reviewed the mission data on the site in Cedar Rapids. It wasn't especially significant in terms of his priority list of targets, but it was the closest Trofimov asset. The type of operation Bolan was about to run was based on the notion of shaking the tree. You targeted the enemy's assets, made a lot of noise, caused a lot of damage and then stood back to see what shook loose. Along the way, some of Trofimov's secrets were bound to be exposed; the facilities, by definition, were somehow dirty, or the Farm's cybernetics staff wouldn't have ferreted them out as suspicious.

Trofimov's reaction to Bolan's incursions would tell the soldier, and by extension the Farm, everything he would need to know. Countless times, Bolan had marched willingly into the jaws of death to see what would try to bite him. This was no different.

The facility outside Cedar Rapids was ostensibly an assembly plant for DVD players. The parts were manufactured abroad, mostly in China, then imported and put together for domestic sale in the United States. The legal details were irrelevant to Bolan, but he was at least vaguely aware that such an arrangement allowed Trofimov to claim the devices were "made in the U.S.A." while achieving the cost savings of foreign import manufacture. There were probably certain import restrictions that were also being circumvented.

What was important about this particular plant, according to reports Price had sent and the data Kurtzman and his people had compiled, was that it had never made any money. Quite the contrary; when the financial records were traced all the way to their virtual conclusions, past several holding and front companies and through more than a few creative bookkeeping tricks, the plant consumed more money than it would if it were operating at a total loss. That meant it was burning through cash a lot faster than ever it could, even if

Trofimov was building DVD players free of charge. While it wasn't unheard-of for a large company to produce a commodity at a loss, to gain market share or build brand loyalty, the degree of financial drain in this case was staggering. It was far too much for the plant to be anything but a front for something else. Bolan intended to find out just what was being done behind the scenes.

When he knew that, he'd be a step closer to learning just who and what this Yuri Trofimov was, and why the man had chosen to make the United States his enemy. Bolan had no illusions. This wasn't an investigation, nor was it a mystery. He wasn't a detective. He was a soldier, and he was performing a soldier's task.

Search and destroy.

CHAPTER FOUR

Yuri Trofimov sat at his desk as the makeup girl swabbed the last of the television makeup from his face. He favored her with a smile full of perfectly capped teeth. From his elaborately styled hair to his tailored suit to his spray-on tan, there was nothing about Yuri Trofimov that was not meticulously groomed, controlled and managed to effect. The man left nothing to chance, and he was very proud of that fact.

Swiveling in his chair, he took in the view from the window overlooking downtown Orlando. Several buildings, not quite as tall as his own TBT headquarters, were still under construction. He had never quite lost the joy he had felt as a boy, watching construction work, and there were times when he watched the cranes below slowly swiveling over the steel skeletons that were taking shape in the shadow of Trofimov's own building. Downtown Orlando had been undergoing something of a commercial revitalization for some months now, though in these turbulent economic times it was anybody's guess how long *that* would last.

There were precious few memories from his childhood that were pleasant ones. Growing up, he had believed he was destined for the navy. He had never known his father; his mother, little more than a prostitute who existed on the kindness of the many men she bedded, had hinted more than once that Yuri's father had been a naval officer. Her indifference to him had set the tone for his early life. He was neither abused nor loved, neither cared for nor hated. The empty ache left him eventually, when he learned to substitute for it other, preferable emotions. Chief among these were anger and ambition.

Young Yuri Trofimov had a gift, he soon learned, when among his peers and even his teachers in school. He had a talent for influencing others, for captivating them with his stories and with the expression of his opinions. People cared about what Yuri Trofimov had to say. They cared about his opinions. They wished to hear him when he spoke. He learned, therefore, that he had power. With a taste of power came the desire for more.

As the infrastructure he had always taken for granted began to crumble, as the ships of the former Soviet navy began to rust in their docks and to sink from neglect, Trofimov gave up the last hopes he'd held of serving in that force. Already, his mind was alive with possibilities, with ways to use his talents both to enrich himself and to extend the power he believed was destined to be his. Power over his fellow men: that was Yuri Trofimov's greatest goal, his greatest hope and his fundamental desire. He began to make plans.

When the time had come to leave the smoking ruins of what had once been proud Mother Russia, he had done so without looking back. Russia could do nothing more for him. The post–Cold War years hadn't been kind to the once-powerful nation and, while the crime-infested world of business in Russia held certain attractions, the market was saturated. Better to move to the West, where untapped, unexploited markets still remained. Trofimov hated the West; he hated it for what it had done to his nation, for the Cold War that had denied Russia its once-proud destiny. He hated the strutting, arrogant Americans who believed they owned the world and could tell everyone within it how to live and what to do. But he also knew that the West was his best hope for achieving his still only vaguely defined personal goals. He swallowed his pride temporarily, which was the hardest thing of all.

The teenage Trofimov had managed to immigrate successfully to the United States, illegally at first, then legally, after a fashion, many years later. He found himself, almost to his surprise, in Florida, and there he realized that his ambition alone wouldn't be enough. He needed contacts. He needed resources. It was all fine and good to know he could influence, control, even manipulate his fellow human beings. There were few enough opportunities to do so when one was penniless and homeless on the streets of an American city.

Trofimov, growing increasingly desperate, had prowled the streets of Miami, increasingly worried that he would find himself among the city's population of street people before much longer. Then came the break he had sought, the opportunity he needed: he saw two men bullying a third, demanding money owed them.

He had crept up the alleyway until he was close enough to hear the conversation. The two men worked for a local loan shark. The third man owed a great deal of money. He grew increasingly combative as the two enforcers threatened him. It quickly became evident to Trofimov that these men were overmatched. The third man was bigger and appeared stronger. As Trofimov watched, the big man suddenly, with no warning whatsoever, punched one of the two enforcers square in the jaw. He kneed the second, dropping him. Breaking into a run, the third man hurried past the very spot where Trofimov stood.

He tripped him.

The big man hit the pavement of the alleyway. He struck his head as he fell. He was either dead or unconscious as Trofimov stood over him, checked his pockets and took his wallet.

"Hey, kid," one of the enforcers said. It was the one who had taken a knee to the groin. "Gimme that wallet."

Trofimov tossed the wallet to the man without hesitation, as if this had been his intent from the start. He regarded the enforcer coolly; the enforcer stared back. Finally the other man said, "What? What the hell you want?"

"I want a job," Trofimov said.

The enforcer seemed to think about that for a moment. He looked down at the debtor and then back to his partner, who was slowly struggling to his feet. "What do you do?" he asked.

"Name it," Trofimov had said.

The enforcer laughed. Eventually he nodded. "Come on, then."

That had been the humble beginning from which Yuri Trofimov built his empire. He had at first worked his way up in the hierarchy of organized crime in Miami, learning the violent ropes. His talent for persuading people, his guile, his natural, snake-oil charm served him well. He moved up within the ranks. When he had enough support, when he had co-opted enough of the organization, he took it over from within, then fought a war with those who disagreed with his palace coup. Finally he ruled uncontested. He leveraged his money and his power into several legitimate enterprises; the boom in consumer electronics and the new Internet age helped him along the way.

When he had the time, he attended college. In business school he learned the formal terms behind what he had found through hard-won and bitter experience. Then, in journalism school, he found the true means of channeling his natural abilities. Always, he branched out, expanded, reinvested. His legitimate empire, on the backs of his criminal enterprises, became truly, remarkably, breathtakingly powerful.

He expanded from electronics into heavy industry, buying shares in the few Russian businesses that showed financial promise, greasing the wheels back home and in the United States with plenty of bribes. When he couldn't use his power or his money to get what he wanted, he knew who to hire. He learned just how much was possible if one sought the services of armed, amoral men, the types of men who fought wars for hire, the types of men who could be counted on to take their money and quietly go about their business. As his ties to such mercenaries deepened, his reach grew. Those who wouldn't bend to the will of Yuri Trofimov often found themselves dead, victims of random street violence, presumed gang shootings or even open massacres whose perpetrators were never caught.

Always, Trofimov was careful to keep his own record, his own reputation, clean. He knew as well as anyone that the government of the United States had its suspicions, but was hamstrung by its own rules. For all its tough talk about homeland security, its posturing and its saber rattling, it didn't have the killer instinct it needed to deal with the likes of Yuri Trofimov. Thus he would continue his work, under their very noses. They would be able to prove nothing. They would never be able to assign to Trofimov the blame for the storm that was to come.

Eventually he bought his United States citizenship. It was easy enough—a bribe here, a favor there, the gentle application of political power over there. He followed the models established by other businessmen before him, never reinvented the wheel if he didn't have to do so. When TBT and its news network finally burst on the scene, Trofimov was more than prepared to take market share by giving his viewers what they wanted. He traded in the sensational, the outrageous, the bloody, the messy. Always, his hatred of the West came through, and it tapped the streak of self-destructive, self-loathing guilt some of his now-fellow Americans seemed to feel about themselves and their nation.

For many men, this would have been enough. Riches. Influence. Swaying the cultural pendulum and affecting the collective consciousness of the most powerful nation in the world.

Yuri Trofimov wasn't most men.

He wouldn't be truly satisfied until the United States, the embodiment of the hated West, suffered as his homeland had suffered. Only when the arrogant United States knew the pain of losing its military might abroad, only when the miserable United States was humiliated on the international stage as the Soviet Union and later Russia had been, only when the United States military—the truncheon with which the Americans beat all around them—was utterly disgraced would Yuri Trofimov be truly satisfied.

And thus he had, using the great wealth and power

available to him, embarked on the elaborate plan that was to be his life's crowning achievement. He was going to destroy the United States military, using the Americans themselves to help him do the work.

He had, of course, no compunctions about breaking the law. He had begun his life as a criminal; laws were for other men, not the rich and powerful like Trofimov. As long as he was smart enough not to get caught, and he had always been smart enough not to get caught, he could do as he willed, pay whom he wished to kill whom he wished. It was the way of things. Simple violence solved many problems. Complicated, crafty, *deceitful* violence…well, that solved so much more. And of what use was power if it wasn't applied, used to shape the world in the way the man wielding that power saw fit? That was, after all, what had first attracted Trofimov to wielding power over others: the ability to manipulate and shape the world by affecting the will of other men and women. He let his hatred guide him. He would shape the world.

He started by infiltrating and then co-opting most of the Peace At Any Cost group. It was the largest and had the most influence on the antimilitary scene within the United States, a fact born out by the copious research his people at TBT News conducted at his direction. It was simple enough to liberate from the group those members willing to take the next step, to use actual violence in fighting the hated American military and what it represented. Trofimov himself had selected the first targets. He had made certain that these baby killers, these returning war criminals, knew that they weren't safe in their own country, weren't safe from the horrors they had inflicted overseas.

He hadn't counted on the American government covering up the crimes, however. This robbed his murders of the impact they were to have. He fought his propaganda campaign on many fronts, including spreading and sensationalizing the reports of the latest high-profile military atrocities, and he manufactured these accordingly when it was required. This helped, but it didn't fully compensate for the covered-up killings of returning military personnel. Then TBT News had run a report on the growing popularity of protests of military funerals, and Trofimov had another stroke of brilliance. He had his PAAC people use their groups to promote more such protests, and when the time was right, he had the elements within PAAC that he controlled break away and begin the killings anew.

Of course, the peace activists were difficult to control, and had no training in violence or the use of weapons. That didn't matter. Trofimov had access to more than enough men and matériel to train and direct these useful idiots. He had called in his mercenaries and made sure they knew what he wanted, then allowed them to run the operations as they saw fit. He still suggested targets, but on the whole, the operation ran without his direct involvement. This was good; it increased the level of plausible deniability he held, further insulating him from exposure, keeping him and his reputation safe while his people brought his will to fruition.

But all of this was just the start. It was a taste of what was to come, the barest tip of the operations his personnel were running. When Trofimov actually stopped to consider the vast scope of the operation, the world-changing audacity of it, it awed even him. It was a fitting life's work, as he saw it. It was an appropriately bold testament to the power wielded by one Yuri Trofimov, and the legacy left behind by the application of that power would be a different world. That world would be one in which the United States military, humiliated and diminished, would have far less power over the lives of every other person on the planet…and thus, the United States, the West itself, would be diminished. That was Trofimov's goal and his life's work. That was, he had decided some years earlier, the true end goal of his life, the end toward which the means of his wealth was working. He would not fail.

He would change the world.

The clearing of a throat broke him from his introspection. He swiveled in his chair again, facing the interior of his office, and steepled his fingers.

Trofimov frowned as he looked over his guests. These men were, truthfully, really more employees than guests, but he prided himself on his cultivated manners, and so he treated them as if they weren't simply hired help. Yuri Trofimov might be nouveau riche in the eyes of what passed for aristocratic society in this part of Florida, but manners were as important to him as all the rest, the trappings and the plans and the plots and the schemes. He was a rich man, first and foremost; he could afford himself a few affectations, could allow himself a few indulgences and even pretenses.

"You just gonna sit there mooning all day?"

Trofimov's frown deepened as he focused on the speaker. Gareth Twain lounged insolently in the nearest padded office chair. Trofimov spared him a withering glance and then scanned the other visitors to his high-rise office. He had taken little notice of them when they filed into the room; now he supposed he would have to deal with them.

One of Twain's people, an agitated Korean, paced back and forth by the door. In the lounge chair on the facing wall, cigarette smoke curling up to the ceiling, Mak Wei watched with feigned indifference. Mak was yet another Chinese operative late of the People's Liberation Army. Trofimov had enough information on Mak and his handlers to know that the Chinese had tried more than once to mount plausibly deniable operations on American soil. Trofimov also gathered that several of Mak's predecessors hadn't fared well, either failing in their missions directly and fatally, or failing only to return to China to face the wrath of their superiors. Trofimov hadn't bothered to look too deeply into this; it would have nettled Mak to discover the probing, anyway, and the man was touchy enough at the best of times. Trofimov supposed he didn't blame him, given just how notorious the Chinese government was when it came to operations of this type.

The shaven-headed Twain, who looked and dressed like a surly stevedore, was head of the many mercenary forces in Trofimov's employ. He performed his work well, and always did as asked with no complaints and no argument. Trofimov imagined he could tell Gareth Twain to drive to the nearest elementary school and shoot dead every child on the playground, and Twain would merely quote a price before calmly leaving to perform the deed. It wasn't clear to the businessman exactly why Twain did what he did, or what the man cared about. Perhaps he cared about nothing; perhaps he had no goals save the earning of money through the relative ease of his casual brutality. It didn't matter to Trofimov—though Twain's arrogant, cavalier manner irritated him. The big, ruddy, bullet-headed Irishman seemed always to be laughing at him, and at everyone else he met. Trofimov imagined that this was because, in his mind, Twain was picturing the murder of every human being he encountered. The Russian could live with that. The money he paid Twain kept the man in check, or at least directed his madness toward the targets of Trofimov's choosing.

The slight, dark-haired, sallow-skinned and physically gaunt Mak Wei was more of a mystery personally, but his personal motivations were irrelevant. Mak was a Chinese operative, and thus he did as he was told. His goals were the goals of his government. In this case, Communist China wanted very much to see the power of the United States diminished, so much so that it was willing to risk running black operations such as Mak's current mission. The agent was funneling Chinese equipment and munitions to Twain's mercenaries, and providing Chinese security personnel of his own to augment Twain's forces. Both men, working in concert, pursued the goals Trofimov set for them. Mak was smart enough to know that Trofimov's master plan was sound but, more important, he knew he had to allow for a certain degree of distance between his government and Trofimov. That meant that whenever possible, he would defer to Trofimov so that his government wasn't directly involved in the violent actions that resulted.

Trofimov had first made contact with the Chinese through diplomatic back channels years before. Communist China was the last of the truly powerful, centralized command nations. If the world were to have a new superpower, it would have to be China; only China was poised to fill the vacuum that would be left by a faltering United States. At first, Trofimov's overtures were rebuffed. As he grew in power and influence, however, China's government began to take notice. Eventually they had assigned Mak Wei to Trofimov, and a very profitable alliance was born. Through Mak, the Chinese supported Trofimov's efforts. When America ultimately fell, it was the Chinese who would benefit. Trofimov knew that the gratitude he hoped would be shown him by the resulting Chinese superpower wasn't guaranteed. That didn't worry him, however. His own power would be as great, if not greater, once America fell. He would be in a position to command China's respect, if not its thanks. The world order that emerged would be closer to the one he desired, and that was really all that mattered to him. In this manner, Mak and his government were also "useful idiots," after a fashion. The difference was simply that they weren't stupid like the peace protesters Trofimov used so easily.

Trofimov finally spoke. "You requested this meeting, Gareth. You tell me what it is you want."

"It isn't what I want," Twain said. "It's a new wrinkle. A new problem."

"Then tell us what it is," Mak Wei said quietly, breathing out a plume of blue-white smoke, "and we can all address it that much more efficiently."

"You've met Kwok Sun." Twain jerked a thumb toward the man by the door. "Poor bugger's gone and lost his brother, hasn't he?"

"Lost him? How?" Trofimov asked.

"Jin was assigned to that bunch out in Wisconsin," Twain said, "handling the PAAC splinter bunch."

"They turned on him?" Trofimov asked.

"Nah, nah." Twain shook his head. "He was ambushed. They moved on the funeral like you wanted. Full kit, armed to the teeth. Only, somebody was waitin' for them. Shot down every one of the civvies, then ran down Kwok Jin and plugged him."

"How do you know this?"

"Paid me an informant in the police department out

there." Twain grinned, as if this were the most brilliant maneuver ever conceived. The man's mannerisms were that of a much less professional killer, and Trofimov knew this for the ruse that it was. Gareth Twain was cunning, vicious and completely pragmatic. He liked to be underestimated. It was habitual with him, Trofimov was sure.

"You are saying your men were intercepted by law enforcement?"

"Are you kidding me?" Twain was suddenly indignant. "First, they wasn't my men, except for Jin. Second, no cop or even Fed, hell, not even a Royal loyal would ha' done as this fellow did. Shot them all down without so much as even a by-your-leave, no warnings, no 'Stop, police,' or whatever the hell else. Just bang-bang-bang, you're all dead, and Bob's your uncle."

"Spare me the colorful argot," Trofimov said. "You forget that I know you're not quite the Irish rube you pretend to be."

Twain frowned, but wisely said nothing.

"This is an unfortunate complication," Mak Wei put in, sucking the last of his unfiltered cigarette down to his stained fingers. "It could indicate that we—that *you,* Trofimov—have finally raised the attention of some governmental or legal entity. The operation could be in danger."

"Not buyin' it," Twain said. "You know who I think it is? I think it's the Mob. Some competing 'interest,' and the kinds of folks who don't mind plugging a few of the other side's boys to make a point."

"That makes no sense," Mak said disdainfully. "Why would a criminal concern care about political protests or political murders?"

"An investment in the status quo, perhaps," Trofimov

offered. "The Mafia and the CIA once worked together in an attempt to kill Castro, perhaps more than once. There are criminals, and there are patriots. They aren't necessarily mutually exclusive."

"Perhaps," Mak conceded. "But you forget, I have knowledge of operations, of actions against United States interests, that you do not. The methods employed are brutal, yes. They are not consistent with the usual manner in which the Americans do things *officially*. Unofficially, my government is quite certain that elements at least affiliated with the United States government are quite prepared to use violence, and to use it preemptively and overwhelmingly to protect American interests."

"What can you tell us about this?" Trofimov asked.

"Only what I have said just now. There are few specifics."

"Well, that hardly helps us, does it?" Twain snapped. "And in the meantime now I've got to watch my back, and yours, and wonder where this trigger-happy goon is going to show next. The entire operation could be compromised."

"Is that a problem, Twain?" Trofimov asked directly. "Are you saying you aren't up to the challenge?"

"Not hardly." Twain grinned wolfishly. "I'm just warning you. It's going to get bloody."

"Then let it get bloody," Trofimov said. "Now go, and do what I pay you to do."

CHAPTER FIVE

The neighborhood around the assembly plant outside Cedar Rapids was fairly sparse and largely industrial. Mack Bolan was grateful for that; it reduced the chances of innocents wandering into the cross fire. He parked his rental truck a block away, scanning the area for threats and spectators. He saw no one.

The care package he had requested from the Farm was in a hard-shell case in the back of the truck. It was a Tavor TAR-21 assault rifle fitted with a 40 mm M-203 grenade launcher. The 5.56 mm modular Israeli bullpup-style rifle, which looked like something out of a science-fiction movie. This gas-operated select-fire rifle had a cyclic rate approaching fifteen rounds per second on full automatic. The compact weapon, coupled with the power of the grenade launcher, was just the thing for the mission on which Bolan was embarking.

The soldier made sure his movements were concealed within the rear of the truck, checked his weapons and slung the Tavor along the side of his body. The weapon wasn't truly concealed, but it didn't need to be. Bolan intended to make a significant first impression, and fast. He slung his OD canvas war bag across his chest on its broad shoulder strap, making sure his extra magazines, explosives and other weapons were in place in the bag and in the pockets of his combat blacksuit. He didn't bother to don his field jacket.

A parking lot fronted the assembly plant. Three or four cars were parked here; none of them was remarkable. Bolan gave them a casual glance as he passed, stopping at the double doors to the plant itself. He pushed one open and quietly stuck his head inside, looking left and then right.

Nothing.

The foyer was empty, the floors a dusty and ancient linoleum that hadn't seen a good waxing in years. Bolan walked through the first set of doors and paused, peering through the gap between the inner doors. Beyond, he could see a fairly typical light industrial area. Workbenches were arrayed across the plant floor, which had a high ceiling and walls dotted with dusty, multipaned windows. Many of the windows were painted over. Fluorescent lights suspended from the high ceiling buzzed and cast a greenish-yellow hue over the interior. At the rear of the floor space, which was at the far end of the building, Bolan saw a sign that read, simply, Office.

The benches held many cardboard boxes, plastic racks and rows of what, from this distance, appeared to be circuit boards. Men in casual street clothes—Bolan looked carefully, but saw no women—were standing among the benches, half-crouched as they bent over their work. Some of them wore magnifying lenses on straps around their heads, presumably for seeing the fine details of complicated work.

In short, the plant looked like exactly what it was supposed to be.

Bolan was mildly surprised by that. He had expected to see something far more nefarious. He started to back out the way he came in, careful to keep the Tavor out of sight behind his leg.

A shadow moved on the other side of the door, and Bolan's combat instinct prompted him to hit the floor. A bullet burned past him. The gunner on the other side of the double doors continued to shoot through the barrier, apparently sighting through the gap between them.

Bolan rolled out of the path of the bullets, bringing up the Tavor, surging to his feet. He angled his fire down, careful to avoid indiscriminately spraying the room beyond the doors, instead triggering a withering blast at knee level. The gunner on the other side of the doors screamed.

The soldier kicked the doors in, stepping over the writhing gunman as he did so. The workers beyond scrambled for cover. Pausing over the wounded man, Bolan kicked his handgun away.

"No one move!" he ordered. "Lay down your weapons and place your hands behind your head!"

Movement from two directions caught his eye. A stream of full-auto fire, the unmistakable, hollow metallic clatter of Kalashnikov rifles, ripped through the space, shredding the components on top of several benches between the shooters and Mack Bolan. The soldier dived and rolled to the side, angling toward a heavy metal rolling toolbox. The toolbox rang like a bell as 7.62 mm fire from the assault rifles ripped into it.

The Executioner fished a flash-bang grenade out of his war bag, considered it and grabbed a second. He yanked the pins from each bomb in succession, then whipped the grenades in opposite directions, toward the points of fire converging on his location. Curling his chin into his chest, he squeezed his eyes shut, opened his mouth and covered his ears.

The searing flashes were accompanied by a deafening wallop. Even though he was prepared for it, Bolan's ears were ringing in the wake of the powerful light-and-sound explosions. He surged to his feet, breaking cover with the Tavor's integrated red-dot sight seeking targets. The first AK gunner had dropped his rifle and was holding his eyes, staggering back and forth in place. Bolan put a 5.56 mm round through his head and made a quarter turn, bringing the second man into line. That man was starting to recover, and clawed for a handgun in his waistband. Bolan burned him down with a short burst.

The soldier checked his six, then each point of the compass, assessing his surroundings. Somewhere, a worker whimpered. Bolan tracked the noise and found a twentysomething man with lanky blond hair, dressed in a flannel shirt and ripped jeans. He was cowering under one of the workbenches. He still wore a wrist strap connected to a ground wire, a precaution against electrostatic discharge.

Bolan gestured with his rifle. "You."

The young man's eyes went wide. He looked left, then right, crouched on his back in a near fetal position. "M-m-me?" he stammered.

"You." Bolan nodded. "How many armed guards?"

"What?"

"Armed guards. Men with firearms. How many in this facility?"

"J-ju…just those two," the young man managed to tell him. "Plus the guy at the door. Jesus, you killed them. You killed them both."

"Stay with me," Bolan said, kicking one of the man's feet with his own combat boot. He didn't bother to point out that he hadn't, in fact, killed the door guard. "Focus, kid. Why were they here? Why attack me?"

"I don't know," the young man admitted. "We…we just work here, man. We just work here."

"Work here doing what? What are you building?"

"How should I know?" the man said, indignant. "They give us the specs and we build the boards. I don't ask. I get paid by the board. I just do my job."

"Get up," Bolan said. "Get the rest of the workers together. Get out of here."

"Why?" the kid asked, pulling himself up, using the workbench for support. He was rapidly regaining his composure; it was dawning on him that Bolan didn't intend to kill him.

"You're out of a job, kid," Bolan told him. "Get the others and get gone. Don't make me tell you again."

The young man did not need any further urging. He ran among the benches, grabbing each of his fellow assemblers, urging them on and even shouting at them when they hesitated. Under Bolan's watchful eye, the workers hit the bullet-pocked double doors and ran for it.

The numbers were ticking down in the soldier's head. One of those workers was bound to call the police, if a silent alarm hadn't already been triggered. He thought it unlikely, though, that there was such an alarm, at least not one connected to local law enforcement. Those whose facilities were guarded by gunmen wielding presumably illegal, full-auto Kalashnikovs probably didn't welcome police involvement in their affairs.

Still, one of the assemblers was probably on a wireless phone to the cops right now. Bolan would have only a little time before the place was overrun.

The wounded gunman was still rolling around on the floor, holding his legs and groaning. Bolan walked up and stood over him, the Tavor held loosely in one hand, the barrel of the rifle pointed at the man's forehead.

"I want to know everything you know about your employers and this facility," Bolan said. "I don't have a lot of time. If you can't tell me anything, your usefulness to me is limited. If I have to hurt you to make you talk, I will." This was a bluff, of course; Bolan, the man once known as Sergeant Mercy, would never torture a helpless, unarmed and wounded man. The Executioner had seen far too many victims of torture and interrogation in the course of his personal war. He would never join the ranks of the butchers who did such things to prisoners. This particular prisoner, however, couldn't know that.

"Don't, man, don't," the gunner said, clenching his teeth through the pain. "I got nothin' here.... Let me—"

The revolver appeared in the man's hand as if by magic, pulled from a holster in his waistband, behind his hip. Bolan triggered a single round from the Tavor into the man's head, the shot echoing across the assembly plant floor.

Searching the dead man's pockets, Bolan finally found something of value: a laminated identity card bearing the corporate logo of a company called Security Consultants and Researchers. The letters *SCAR* were emblazoned in heavy block letters across the bottom of the card, which also bore the man's name. Bolan took a moment to remove his secure phone, snap a digital photograph of the card and transmit the image to the Farm. He took and sent a picture of the dead man, too, for confirmation of ID if nothing else.

There wasn't much more time. Bolan began to move among the assembly tables, snapping photos of the components he saw waiting there. These, too, were transmitted automatically to the Farm for analysis. He gave the rest of the room a cursory search, then paused outside the door to the office, ajar by perhaps two inches.

Standing to one side of the threshold, he reached out and gave the door a push. As he yanked his hand back, a shotgun blast ripped through the flimsy hollow-core door, throwing splinters in every direction. There was the unmistakable sound of a pump-action shotgun being racked. A second blast, deafening in the close quarters, followed the first.

Bolan wasted no time. As the gunner beyond desperately racked his pump shotgun again, the soldier planted a combat-boot sole in what was left of the door, shoving it aside as he plunged through. The man standing in the cluttered office looked up in stark terror as the soldier hurtled toward him. Bolan slammed the butt of the Tavor into the shotgunner's head. He collapsed without a sound. The shotgun hit the floor, its action still open, another round from the tubular magazine waiting to be pushed into the chamber.

The man was dazed but not completely unconscious. Bolan propped him up against the scarred wooden desk that dominated the little office. A name tag on the man's stained and rumpled white, button-down shirt read Hal West, Manager. He didn't have the look of a professional; he looked like exactly what he was, the manager of a mechanical assembly plant. Bolan searched the man's pockets and turned up a wallet, a pair of car keys and a few other personal items. Bolan found a pair of glasses in a vinyl case in the man's shirt pocket. He took these out, unfolded them and placed them on West's face.

"West," Bolan said. He snapped his fingers in front of the man's face a few times.

"Wha…?" West sputtered.

"West," Bolan said more forcefully. "Wake up."

"Who… who are you?" West managed to focus on the soldier.

"I'm with the government," Bolan said. He risked flashing his Justice credentials. It was a test, and he wasn't disappointed. West's eyes went wide and he visibly paled.

"You… you're…"

"That's right," Bolan said. "You just took a shot at a government official."

"I'm sorry!" West blurted. "I didn't know! I thought… I mean… I thought you were…"

"Slow down," Bolan said, though he was keenly aware that his own time was running out. He would have to move fast if he wanted to get out of the building before becoming entangled with the local law.

"They just told us to keep an eye out," West stated. "They said if anyone ever showed up and got violent, it was the terrorists. We couldn't trust the workers, of course, but I brought the shotgun in from home, kept it here in the office."

"Terrorists?" Bolan asked. "What terrorists?"

"You don't know? That isn't why you're here?"

"Why don't you tell me," Bolan said.

"The parts—" West gestured toward the wrecked door "—the assemblies. We're making transmitters."

"Transmitters," Bolan said. "Not, say, parts for DVD players."

"No, no," West said. "That's the cover. That's what they told us to say if anybody asked. They said it was top secret. The folks on the floor didn't know, just management. Just me."

"Who is 'they,'" Bolan said, "and what *exactly* did they tell you?"

"Consolidated Funding and Liability," West said. "That's who pays us, anyway. That's who hired me to run this place. They told me it was top secret, told me I would be helping my country. They said the transmitters are used by the Department of Defense. Missiles or something, hell, I don't know. I didn't need to know. The components showed up, and the plans were given to me, and my people just put the boards and everything else together. We didn't need to know. It was better if we didn't, they said."

"Who at this Consolidated Funding and Liability did you actually talk to?" Bolan asked.

"Some guy." West shrugged. "He said his name was Richard Smith, which I thought was strange."

"Why?"

"He was Chinese," West said. "Or Japanese, or Korean, or whatever. Beats me. But he had an accent and didn't look like a Richard Smith to me. But I figure, the government, it has its secrets and its reasons."

"How were you contacted to take this job?"

"I just answered an ad in the paper," West said. "They told me I was hired, and then told me I was sworn to secrecy, and told me it was my patriotic duty not to tell anybody what was really being built here, because it was for defense. Of course, man, why wouldn't I? I love my country. I'd never sell it out."

"How did they know they could trust you?" Bolan asked.

"I guess they must have looked at my records," West said. "I mean, I just assumed I have a file somewhere, you know? And they paid me a ton of money. A guy would have to be crazy not to take that deal. Six figures to watch the factory floor and not tell anybody we're making transmitter parts. Seemed okay to me, and I'm as patriotic as the next guy. They arranged for the security guys, too. I figure they're like, what, contractors, like those guys in Iraq, right? Those company guys who go over and guard convoys and stuff. They never talked much and I didn't ask. Why did you shoot them?"

"Because they were trying to shoot *me*," Bolan said. "West, forget everything you were told. This wasn't a government facility. You've been duped, plain and simple."

"I...what?"

"You weren't protecting a government secret," Bolan said. "I have my suspicions, but let's just say you were working for the other side."

"Oh, God," West said. "You're kidding. What, like terrorists?"

"It's difficult to say," Bolan said. "Don't worry about it. Cooperate and everything will be fine." He stood and helped the still-wobbling West to his feet. "Leave that shotgun right where it is. I suggest you get out of here and wait for the cops. Tell them what you told me. Are there any schematics or plans here?"

"Oh, God," West said, ignoring the question. "Oh, God, I tried to shoot a cop."

"I'm not a cop," Bolan said.

"You might as well be!" West said. "Look, man, you gotta help me. You gotta make them understand when they get here. I was just trying to do my patriotic duty, man. The owners said that ecoterrorists might show up and want to take us down, something about lead in the circuit boards. I didn't ever figure it come to that. Man, man, you gotta help me. I wasn't trying to kill a cop, honest!"

"I'm not a cop," Bolan said. "Listen to me. Are there any schematics or plans here, any data on what you were building?"

"I've got them," West said. He rummaged absently around on his desk before producing a flash drive, which he handed to Bolan. "This should have all the latest designs on it. They haven't changed much. Everything's very much at the component level. No real way to tell what these go into, or what they do beyond the most general."

"All right," Bolan said. "You should—"

"You! In the building!" a voice amplified by a megaphone shouted from outside. "Come out with your hands up!"

"They're here already!" West said. He bolted before Bolan could grab him.

"Wait!" Bolan said.

"I have to make sure they understand!" West called, running. "I'm no cop killer!"

Bolan took off after him, but as West hit the double doors, the soldier had one of his battlefield premonitions, a flash of instinct. As he threw himself to the side of the doors, catching a glimpse of West running outside through the outer pair, he realized what had tipped him off. There had been no sirens.

The automatic gunfire cut down Hal West. Bringing up the Tavor, Bolan quickly loaded a 40 mm grenade in the launcher mounted under the barrel.

He waited for a lull in the gunfire, indicating the men outside were reloading. The Executioner had expected them to stagger their fire, but they were apparently overconfident in their numbers. He risked a quick peek around the edge of the doorway, through the mess of what had once been both sets of double doors.

Two gray Suburbans were parked out front. The men firing from behind the cover of those vehicles wielded M-4 assault rifles, dripping with accessories. Every weapon had an elaborate red-dot aiming system, foregrip, laser and flashlight pods, and a variety of other add-ons.

"There!" one of the armed men pointed in Bolan's direction. The soldier ducked back behind cover as 5.56 mm bullets chipped away at the battered door frame.

He'd seen enough. He thrust the snout of the Tavor and its grenade launcher through the opening, trusting to luck and his own speed to prevent the weapon from catching a round, then he triggered it.

The grenade caught the lead Suburban, blowing apart the first quarter of the vehicle and sending hot shrapnel in every direction. As the explosion died away, the soldier could hear the screams of his enemies. There was more than one wailing voice. At least two, perhaps more of the shooters had been caught in the blast.

He reloaded the grenade launcher, then repeated the same rattlesnake-fast movement, shoving the nose of the weapon into the gap of the doorway and triggering a second grenade. The explosion, like the one before it, brought a wave of heat pressing through the shattered double doors. Bolan waited and was rewarded with a secondary blast of some kind. Something in one of the damaged vehicles, perhaps extra fuel, perhaps explosives, had caught and detonated.

Sparing the corpse of Hal West a final glance, the Executioner walked out into the flaming hellscape.

Bodies were scattered in and around the two burning vehicles. Some of the shrapnel had damaged two of the nearby parked cars, shattering their windshields and flattening a tire on the closer vehicle. Bolan checked each of the dead men, making sure no one was playing possum. He found only one man still alive, lying on his back behind one of the shattered trucks, staring into the sky trying to breathe with a collapsed lung. His shirt was soaked through with blood. An M-4 lay on the asphalt nearby, forgotten.

Bolan stood over him. He aimed the Tavor at the man's head, one-handed.

"You're…one…tough bastard," the dying man gasped.

"Who do you work for?"

"Card's…in my pocket," the man said. Evidently, as death approached, he felt no compelling urge to remain loyal to his employers.

"SCAR?" Bolan asked.

"Yeah," the man wheezed. "Was…Army."

"And now you're a mercenary," Bolan guessed.

"Yeah." The wounded man's voice was growing weaker.

"Why?" Bolan asked. "What's going on in there? What are you protecting?"

"Beats…hell…out of me." The man grinned. "They…pay."

"Was it worth it?" Bolan asked.

The dead man stared up at him, unseeing. He would never answer that or any other question.

The Executioner shook his head. They fought for money, and they died for nothing. He had seen it countless times.

Shaking his head again, the soldier shouldered his weapon and hurried back to his vehicle. There was much more work to be done.

CHAPTER SIX

Mack Bolan found the Ford Explorer waiting at the pickup and drop-off area just outside the terminal of Kansas City International Airport. He carried his heavy weapons and gear in a large duffel bag, while his canvas shoulder bag was slung under his field jacket. His personal weapons were concealed within the jacket. Flying Air Grimaldi had its benefits; he could, between the private plane and his Justice credentials, bypass any and all security in the airport. It wouldn't do to have some overeager TSA official discovering automatic weapons and grenades on Bolan's person and in his carry-on.

Agent Jennifer Delaney was prettier than her photograph. She was dressed in a silk blouse, a pair of jeans with hiking boots and a well-cut brown leather jacket that almost hid the bulge of the sidearm on her belt. Bolan looked her over as he stowed his gear on the rear seat of the truck. As he climbed in, she was programming the GPS unit.

"Where to, Soldier?"

Bolan stopped short and eyed her.

"Oh, come off it." Delaney smiled, flashing white, even teeth. "It practically radiates from you. If you're a Washington desk-rider or even a legal eagle, I'd be very surprised. You're military or ex-military."

Bolan pulled on his seat belt, looked over at her and stuck out his hand.

"Matt Cooper," he said. "Justice Department."

"Uh-huh," Delaney said. She smiled again. "Have it your way, Cooper. Agent Jennifer Delaney, FBI." She shook his hand. Her grip was surprisingly firm. "So, Agent Cooper. Or is it…Captain? Major? Colonel?"

"Agent will be fine," Bolan said, almost laughing despite himself. He hadn't been read so easily in a long time. Delaney's head was screwed on right, that much was certain. "You and I both know it's probably better if you don't pry too deeply."

"Which is why I'm getting my digs in now," Delaney admitted. "We can continue this witty banter on the road. Where to?"

Bolan rattled off the address. "We'll want to take 152."

Delaney finished entering the address on the GPS. "That's not too far. But far enough out of the city that we may have more privacy than we might like."

"Privacy is good," Bolan said. "Cuts down on people who might get caught in the cross fire."

"'Cross fire'?" Delaney shot him a sidelong glance as she drove. She guided the Ford easily through the busy traffic exiting the airport.

"You were informed of the nature of this operation?" Bolan countered.

"I was told Justice is conducting an investigation into Trofimov, and that there's evidence Gareth Twain is working with Trofimov in some sort of terrorist campaign."

"That about sums it up," Bolan told her. "Officially, the government can't just break down Trofimov's door and waterboard him until he talks."

"Sure it could," Delaney countered.

The soldier paused, watching the traffic rush past. Delaney drove well, moving in and out of the available openings with efficiency and purpose. "Well, all right," Bolan admitted, "but if that happens too soon, we run the risk of getting to the bottom of everything Trofimov is doing. To shake the tree, we have to leave the roots alone…for now."

"Which means?"

"Which means, as you've probably been told already, I have a list of targets. I intend to visit each of those targets in turn. At those locations, I intend to break things. When enough important things get broken, Trofimov and those working for him, including Twain, will get agitated and expose themselves. Then I take them down and put an end to whatever threat Trofimov represents."

"'Break things,'" Delaney said. "You're running a series of armed raids."

"Yes."

"Who's your team? Will they be meeting us?"

"We are the team," Bolan said. "Unless you want to back out now. I'm going to warn you, Agent Delaney. Things are going to get hot." He turned from the window and gave her a hard look. "Are you prepared for that?"

She returned his gaze evenly. "If it means I get Gareth Twain, then yes."

"He's not my priority," Bolan told her. "But I've already faced one of his people, according to the man's background file. Twain's past, his method of operation, it fits. If he's here at all, it's likely we'll encounter him eventually. When we do, he's going to be gunning for us."

"Fair enough."

"You're armed?" Bolan asked, knowing the answer.

"Of course," Delaney said quickly. She shot him a look. "Glock 23, .40 caliber."

"It's a start," Bolan said. "What can you handle?"

"Name it," Delaney said. "Every department has its gun nut. I guess I qualify."

"Good," Bolan said.

They traveled in silence for a while. Finally, Delaney said, "So. Are you going to tell me what outfit you're really with? Or were with?"

"No."

Delaney sighed. "All right, Cooper. Keep your secrets. I don't care, as long as I get Gareth Twain."

"Fair enough," Bolan echoed. "It sounds personal."

"It is." She looked at him again, then back to the road. "Gareth Twain killed someone who meant a great deal to me. The Bureau wants him, but I want him more. I've stayed on the case for that. Hell, I've stayed in the Bureau for that. I'd have left otherwise. I had to call in a lot of favors and burn all my bridges to do it. They wanted me off and I had to fight to stay with it, fight to get justice. Can you understand that?"

"Yes," Bolan said. "I can."

"I have to get him, Cooper. I have to bring Twain in, or take him down. I know your investigation of Trofimov is the real focus—"

"It's not an investigation from my perspective," Bolan interrupted. "It's intelligence. Intelligence for a war, a counterwar, against whatever terrorist operations Trofimov is running."

That silenced Delaney for a moment. "I…" she started. "I know that's more important, both objectively and to the people you work for or with," she said. "But,

Cooper, I've tracked him for so long… I can't fail. I *can't*. Twain can't be allowed to go on killing. That's my reason for being here. Do you have a problem with that?"

"Not if it doesn't get in my way," Bolan said. "I can respect your motives, Agent Delaney. I really can. Just stay with me. I've done this sort of thing before."

"Why am I not surprised?"

"Follow my instructions. Don't question me, especially under fire. I'll do right by you. The rest will fall into place."

"All right," Delaney said, considering that. "Understood."

"Be aware that there is a very good chance we'll encounter resistance," Bolan warned her. "At the previous target, there was a noncombatant work force guarded by paid security personnel. These were professionals unafraid to pull triggers first and ask questions later, if at all. After I neutralized the shooters on-site, I had to contend with a sizable backup force. Whether they were called by one of the guards before or during the firefight, or whether they were responding to some silent alarm triggered by a security breach, I don't know. It doesn't matter. What does matter is that we may encounter the same, or worse, here. When the gunfire starts, don't waste time trying to negotiate. The people we're dealing with aren't interested in talking."

"Understood," Delaney repeated.

They rode the rest of the way in silence. Finally they neared the target address. Bolan didn't have to tell Delaney to park the SUV some distance away, down the block. The neighborhood was closely packed and industrial. Corrugated-metal buildings and concrete-block boxes dotted with windows and metal overhead doors were stacked two and three deep. There was only a little traffic on the roads leading into the industrial area, which made sense. They weren't on a major traffic artery and the only people coming and going through here would be, largely, those with business somewhere within.

They stepped out of the SUV, and Bolan once again shielded his movements by turning his back outward within the open door of the truck. Delaney, close enough to see inside from the driver's door, did a double take as Bolan checked the 93-R machine pistol.

"That's a serious piece of hardware," she said.

"You're not the first to say so," Bolan replied with a grin. When he checked the Desert Eagle, however, making sure a round was chambered, Delaney tensed up.

"What?" he asked.

"That cannon." Delaney nodded at the weapon. She press-checked her Glock as she spoke, using the shelter of the vehicle's interior as Bolan was doing. "Twain carries one just like it. Or he did."

"Good to know," Bolan said. He opened the rear door and grabbed the duffel bag. The Tavor with its grenade launcher, loaded magazines and bandolier of 40 mm grenades was secure and waiting.

"I have a little something in this bag for you, too," Bolan said as Delaney fell in step next to him. "Heckler & Koch MP-5 K. I had it sent with my rifle as a backup, just in case."

"An MP-5 is your idea of backup?" Delaney scoffed. "What's the primary piece?"

"Israeli TAR-21," Bolan said. "Heard of it?"

"I have, but I've never seen one." Delaney looked wistfully at the duffel bag.

"You'll get your chance," Bolan promised. He removed the MP-5 from the bag and handed it to Delaney, with several loaded spare magazines. The woman shoved the magazines in her belt and put the MP-5 under her jacket, somewhat awkwardly. She looked around as she did so, but the street was empty.

"Uh, Cooper?"

"Yeah?"

"Why are we just walking down the street toward the target?"

"Role camouflage," Bolan told her. "Act like you belong and nobody notices you. We're just a couple out on the town."

"In the industrial district."

"Different couples, different tastes."

"You must be a hot date," Delaney joked.

Bolan stopped as they neared the target address. It was a large prefabricated steel building, a metal box with a high, curved roof that looked like countless other similarly cheap structures. "This is it," he said. "Take the back. Assuming there's a doorway, cover it. Wait for me to come to you. If it hits the fan, stay low and cut down anything headed out that's armed and not me."

"You don't want me to come in and back you up?"

"Better if you don't," Bolan said. "One less variable to keep track of."

"If there are armed security personnel inside just waiting to blow the head off any intruder," Delaney pointed out, "how does walking in the front door help?"

"It worked at the last target."

"Didn't you say they tried to kill you?"

"Well, yes," Bolan said. "That's why it worked."

Delaney muttered something that might have been a curse. She hurried around the side of the building, still awkwardly hiding her MP-5. Bolan watched her go. He was going to like Delaney.

Walking up to the front doors of the facility, he tried the handles. The steel doors didn't budge. There was no signage on the front of the building, no indication of who or what operated within. He looked left, then right, then removed a small, lightweight pry bar from the canvas war bag slung over his shoulder. This he inserted into the gap between the two doors, pressing with gradually increasing force.

Something inside the lock mechanism gave with a metallic twang. The Executioner eased the door open and looked inside.

Nothing.

The corridor bore several dusty material safety warning signs. Bolan ignored these, but the smell was harder to ignore. The corridor reeked of chemicals that reminded him of a rendering plant, only more metallic, more…synthetic.

He passed a series of offices divided by translucent plastic partitions, then reached another set of metal fire doors. The chemical smell was growing even stronger. These doors weren't locked. Bolan pushed the left-hand door wide, dropping his duffel silently on the opposite side of the door. He withdrew the Tavor and its bandolier of grenades, throwing the bandolier over his shoulder.

"Vince, that you?" A voice came from around the corner. The interior walls were drywall partitions, the type of permanent cubicle-style walls that could be cheaply thrown up and painted within a prefab building like this. Sound echoed off the walls, making it difficult for Bolan to place the location of the speaker. When the unseen man called for Vince again, Bolan responded.

"Yeah. Over here."

"Vince?" The voice was even closer. "You don't sound—"

"No," Bolan said as the man rounded the partition and almost ran into him. "I don't."

"Oh, Jesus." The man wore a protective chemical suit. His hood was off, however, revealing a sallow, hangdog face under a mop of dark brown, curly hair.

"Wrong again," Bolan said. He gestured with the deadly, futuristic-looking Tavor. "Don't scream. Don't make any sudden moves. Nod once if you agree."

The man nodded.

"Name," Bolan ordered.

"Jason," the man said. "Jason McKinley."

"Well, Jason," Bolan said, "we're going to take a tour of the facility. You're the tour guide."

"Hey, man, that's fine. Only, we don't have any money here."

"This isn't a robbery," Bolan told him. "Quickly, now. How many people in this facility?"

"What? No, man, nobody. Just me and Vince are here, cleaning up."

"Cleaning up what?"

"I'll show you, man." McKinley gestured toward the plastic sheets covering the corridor opening behind him. "But you might want to put on a mask. It's still pretty rank in there."

"We won't be staying long," Bolan ordered. "Now move. Try anything and I'll shoot you."

"I believe you, man." McKinley nodded vigorously. "Come on, this way."

Bolan followed his reluctant guide through the plastic sheeting. The room beyond was clearly the width and height of the building itself; no partitions carved up the large, open space. There were several metal vats arrayed along one side of the space. From these, conveyor belts led to a series of ramps that terminated in chutes at the opposite wall. There were also small track cranes running across the upper portion of the open space. Scoops attached to chains dangled from these, rusty and mute.

"Where do those chutes go?" Bolan asked.

"Outside, of course." McKinley looked at him strangely. "You don't have any idea what this is, do you?" He gestured. "Why would you try to rob the place if you didn't know?"

"I told you," Bolan said evenly. "This isn't a robbery."

"Then what?"

"You tell me," Bolan said. "What do you do, and why are you here?"

"I'm with MatrixEarth," McKinley said, as if that explained everything. When it had to have been obvious to him, from the look on Bolan's face, that it didn't, he went on. "We're an environmental consulting firm. Vince, that's my project manager, and I are assessing the environmental impact of the operation here."

"What was the operation?"

"That's a good question," McKinley said. "I thought maybe you knew and were coming to knock over your former business partner, the crook."

"Explain," Bolan said, growing impatient.

"We're under contract from the county," McKinley said. "The company that owned this joint pulled up stakes about a week ago. Left behind a big mess, and a lot of permits unfiled and unpaid for. The landlord about had a heart attack when he saw this place after they were done with it and let their lease drop."

"Who was leasing the building?"

"Beats me," McKinley said. "Vince talked to the landlord, but I don't think they got to that level of detail. Say, uh, could you stop pointing that gun at me?"

"We'll see," Bolan said. "Show me what you've found."

McKinley, looking irate but still afraid, moved to one of the vats. There were several pieces of metal lying on the floor. He picked one up in his heavily gloved hands.

"See this?" McKinley said. "This is a piece of stainless steel. There are a couple of leftover boxes of these test pieces in a storage room off the main corridor." He pointed with his free hand, back the way he and Bolan had come. His feet echoed on the stained, poured-concrete floor as he went to the conveyor belt. He picked up another piece of metal. "Do you see the color difference?" He held up the two ingots of steel.

"Barely," Bolan said.

"It's faint, but it's visible." McKinley dropped the first piece of steel. It hit the concrete and rang like a bell. Bolan briefly scanned left and right, mindful of a trick. McKinley caught the soldier's movement and froze.

"Hey," he said. "I'm just making a point, here."

"Go on," Bolan said.

McKinley held the second piece of steel in both hands. He twisted and the metal snapped like a piece of balsa wood. He dropped the pieces to the floor. They made much less sound when they struck the concrete.

"That," McKinley said, "is a piece of the same metal. Each test piece is marked with a serial number. Those two bars started life as the same batch of stainless steel."

"Yet one of them now breaks like it's nothing."

"You see why the county is freaking out," McKinley said proudly.

"I'm afraid I don't."

McKinley made a disgusted noise. "Don't you understand, the vat's there, the assembly line here. The hoist's up there. It's a line for soaking and shipping a product."

"Soaking and shipping. You mean whatever they were bringing in was being treated with chemicals that can do...that—" Bolan nodded to the broken steel bar "—and then shipped out through the chutes?"

"Seems to have been," McKinley said. "Look, I don't know who you are or why you've come armed for World War Three, but I'm guessing you really aren't a disgruntled business partner looking for payback."

"No," Bolan said. "Justice Department."

"*Justice* Department?" McKinley blanched. "It's worse than I thought. Originally the county called us in because they were worried about groundwater contamination. The folks who skipped out on the building owner's lease also weren't too concerned where they dumped waste chemicals, you know? The owner was worried about the value of his property, which is why he called the county, but when their assessor took one look at the mess here and out back, they called us in. Vince and I have been crawling all over the place ever since. But I had no idea this was so bad it was federal."

"It might be," Bolan said, being deliberately vague so McKinley could supply an explanation with which he would be satisfied. "Let me have one of those pieces of treated metal."

"Sure," McKinley said. He handed over half a broken bar.

"I want your contact information," Bolan said. "Someone will be contacting you to find out what you've learned about the chemicals stored here. I'll also want the building owner's name. You'll get a call asking you about what you've told me, and whatever other data your company has on hand regarding this site. I suggest you answer the questions asked without argument."

"Hey, man, no problem." He started shrugging out of

the top half of his suit, letting it dangle from its built-in belt cinched around his waist. From his shirt pocket he produced a business card. "Here you go. Everything you need to contact us is there."

"All right," Bolan said. "Point me to the rear door."

"That way," McKinley said, jerking his thumb over his shoulder.

"I was never here," Bolan said without looking back.

McKinley let out the breath he had been holding. The Executioner heard the exhalation from across the room.

At the rear of the building, he found Delaney and another man in a chemical protection suit. They appeared to have been chatting amiably.

"Vince, I presume," Bolan said.

"Yeah," Vince said. He was younger than McKinley, with stronger features, and a crew cut that didn't hide his male pattern baldness very well.

"You didn't shoot him," Bolan said to Delaney.

"He wasn't armed." Delaney shrugged.

"Uh, what's going on here?" Vince said, taking in the assault rifle Bolan carried.

"Your friend inside can fill you in," Bolan told him. He nodded at Delaney. "Come on. We've got to move." He pulled out his secure satellite phone and hit the speed-dial button that would connect him to Grimaldi.

"Yeah, Sarge?" Grimaldi answered on the first ring.

"Have the Farm arrange for a local courier to make a pickup," Bolan said. "I've got something they need to analyze."

"Will do," Grimaldi said. "Any fireworks?"

"None so far," Bolan said. "It looks like we got here after the party was over."

"It happens, Sarge," Grimaldi said. He closed the connection.

"So far," Delaney said, looking up at the soldier, "this hasn't been the hot date I was expecting."

"Don't worry," Bolan told her. "We're just getting warmed up."

CHAPTER SEVEN

Delaney drove the rental truck—a GMC, this time—that had been waiting for them at Little Rock National Airport, also known as Adams Field. They were headed to the central business district, a little more than two miles from the airport. Grimaldi had wished them luck after spending most of the relatively short flight from Kansas flirting with Delaney. The legendary womanizer had made little headway, but Bolan suspected he hadn't really been trying. It wasn't that the pilot's most wolfish days were behind him; it was simply that he was too polite to push it with a government agent assigned as liaison or observer to Mack Bolan's mission.

Bolan had placed a call to the Farm the moment the Gulfstream V's landing gear had cleared the tarmac in Kansas. Price had filled him in without preamble.

"We traced the phone number you got from the Patriotism Riders," Price had told him. "Bear had to guide his people through some pretty tricky maneuvers, but eventually we pinned down the real source. The call was electronically routed and disguised, but we ran it down to an executive training facility in Little Rock, Arkansas."

"Executive training," Bolan repeated.

"Supposedly," Price said, "it's the sort of place corporate managers, CEOs and other executives go to learn leadership skills, play teamwork games and take seminars on the latest management theories."

"All right," Bolan said. "Can it be traced to Trofimov?"

"Not so far," Price told him, "but I would recommend penciling it in on your schedule anyway. We've traced the real owners of the facility. The virtual money trail leads back to Security Consultants and Researchers, your trigger-happy security outfit. Once we had the in, Bear started cavity-searching their networks. This SCAR's employment rolls reads like a who's who of soldiers of fortune."

"Mercenaries training business executives?" Bolan asked.

"There's more," Price said. "We've established a link between disbursements made through SCAR to its management, and payments wired to accounts held by Gareth Twain."

"So Twain runs SCAR, and SCAR is…what, cover for Twain's mercenaries in the United States?"

"Looks that way," Price said.

"If they're with Twain, and Twain is working for Trofimov, I'm going to stir them up in a big way with each new hit. They're going to keep coming at me," Bolan said. "Can Hal move on them from Washington, maybe have their assets seized and their people rounded up?"

"He's trying." Price sounded frustrated. "But it's slow going. It's going to take some time to get official buy-in at a level high enough to permit us to roust that many individuals on American soil, preemptively and without legally obtained proof."

"I understand," Bolan said. "Let me know if that changes. You received the contact information I transmitted, for this environmental consulting firm?"

"We're following that up now," Price confirmed. "I'll get an analysis of the sample you forwarded as soon as possible."

"There's no chance we were wrong about that site?"

"No," Price said. "It was definitely a Trofimov holding."

"Then we've got serious trouble there," Bolan said. "Whatever they were working on, they've already done it, and we need to know what and why. What about this 'massacre,' any news on that yet?"

"Still nothing, Striker." Price sounded almost apologetic. "At least three different government agencies are working on enhancing the tape, to no effect yet. No one has turned themselves in within the military. The call has gone out to find the people responsible, but so far they're ghosts."

"Which makes me wonder," Bolan said.

"You and me both," Price agreed. "Trofimov's news network has gone to an overdrive cycle, playing highlights from the video every twenty minutes during its regular news clip recaps. Protests have broken out in several countries, and two different American allies have come under halfhearted attack. No casualties there, and in both cases the attackers were repelled, but it's a disturbing trend. Basically, Striker, there's nothing we can do about that right now."

"All right. What about the 'transmitter' components in Cedar Rapids?"

"Analyzing now," Price said.

"The locals bend Hal's ear for him?"

"The usual amount," Price said. "They weren't happy

to have bodies and burning vehicles show up on their doorstep, but Hal handled it. As for the data you recovered and the components you sent to us, Aaron says he's onto something but wants to confirm it first. We'll let you know as soon as he's ready. He does have some good news for you, though."

"I could do with some."

"Once we knew to target them," Price explained, "it was apparently very easy for Aaron to compromise SCAR's computer network. We've got you a gold ticket through the front doors. They'll be expecting you."

"You're certain?"

"Absolutely. Walk right in the front."

"That hasn't gone so well in recent memory." Bolan's grin was not visible through the phone, but he imagined Price could hear it in his voice. "All right, Barb," Bolan had told her. "I'll stay on it."

"We'll do the same."

"Striker out."

Now Bolan and Delaney were headed downtown to the location of this training facility, which was apparently far more than it seemed. Delaney had been quiet on the flight to Arkansas, apart from her conversation with Jack Grimaldi. Bolan didn't pry. Her thoughts were her own, and he imagined he knew what she might be thinking. No doubt she was thinking about finally getting revenge on Twain. Justice for a dead FBI agent, and personal revenge for Jennifer Delaney, were one and the same, in this instance. Bolan understood the twin drive for revenge and justice only too well. And, after Twain was down or dead, what then?

There were no easy answers to such questions, beyond the very obvious. Good men and women often became obsessed with bringing violent criminals to justice. All those men and women could do, once justice was done, was live with the actions taken to that point— and go on with own their lives as best they could.

"This is it," Delaney announced. She pulled the SUV into the entrance to the training center's parking lot. There was a metal gate bar across the entrance, next to a small guard hut. The bored guard within looked at them.

Delaney rolled the window down. Bolan leaned over her and said through the open window, "Cooper."

The guard checked his list and, without a word, pressed a button to raise the gate bar. Delaney drove through to the parking garage below the building.

"I can't believe that worked," she said.

"It hasn't worked yet."

They were already wearing their weapons concealed. Bolan left the Tavor in its duffel, safely stowed in the rear of the vehicle. He had his 93-R and Desert Eagle under his field jacket, of course. They had rigged a shoulder harness from which Delaney had slung the MP-5 K, ready to go under her right arm. It was covered by her jacket, but only barely.

The two of them crossed the parking garage. There was an elevator with only one button on its control panel. Pressing it brought them to the lobby of the training center. A man in a uniform emblazoned with the SCAR logo sat behind a raised reception area. His right hand wasn't visible under the desk.

"Can I help you?" he asked. His tone was cordial, but his eyes were hard. Bolan pictured him curling his fingers around the grip of a handgun, or perhaps a submachine gun, mounted somehow behind or under the desk.

"Cooper," Bolan said. "I believe you're expecting me."

The guard visibly relaxed. "Yes, Mr. Cooper," he said, double-checking his computer terminal. "We have

you in Room 1C. It's just down that hall to your right."
He pointed. The lobby opened up into corridors leading
left and right. The floors were polished, but not made
of expensive stone. The decor itself was reasonably con-
temporary, but nothing ostentatious. This place, like the
assembly plant in Cedar Rapids, looked from the
outside to be just what it was. Bolan, however, wasn't
fooled.

They passed several rooms that were obviously set
up for training classes. In one, a human-shaped
dummy sat in a room whose floor was padded with
vinyl mats. It would have been a fairly typical physical training setup except that the dummy was dressed
in a cop's uniform. Posters on the wall were emblazoned with slogans. These ranged from the benign—
Murphy's Laws of Combat—to the disturbing, such
as a list of misleading statements to give police in the
event one was caught in the commission of a violent
crime.

Another room they passed held tables with what
appeared to be bomb-making materials. An easel near
the front of that room contained detailed instructions for
assembling a pipe bomb.

"Cooper," Delaney whispered, "this is a full-on
terror camp!"

"Possibly," Bolan said. "But remember, if this SCAR
outfit is owned by Twain, it's both more and less than
that. More, because of the scale of the viciousness that's
likely to come out of this, with Twain heading it. Less,
because Twain has no political affiliation and thus no
cause to support. These aren't terrorists. They're mercenaries in the truest sense of the word. Well, mercenaries in training, from the look of this place."

"It's like a finishing school, then," Delaney said.

"Put the final polish on the worst human beings money can buy."

"Something like that, yes."

They walked down the hallway, taking in another couple of classrooms bearing obvious course work in mayhem, until they found Room 1C.

"Delaney," Bolan said quietly, "it's about to get hot. Hit the deck when the shooting starts."

"Like hell," she swore.

As they entered Room 1C, Bolan was only too aware of the eyes on them. At least two dozen men, all of them looking like experienced hardcases, lounged, sat or stood around the room, which held a whiteboard, a desk at the front of the room and several rolls of folding metal chairs.

The men in the room were all wearing SCAR uniforms.

Bolan ran his experienced eye over the trainees. They didn't all appear to be ex-military, but many of them had the look—though, of course, that was no real test. He'd certainly seen plenty of exceptions within the armed forces. Still, it was obvious he and Delaney had just walked into a room full of sharks. He looked down on the desk. Someone had printed an agenda for the class, if that's what this was. Bolan picked it up and looked at it.

M. Cooper, it said. *Guest lecturer, Understanding Counterterrorist Tactics.*

So. Kurtzman had a sense of humor, after all.

There was a chance these men weren't hired murderers. There wasn't much of one, but it was possible. Mack Bolan wouldn't take an innocent life, nor even the life of a not-so-innocent man if that man wasn't a combatant. He crumpled the paper and tossed it into a nearby wastebasket. Then he looked out at the crowd of hardcases watching him intently. More than a few eyes were on Delaney, of course; she would turn heads among any crowd of men, much less these.

"Good afternoon," Bolan said. "I have a confession to make. I'm not really here to lecture on counterterror tactics."

The trainees didn't stir. No doubt they thought this a clever opening to a lecture on that very topic. Bolan reached into his jacket and withdrew the Beretta 93-R, flipping the selector switch to 3-round burst as he did so. "This is a machine pistol. I'm a government agent, and all of you are under arrest."

Delaney, without prompting, pulled her jacket back and brought the MP-5 up and on target. She slapped the weapon's cocking knob for emphasis.

"What the hell?" one of the trainees muttered. "That ain't cool, pointing guns at us."

"Isn't it?" Bolan asked. "I imagine a few of you have pointed guns at others before. Now, I want to know everything you lot know about Gareth Twain. I also want to know what you can tell me about Yuri Trofimov. And I'd like to know exactly what goes on in this facility. Once we've got that all squared away, you can list for me the various crimes for which many of you are sure to be wanted. Now, who wants to start?"

"Up yours!" one of the men shouted. "Kill 'em both!" As he dragged a revolver out from under his shirt, from the waistband of his pants, Bolan triggered a 3-round burst that sent him toppling in his folding metal chair.

Chaos erupted.

Bolan broke left, Delaney right. The men in the chairs in front of them started going for concealed weapons of their own. Bolan charged their ranks, putting himself into the thick of the action, to Delaney's consternation. She leveled her MP-5 but couldn't take a shot, as Bolan waded into the enemy.

A bullet seared the air in front of her face. She ducked behind the desk, slamming her shoulder into it hard, rolling it over.

Bolan had no intention of seeking cover. He pulled the Desert Eagle left-handed and fired both guns into the crowd of mercenary trainees.

Moving among the men like the grim reaper, he played them off one another, throwing brutal kicks into knees and stomping ankles when one of the enemy got too close. As he turned and moved among the writhing crowd, he put bullets where they were the most lethal. First one, then another, then another man went down with a slug in his brain, as the Executioner danced a deadly dance among the armed killers.

Delaney could only wait from cover as her partner took apart the killers.

Bolan used the crowd's numbers to line up the enemy, instinctively putting himself at the "corners" of the engagement. It was a tactic as old as time, a method of warfare Sun Tzu had written about centuries before. By stacking his enemies on top of one another, the ones in the back had to fight their way through the ones in the front, or their weapons were ineffective. Bolan, firing into the stack of enemy from without, had no such problem. He dropped man after screaming man. The enemy gunfire never once came close to him; the shooters simply never got that organized. Delaney, using the desk for cover, actually was in greater danger, as the shooting from the knot of confused gunmen threw hot lead in random directions. Her desk caught a few rounds before the gunfire finally died down.

She came up from behind the shelter of the desk, weapon ready. Bolan was standing over the dead men, a gun in each hand.

An alarm began to sound from speakers set within the walls.

The door burst open to reveal a man firing a shotgun on the run, the same man who'd been at the front desk. Bolan, without even ducking, tracked the man with the Beretta and pumped a 3-round burst into the center of his chest. The gunman was dead before he finished falling.

"Holy shit, Cooper," Delaney said, looking at him.

Bolan shot her a look. "Come on," he said. "They'll be on the move. Let's see what's beyond this classroom." He headed for the exit in the far wall.

No sooner had he thrown open the door than a blast of automatic gunfire sent him diving back into the room.

"They're in the corridor beyond," Bolan said.

"Now what?"

"Pretty basic tactic, really," Bolan said. He retrieved a pair of flash-bang grenades from his war bag and pulled the pins. "Open the door for me."

Delaney pulled the door open, dodging another blast of gunfire. While it was open, Bolan chucked the flash-bang grenades down the hallway. He could hear them bounce against the walls and down the carpeted corridor.

"Close your eyes, open your mouth and cover your ears!" he ordered. He had just enough time to see Delaney obey before he squeezed his own eyes shut. The actinic blasts of the flash-bangs came a moment later.

"Go, go, go!" Bolan ordered. Then he was up and into the hallway, tongues of flame discharging from the barrels of both guns as he marched down the corridor and brought death to the mercenaries opposing him. Delaney followed, covering him as best she could.

First one, then a second man in a SCAR uniform broke cover from around the corner of the next leg of their journey. Bolan shot the first man in the face. The second was craftier and dropped low to the floor. He triggered several shots from a Glock before Delaney put a .40-caliber bullet from her own handgun into the man's forehead.

"Good shooting," Bolan had time to say. Bullets chewed up the carpet to either side as they were forced back again.

"We can't be far from the exit," Bolan said, calculating their travel through the building based on their point of entry and the distance covered. "They're fighting awfully hard."

"Because we've seen what goes on in here!"

"Maybe," Bolan said. He waited for a break in the shooting, then threw himself into the hallway beyond. Both arms extended, he fired in two directions, catching the mercenaries off guard and sending them to their final rewards. He landed on the floor with a bone-jarring thud, rolled out of it and came up on his feet once more, pistols practically smoking.

The corridor terminated in direct access to the parking garage's upper level.

"Come on!" Bolan said. "This must be what they were protecting."

On the other side, the air stank of diesel. Bolan took in the cargo van parked to one side of the doorway. He reloaded and holstered the Desert Eagle, then reloaded the Beretta, using it to lead the way as he checked the van.

"Clear!" he said after checking the driver's door.

"Clear," Delaney said. "But, Cooper, you'd better get back here and look at this!"

Bolan joined her. The rear doors of the van were open, where they'd been left. Inside the van were dozens and dozens of clear plastic bags full of crystalline powder.

"Is that what I think it is?" Delaney said. "My God, Cooper, do you realize how much is here?"

"Crystal meth," Bolan said.

They both heard the squealing tires on the level below.

"No time!" Bolan shouted. He jumped into the back of the van and ran forward to the driver's seat. Delaney leaped in after, managing to pull the rear doors shut as Bolan turned the key that had been waiting in the ignition. The big van roared to life. The soldier sent it fishtailing backward and around, scraping the concrete barriers on either side of the parking garage.

The van bounced and sparked as Bolan sent it roaring too quickly down the ramp leading to the next level. When there was nothing to see there, he pushed the pedal even farther to the floor. The monster engine roared, dragging the ungainly cargo van even faster through the depths of the garage. They bottomed out at the enter-and-exit level, spraying a shower of sparks and taking several thousand miles' worth of wear off the underside of the vehicle.

They were moving just fast enough to see another vehicle, a Chrysler minivan, flying out the exit to the parking garage. Bolan pressed the accelerator to the floorboards and pursued, the vehicle punching through the metal gate bar as it descended.

The chase was on.

CHAPTER EIGHT

Delaney fought her way into the passenger seat despite the swerving and bucking of the stolen van. She pulled on her seat belt.

"Cooper, are you trying to get us killed?"

"Just hang on," he told her.

Traffic was heavy. The Chrysler swerved in and out among the other vehicles, trying desperately to lose its pursuers. Bolan knew he would have to walk a fine line. Push too close, and whoever was in the fleeing minivan might decide to start shooting. While it was unlikely that such resistance would slow Bolan in tailing the other vehicle, it would endanger innocent lives, and that he couldn't tolerate. So he held back, maintaining just enough distance between himself and the other vehicle so that the enemy driver would feel like he was gaining ground.

"What are we waiting for?" Delaney asked. It wasn't a challenge; she was simply curious, knowing enough about pursuits of this type to understand Bolan was applying strategy.

"We need some combat room," Bolan said. "When

we hit an open stretch, somewhere without a lot of people around, I'll try to pit them. We've got the heavier vehicle. We just need to get up on them before they spray the neighborhood with a lot of unnecessary gunfire."

Delaney nodded.

They kept up the chase for several more minutes. Traffic was getting thinner as they moved away from downtown. It became obvious that the minivan's driver was heading toward an on-ramp to the nearest multilane highway.

"Okay," Bolan said. "Now. On the ramp."

"Are you sure this will work?"

"We've got weight on our side," Bolan said. He floored the accelerator.

The van shot forward, its big engine roaring in response. The soldier clipped the rear side panel of the minivan as the smaller vehicle began negotiating the curve of the ramp. The maneuver spun the Chrysler around and planted it against the guardrail.

One man wasted no time, throwing open his door and jumping out, then from the ramp to the road below it. He stumbled from the high drop, but was up again and running, apparently uninjured.

"Dammit," Bolan said. He brought the van to a screeching halt on smoking tires and squealing brakes. He pointed. Another man was trying to climb out the open window of the passenger door. The door itself was jammed shut against the concrete butting against the on-ramp.

"I'll get him," Delaney said. She ran for it, Glock drawn.

The man Bolan chased was full-on sprinting across the multilane highway, trusting to luck or fate to get him through. Bolan poured on the speed, narrowly missing being struck by an eighteen-wheeler as he gave chase. He couldn't simply shoot the fleeing man; he needed him alive to answer questions, if at all possible.

Judging the distance, Bolan caught him in a flying tackle. The two men rolled over each other, and when they stopped, Bolan had a knee in the man's chest and his Beretta in his face.

"Move and you die!" Bolan said forcefully.

The Asian in the SCAR uniform began to swear in Mandarin. Bolan knew just enough of the language to recognize it for what it was.

"English," he said. He squinted through the cloud of road grit raised as another eighteen-wheeler roared past. The driver honked the truck's air horn. It was possible he thought Bolan was up to no good and was even now calling the cops. Or he might have been expressing his support for what appeared to be an act of citizen-dispensed justice. Then again he might just have been expressing his disgust at narrowly missing two people rolling around on the shoulder of a major highway. Bolan didn't know and didn't care, though it was possible he and Delaney would have local law enforcement on the scene before too long.

"Die, Yankee," Bolan's captive said in heavily accented English.

"Haven't heard that one in a while," Bolan said.

The man the Executioner presumed to be Chinese stared at him with undisguised hatred. Bolan rolled him over and secured his wrists with plastic riot cuffs from his war bag. Then he pushed him up against the concrete barrier on the side of the road and frisked him. The man was carrying absolutely nothing, not even a gun. His pockets were empty. Very likely, the man had left a gun back in the van.

"Come on," Bolan said, dragging the man to his feet. "We've got a long walk back."

When Bolan and his prisoner finally reached the on-ramp, a marked police car was rolling up. A second was already parked, and the officer was setting out road flares.

"Did you call them?" Bolan asked his partner, dragging the Chinese prisoner forward.

"No," Delaney said. "Somebody else must have. Passing driver or trucker."

"My thoughts exactly." Bolan nodded. "What have you got?"

"Body," Delaney said. "You're a bad influence on me, Cooper. I'm racking up quite the body count today." She pointed. The dead man was still half in, half out of the front passenger window. A snub-nosed revolver lay on the pavement nearby. "He pulled a gun as I approached and took a shot at me. I had no choice."

"No," Bolan said, "you didn't." He jerked his chin toward the nearest police officer. "They give you any static?"

"No," Delaney said. "I told them it was an FBI matter and showed them my ID. That was enough, for now."

"It probably won't stay that way," Bolan said. "But one problem at a time. Let's take this character back to the training center. We can question him there and mop up."

"Did you forget the pile of bodies you left behind?" Delaney asked. "That place will be crawling with cops, coroners and detectives, if anyone called in the gunfire."

"Yes," Bolan said, "but that can't be helped, and my boss spends enough time making nice with the people whose jurisdictions I fight my way through. I want to make sure we haven't missed anything, and I have enough clout to hang on to the prisoner until we're done with him."

"It's your show," Delaney said. "Oh, Cooper, I checked this vehicle." She pointed to the minivan. "It's full of meth, too. The sheer quantity of it is amazing. I've worked joint drug task forces with the DEA before. This is just an astonishing amount. We're in regional distributor territory here, not just individual or even organized crime at the dealer level."

"Which raises more questions," Bolan said. "Why would Twain's mercenary training facility also be moving vast quantities of meth? Is it the source of their funding? And where was this meth headed, if it was being loaded and moved?"

"Maybe they were accepting a delivery, rather than making one," Delaney said. "We don't know the vans were going to leave with the meth aboard. They might have just been convenient when your boy and mine—" she indicated the dead man "—decided to make a run for it."

"Possible," Bolan said, "but not likely. This quantity of meth would take a year to move in a city this size. I think it's more likely it was outgoing to some other point in a network. As you said, a distributorship."

Delaney sighed. "Nothing's ever easy, is it, Cooper?"

"No," Bolan said. He removed his phone and snapped pictures of the dead man and the prisoner, then transmitted them to the Farm.

They were able to secure the cops' permission to leave the scene, after Delaney gave one of the officers her card and assured him the Bureau would take full responsibility. Bolan, even as he overheard that, wasn't so sure the FBI would be happy to sign on to this mess, but if Delaney wanted to use her influence and her employer to make the mission easier, so much the better.

The Chinese man became agitated and violent when

they tried to put him in the cargo van. Bolan finally struck him on the back of the head with the butt of his Beretta. The dazed man offered little resistance as Bolan rolled him into a rear corner of the van and secured his feet with a plastic zip tie.

"I really, really want to know what agency you're really with," Delaney said, watching him.

"Yeah?" Bolan grinned. He didn't rise to the bait.

They got back to the training center just in time to be stopped at a police cordon. As Bolan had predicted, the locals weren't happy about the mess inside, but Bolan made good use of his Justice credentials, and Delaney was there to back him up with her FBI identification. Finally the officers in charge allowed Bolan and Delaney to pass with their prisoner. Bolan had Delaney guard the man in an upper-floor conference room while he swept the building, moving from room to room. Apart from gear and demonstration aids that made it obvious the men training here were learning nothing about business and everything about being successful mercenaries and even terrorists, Bolan found nothing of interest and, more important, found no more SCAR personnel lurking. He joined Delaney in the conference room.

"There's nothing here," he said. "At least, nothing I can find quickly. My people haven't found anything in their computer network, the same one they breached to get us in, or they'd have told me by now. All we have is him." He nodded to the prisoner.

The man sat uncomfortably in an office chair, his hands still strapped behind his back. The strap securing his feet had been cut when they pulled him out of the van, to allow him to walk.

"Are you going to…?"

"No, but he'll think I am," Bolan said quietly. "Follow my lead."

Bolan grabbed a folding chair from a stack against the wall, reversed it and sat in front of the prisoner. "We have a problem."

"I tell you nothing," the prisoner said in English.

"I don't doubt that," Bolan said. "But we still have a problem. This facility housed quite a few armed men who had no compunctions about killing two people at the blink of an eye. On top of that, you're running a significant crystal meth distribution operation. You remember the crystal meth, don't you? It was in the van you were driving, and in the one you left behind."

The prisoner stared balefully but said nothing.

"It's clear to me," Bolan said, "that we've happened on something that is rapidly developing." He made a show of looking at his watch. "Now, we're on a very tight schedule." He reached for the butt of his holstered Desert Eagle. The rest of the script was fairly standard. He would draw the gun and bluff his way through, making the prisoner believe he was ready to put a bullet through the man's forehead.

His secure phone began to vibrate. The pattern was the urgent ring the Farm rarely used. It meant, essentially, "Drop everything and answer now."

"Watch him." Bolan nodded at the prisoner. He stood and walked across the conference room, putting the phone to his ear. "Cooper." Using his code name would signal that there were others listening to his side of the conversation.

"Striker," Price said, "we got an identification from the picture you sent. Your prisoner is Kam Chen, twenty-eight. He's Chinese special forces. Declared dead two years ago in a training accident outside of Beijing."

"Special forces?" Bolan said quietly. "No indication of mercenary work?"

"None," Price said. "From what we can tell he was a decorated soldier before his 'death.' We want to know what a Chinese special forces operative is doing mixed up with your hired guns in the United States."

"Yeah, me, too," Bolan said.

"Cooper," Delaney interrupted, calling to him. "There's a puddle of blood on the floor."

Bolan's head whipped around as he put two and two together. "Delaney! Get back!"

Kam Chen launched himself from the chair, tackling Delaney and knocking her to the floor. Blood streamed from his wrists; he had worked his way ruthlessly through the riot cuffs. He threw a series of rapid-fire kicks, beating Delaney back and down, doubling her over.

The Executioner waded into the fray.

It would have been simplest to shoot the man, but he was still the only link they had to the operation here. Bolan threw a brutal front kick at the man's midsection, but Kam slipped it easily, bashing Bolan's leg away with a double forearm block of his own. Bolan pressed the attack, but while he was more powerful, Kam was faster. The Chinese operative managed to grab Bolan's wrist and apply a wristlock. The Executioner went with it, allowing his adversary to take him to the floor and attempt to wrap one leg around him. As the man was focused on his maneuver, Bolan drew the Boker Applegate combat dagger from his waistband.

Kam suddenly froze. The wide, double-edged, spear-point blade was pressing against his neck.

"Now," Bolan said, "let's talk. Delaney!"

"Here," Delaney said. She was breathing heavily

but standing. She had drawn her Glock and was covering Kam.

"Keep our friend honest while I get him arranged." Bolan removed a small first-aid kit from his war bag and wrapped the Chinese operative's bloody wrists. Then he guided the man to the folding metal chair. Double-cuffing each wrist and ankle, Bolan secured the prisoner to the chair. "All right," he said to Delaney. "Grab me another chair." He sat on the replacement chair that Delaney brought him, facing the Chinese agent.

"Cooper here," he said, raising his phone to his ear once more. "Still with me?"

"Striker!" Price said, sounding worried. "Are you all right? What happened?"

"Nothing we couldn't handle," Bolan said. "I need to know something. Does Kam Chen have a family?"

There was a pause while Price checked the intelligence file. "Yes, according to this. Parents. Two brothers. A niece and nephew."

"Good," Bolan said. "I'll be in touch." He closed the connection and gave Kam a hard look.

"You work for the Chinese government," Bolan said. It wasn't a question.

Kam glared but still said nothing.

"We know that you were special forces in China until you were reported dead. Now you're here, mixed up with Twain's mercenaries. Care to explain that?"

"I tell you nothing," Kam said again.

"I don't think you understand," Bolan stated. He took no particular pride in the threat he was about to make, but it was necessary. "You'll quite probably die before you tell me anything if I try to force you, but I'm not holding the threat of death over you. I'm threatening you with *life*."

Kam looked at him, confused.

"How does a big, televised show trial sound to you?" Bolan said. "I can think of a few networks who would love to have an international spy scandal to take some ratings from their competition's lead story. I know the people in government who can make that happen. Imagine the reaction of your handlers back in China, Kam, when your face is splashed all over the news. 'Chinese operative found working with drug runners in American city.' I bet we could work that into quite the thriller, if we tried. The Chinese government sponsoring traffic in illegal drugs in the United States. Your nation needs the United States and the rest of the West, Kam. Can it really stand another scandal? Let's run down the public relations list in the last few years. Allegations of human rights violations at the Beijing Olympics, including the quick cover-up of the stabbing death of an American visitor during the Games. The exporting of tainted consumer products. And not so long ago, the holding of an American aircrew as de facto hostages while their high-tech plane was dismantled and reverse-engineered."

"You… What do you want?"

"I want you to tell me where those drugs were going," Bolan said, "or I'll have you remanded to federal custody and I'll make sure everyone in both our nations knows what you were doing here. The shame of being caught would pale in comparison to being the pawn at the center of a political chess game, wouldn't it? I don't imagine the people you work for would be too happy about that."

"What you offer me?"

"Tell me about the drugs, and I'll have you quietly taken into custody. Your people will never know you talked. They'll probably assume you're dead. And I won't insult you by asking you to tell me why a Chinese special forces soldier is working with hired-goon trash in middle America. I know you'll die before you tell me that. So take the deal. It's the only one you'll get."

Kam stared at Bolan, then at Delaney. He licked his lips.

"Think about your family," Bolan warned.

"All right." Kam shook his head. "All right. I tell."

Bolan thought he heard Delaney trying and failing to suppress a sigh of relief.

"Where are the drugs manufactured?"

"Some here. Some not here. I do not know. Shipments come. We send by van to airfield, then to Houston."

"Houston?" Bolan repeated. "The drugs are going to Houston?"

"Yes," Kam Chen said, sounding tired. He rattled off an address. "Hangar. Near main airport. Private owned. Drugs shipped there. End of my involvement."

"I have to make another call," Bolan warned Delaney. She aimed her Glock at Kam's head, taking a step away from the man. She was taking no chances this time.

Bolan dialed the Farm. Price answered his scrambled, multiple-routed call on the first ring.

"Cooper," Bolan said again. He recited the address Kam had given him. "This address isn't on the target list. Can you check it for me?"

"Looking," Price said. He heard her fingers flying over a keyboard, then Kurtzman's deep voice rumbling in the background. Stony Man's mission controller and the head of its cyberteam continued to confer for a few minutes before Price came back on the line.

"Yes," she said. "It's a minor piece of property owned by a holding company that is in turn owned by Trofimov's network. A private hangar attached to the George Bush Intercontinental Airport. The airfields in Houston comprise the fourth-largest airport system in the country, Striker, and the sixth biggest worldwide. It would be a great place to hide in plain sight. We didn't flag it before because there was nothing particularly unusual about activity there. There was no indication that Trofimov even uses the site regularly. A man of Trofimov's wealth typically maintains several locations like that, to give his private jet a place to stage and be serviced."

"All right," Bolan said. "Contact Jack, give him the data, tell him to get us ready to fly to Houston. Also, I need you to bury Kam Chen in the system somewhere. Have the locals pick him up and transfer him to federal custody however you see fit, but then make sure he finds his way into one of our black-ops holding facilities pending a prisoner transfer, or something."

"Can do," Price said. "But why?"

"Just keeping my end of the bargain," Bolan said. "Cooper out."

Delaney was looking at him strangely. She shook her head.

"What?" Bolan asked.

"You're a complicated man, Cooper," she said.

CHAPTER NINE

"All right, Sarge." Grimaldi's voice came over the intercom from the cockpit. He affected a Texan drawl. "Welcome to Houston, good buddy." In his normal speaking voice, he said, "I'm taxiing us now. We're as close as we can get. I've arranged for a shuttle from the terminal. It's just transportation. They don't know you. They think the both of you are real hot VIPs, in fact. The shuttle van will take you across the airfield and drop you not too far from the private facility you're targeting."

"Good work, Jack," Bolan said. He was once again cleaning and reloading his weapons.

Delaney had spent the flight staring out the window, occasionally looking over at him thoughtfully. "You heard?"

"Of course." Delaney nodded. She made sure her MP-5 was tucked under her jacket and her spare magazines prepared. "I didn't realize I was signing on for war when I pressed to be assigned to this Justice operation," she commented.

"You signed on to get Twain, didn't you?"

"You know I did."

"Then you signed on for war. That's what justice is, Agent Delaney. In this world, in these times, if you seek it, you're accepting and pursuing total war."

Delaney had nothing to say to that.

They picked up the shuttle as planned, Bolan carrying the duffel bag containing his Tavor, once again bearing his canvas war bag over his shoulder under his field jacket. As they rode, Bolan produced a pair of earbud transceivers.

"These are communications units," Bolan said. "Very small, very powerful. Difficult to jam and almost impossible to pick up unless you know exactly what frequency you're looking for. Put it on and we'll be able to stay in touch. It'll pick up a whisper and anything louder, but will cut out automatically above its decibel threshold."

"So I don't have to worry about you blasting away in my ear when the shooting starts," Delaney said.

"Exactly."

"What do you think we're walking into here, Cooper?"

"Hard to say, beyond the obvious," Bolan said. "A meth ring, maybe. Could be we've found a portion of the illegal empire behind Trofimov's legal assets. Maybe that's why the man has so many facilities that seemingly do nothing, yet generate funds on the books. Could be wide-scale money laundering for a criminal enterprise."

"If that was all it was, would you be involved?"

"No," Bolan said. He saw no reason to lie. "That's something any number of government agencies, including yours, could look into. This is more. Trofimov is mixed up in the killing of American soldiers and their mourning families and friends. He's using the corpses of American soldiers and their families to wage some kind of political war. I want to know exactly what he's doing and I want to stop him."

"You want him as bad as I want Twain."

"Worse."

Delaney nodded. "I think we understand each other."

"We do."

When they were in sight of the target hangar, they stepped off the slow-moving shuttle van while it was still moving. Walking briskly, they covered the distance to the hangar and skirted the side, angling for a secondary entrance. Their luck held; no one saw them or challenged them.

Once in the shadow of the hangar, Bolan pressed himself against the wall on one side of the door, indicating that Delaney should do the same. He tried the door with one hand, but it was locked.

"Figure it's wired for an alarm?" Delaney asked.

Bolan gave it a casual glance. It was an old, rusted steel door; there were no telltale signs or contacts that he could see. That meant exactly nothing, but it was a risk they would have to take. "Not sure," Bolan said. "We're going to find out." He set the duffel bag on the cracked pavement by the door and removed his pry bar from his war bag. The door's lock gave easily. The hinges didn't even squeal as he eased the heavy metal door aside.

The soldier looked inside through the crack in the doorway, conscious of Delaney pressed close behind him.

"Holy shit," Delaney said from over Bolan's shoulder.

The hangar boasted two rows of what appeared to be U.S. military Hummers. There were racks of M-16s and stacks of crates, many of which appeared to be munitions. The hangar looked, to Bolan, like a typical staging area for a military operation.

There was nobody in evidence.

"Come on," Bolan said.

They entered the hangar. Bolan crossed the floor to the first stack of crates and checked it. He found ammunition—and in one crate, disposable M-72 LAW antitank rockets. Delaney rejoined him after checking the perimeter of the hangar. "There's all kinds of stuff here, Cooper. Weapons, food, spare parts for the vehicles. I found one crate full of uniforms." She held up a BDU blouse. The digital camouflage was of the most recent Army pattern. As she looked over Bolan's shoulder her eyes widened. "Are those what I think they are?"

"Yeah." Bolan nodded.

"What is all this?"

"The hardware, the uniforms…it's all government issue," Bolan said. "Come on, let's keep looking."

The rear of the hangar was divided into office space. Here, they encountered another locked door, this time with a simple hasp and padlock. Bolan's pry bar made quick work of it. Inside the otherwise empty room, they found stacked, impact-resistant plastic crates.

"These are designed to withstand being dropped by parachute over a target zone," Bolan explained. He pried open the seals on the topmost crate.

The container was filled with bags of white powder.

"Check one of those others," he instructed, handing the pry bar to Delaney.

She followed his instructions and whistled when she looked inside her container. "Cooper, I think this is more crystal meth."

"And what I've got here," Bolan said, drawing the Boker knife, poking its needle-sharp tip into one of the plastic bags and examining the residue on the blade, "appears to be heroin."

"I don't get it," Delaney said. "Why fill a private hangar with military gear and drugs? Have we stumbled on a covert U.S. operation?"

"Unlikely," Bolan said. "If it was, my people would know."

"I envy 'your people' their certainty," Delaney said.

"Come on," Bolan said. "Let's get out of here." He was taking photos with his phone as he moved, catching the various pieces of equipment and staged supplies.

"Right behind you," Delaney said.

As they neared the side entrance, they heard the truck pulling up outside.

"Back, back," Bolan said. "Toward the front."

"No good!" Delaney whispered. The main doors to the hangar were parting; a charter bus was waiting outside to pull in. "We're caught between them!"

"Then we've got only one option left," Bolan said, pulling the Tavor from the duffel bag and letting the bag fall.

Delaney nodded, swallowing hard.

They moved into the center of the hangar, among the rows of vehicles and stacks of crates. The bus was disgorging men who wore U.S. Army uniforms like the ones Delaney had found. More uniformed men, carrying OD metal ammunition boxes, were coming in through the side entrance.

"Hey!" someone shouted. "Who the fuck is that?"

"They're armed!" another voice called.

"Justice Department!" Bolan shouted. "This is a lawful government action! Place all weapons on the floor."

The first gunshot chipped the concrete near his feet.

"Go!" Bolan shoved Delaney away from him. They couldn't afford to bunch up; they had to stay mobile, maintain distance between each other.

Delaney's MP-5 chattered.

A wall of sound and barely perceptible heat closed in around the Executioner.

To be surrounded by people firing automatic weapons was an experience no soldier quickly forgot. The deafening wall of noise, the muzzle blasts, the ejected shells, the smell and the smoke of the discharged rounds… It was an almost overwhelming experience, especially the first time. Mack Bolan was no green recruit. He had been in the midst of battles as fierce as this one many times, but still, it was like walking into hell, and there were no guarantees he would be walking out again.

The enemy closed in, firing M-16s they had been carrying with them, though in a few cases the uniformed enemy grabbed at the staged crates to obtain weapons or ammo. Bolan could only process these fleeting images as he ran from point to point among the staged supplies, using the crates and trucks for cover.

Bolan fired a grenade from the Tavor's launcher into the far end of the hangar. When it exploded, several men screamed. Blasting away on full-auto, the Executioner worked his way from crate to crate, nearing the one he sought. The enemy fought with no real cohesion, no real plan, and Bolan wondered about that. It was obvious they were not U.S. military personnel; no Army unit would have attacked him like that. They'd have taken him prisoner and demanded to see his credentials if they hadn't believed him.

There was a darkening suspicion coiling in Bolan's gut that was increasingly hard to ignore.

When he found himself once more at the crate with the LAW rockets, Bolan broke cover long enough to grab one, open it, heft the weapon and take aim at the bus near the front of the hangar.

"Delaney," he said, knowing her earbud transceiver would pick up his words.

"Yes?"

"Get down. Brace yourself."

"I was afraid you were going to say that."

Bolan pressed the firing switch and the antitank rocket streamed across the space between the Executioner and the bus. When it hit and detonated, the warhead ripped open the large vehicle as if it were made of aluminum foil. The blast was staggering. Several of the armed men nearby were thrown flat, stunned. Shrapnel shredded several more.

The soldier pushed himself up and into the carnage left in the rocket's wake. He walked quickly among the scattered gunmen. Each time a man recovered enough to point a gun at him, Bolan triggered a burst from the Tavor. He began working his way to the back of the hangar, heading toward Delaney.

"You all right?" Bolan asked.

"I think I'm deaf," Delaney complained. "But yes, I'm all right."

"Resistance?"

"Minimal, now," Delaney said. "I shot a couple who were still trying to get a bead on me."

"I'm coming to you," Bolan said.

"I'll meet you."

They reached each other perhaps two-thirds of the way back. A stream of 5.56 mm bullets briefly sent them in two directions, as they both triggered return fire. The man who had been lying in wait for them took rounds in the chest and throat. He toppled back behind the fallen stack of crates he had been using for cover.

"We've got to check the trucks carefully," Bolan said.

They approached the line of Hummers, two of which

had been damaged in the fighting. The rear of each vehicle was covered with a tarp, which meant anything and anyone could be in the cargo area. Bolan removed two incendiary grenades from his war bag, which he handed to Delaney.

"Start from the far end of the line of vehicles," he whispered. "Plant these in the first and third truck from the end. I'm going to do the same from the other side. Be prepared to move fast."

Delaney looked grimly at the bombs but said nothing. She nodded.

Pulling the pins and watching the spoons spring free, Bolan sprinted to first one Hummer, then another from his end of the line. He dropped the incendiaries into the target vehicles.

"Holy shit, grenade!" someone in the second vehicle shouted.

Then the bombs blew.

The initial flash bursts of the grenades were followed by an orange-red glow as the Hummers became sudden infernos. A pair of burning, screaming men leaped from the rear of the nearest vehicle. Bolan put a mercy round into each one, sighting carefully with the Tavor's red-dot scope. Farther away, Delaney blasted a shooter who charged out of the Hummer with his clothes on fire and his M-16 spitting rounds.

"Back off, back off!" Bolan called. He wanted to put some distance between them and the flaming trucks. "Take no chances. Shoot anything that moves. We've broken them, but there's no telling how many could be hiding."

Delaney said something that Bolan took to be assent. He circled around, coming up on the opposite side of the hangar. Moving quietly, the sound of his footfalls easily masked by the crackling of flames and the distraction of the billowing smoke filling the hangar, he wasn't surprised when he almost stumbled on one of the gunmen. The man had a cell phone to his ear.

"I said we're under attack!" he was saying. "Is Stilson in the air? Good, send him in hot! Dammit, now! It's a goddamned army! Come in now! If it's moving, it's probably not one of us, so blow it away! Did you hear me? I said come in now!"

"Put it down," Bolan ordered as he approached the man, who was sitting on the floor of the hangar with his back to the stack of bullet-pocked crates.

The gunner, who Bolan could now see had a piece of shrapnel in his leg, looked up at him.

"You're too late, you son of a bitch." He grinned through his bloody teeth. His lip was badly split; he'd apparently taken some shrapnel to the face, too.

"Who is Stilson?" Bolan asked.

"You're about to find out."

"What is this operation?" Bolan said. "You're not with the military."

"Figure that out on your own, did you?" The man smiled. His hand moved behind his back.

"Don't," Bolan said.

The Beretta M-9 came up in the man's hand. Bolan pressed the Tavor's trigger and put a single 5.56 mm round in the man's brain.

"Delaney!" he said. "I found one, apparently in contact with the outside. We're about to have company, nature unknown."

"It's here!" she said. "I'm at the front. You'd better come see this!"

The soldier left the dead man behind and ran for the

main doors of the hangar. They were intact and even now sliding apart on automatic, motorized pulleys.

"Can we stop the doors?" Bolan said.

"I don't see any controls on this side," Delaney said.

Bolan assessed the situation and then brought the Tavor to his shoulder. Sighting carefully, he put a burst into each of the pulleys connected to the doors. They stopped with a six-foot gap between them. Through this gap, Bolan could see the tarmac outside.

"You weren't kidding," he said simply.

A pair of heavy canvas-covered troop trucks, painted in Army camouflage rumbled toward them from across the tarmac. In the sky above, the trucks were being paralleled by an OH-6 Little Bird helicopter. The nimble little Loach, as it was often known, sported a pair of rocket pods and what appeared to be a light machine gun on one landing skid.

"Grab me two more of those rockets," he said simply. "No, make that three." Delaney hurried to obey.

If the drivers of the trucks realized they were hurtling toward their doom, they didn't show it. Bolan calmly opened another LAW when Delaney handed it to him.

"Watch my back," he said. "There's no telling how many of them are still circulating inside here, holding back or playing possum."

"Understood." Bolan looked at her carefully. She was shaken, but holding together. That was good. He'd had no doubts about her mettle.

The Executioner shouldered the LAW, aimed and pressed the firing switch.

The first rocket impacted the center of the lead truck's grille. Parts of the engine and cab flew in every direction. Bolan threw down the spent launcher and picked up a second LAW, popping it open and firing as quickly as he could shoulder the weapon and acquire the target. At the last moment, the driver of the second truck swerved, and the rocket hit the tarmac close by. The explosion rocked the vehicle onto its side, where it squealed and groaned to a halt in a shower of sparks.

The Little Bird began spraying the front of the hangar with its machine gun. Bolan was forced back, clutching his third rocket. Rounds chewed through the hangar roof leading up from the doorway, raising a billowing cloud of dust and spraying fragments of the hangar floor.

Bolan raced toward the rear of the hangar. "Come on!" he said. Delaney fell into step with him, pausing only just long enough to drill a wounded gunner who was pulling himself up from behind one of the fallen crates, aiming an M-9 in their direction. The man's head snapped back and he fell without a sound.

"Nice shooting," Bolan said. "Come on, we've got to work our way around and out while they're still confused."

"That chopper—"

"I know. It's a problem. Watch yourself. Whoever these people are, they're playing for keeps."

The chopper shifted position, angling over the roof of the hangar. Bolan looked up.

"Move!" he shouted. He shoved Delaney forward, forcing her to run. The Loach dipped its nose and began strafing them from above. Machine-gun bullets roiled the air behind them, and Bolan and Delaney ran for their lives.

"Break now!" He shoved Delaney again, this time to the left, and threw himself to the right. The rain of hot lead passed them by as the chopper pilot's forward momentum carried him beyond their position. They had only seconds. The pilot would wheel around for another run in less time than it would take them to think about doing it.

Rounds continued to rain down, punching holes in the roof of the hangar. Bolan was impressed by the pilot's ruthlessness. The Loach's jockey had no way of knowing if any of his comrades were alive and kicking inside, but regardless he was gunning for the intruders with all he had.

It was too bad for him that all he had wasn't going to be enough.

Bolan deliberately ran for the shattered, half-open main doors of the hangar. "Stay low and back there," he said, his transceiver carrying his words to Delaney despite the din of the chopper and its machine gun. It was only a matter of time before the chopper pilot realized he was making no headway. When that happened, he would back off to a safe distance and fire his rockets, keeping the Little Bird clear of the blast that was sure to result, especially if some of the munitions in the hangar detonated. Bolan didn't intend to give him the chance.

The smoking ruins of the two wrecked trucks were billowing flame and clouds of oily black smoke, which was drifting in through the front of the hangar. Bolan saw figures moving amid the smoke. The survivors from the trucks were regrouping and moving in.

The chopper buzzed the ground troops, the pilot hot-dogging to show he had the situation under control. Then he steadied, gained altitude and dipped the nose of the aircraft once more.

This was it.

The Executioner stepped into the middle of the ruined hangar doorway. He dropped the Tavor, brought the LAW to his shoulder, compensated for the angle and pressed the launcher's firing switch.

In the last moment, the pilot saw his mistake. The nose of the helicopter turned a fraction of an inch. The antitank rocket slammed into the curved snout of the helicopter, detonating after it bored through to the engine compartment.

The Loach blew apart in a spectacular fireball, spraying the men on the ground with flaming pieces of wreckage. One man was impaled by a fragment of the main rotor. He screamed his last with the blade of the rotor jutting from his chest.

Bolan retrieved his rifle, crouched and began firing methodically into the remaining gunmen. The red-dot scope of the Tavor was perfect for the distance and the conditions. He acquired each target in turn, his surgically placed 5.56 mm rounds dropping each man with a head shot here, a throat shot there. The Executioner burned through one magazine, reloaded quickly and fired out half of the next.

He stopped when the enemy stopped moving.

Bolan stood. Delaney was crossing the hangar, MP-5 up and ready, staring at the carnage that had erupted so suddenly, the war zone that had enveloped them so abruptly. He looked at her, and back at the dead men on the tarmac. The tail rotor of the Loach had embedded itself in the paving near the doorway. It was bent and scorched. Not far from that, an M-16 rifle had been discarded or propelled. The plastic stock was shattered.

In the distance, the sirens of emergency responders and, most likely, law-enforcement vehicles wailed in chorus. That, too, was very familiar. Bolan had heard it many times before.

"Holy Mother of… Cooper," Delaney breathed, standing next to him. "What have we done?"

"What we had to do," Bolan said, looking at her. "And there'll be more. Count on it."

Delaney could only stare at him.

CHAPTER TEN

"You don't want to know," Hal Brognola said over the secured, scrambled satellite phone transmission, "just how many people have tried to take a bite out of me in the past few hours."

"You always say that," Bolan said evenly, standing in the wreckage of the hangar, watching the locals and a small army of Feds crawl over the scene. They had been cooling their heels at the scene here for at least four hours, while emergency crews put out fires and bodies were tagged, bagged and hauled away. Delaney was answering another batch of questions, speaking to several different uniformed and plainclothes law-enforcement officers. The group included several representatives of the Transportation Security Administration, as well as the DEA. The TSA officials, in particular, weren't pleased. Delaney's FBI credentials were getting a real workout, just as Bolan's Justice ID had. When word had come down that someone in Wonderland was pulling strings hard on behalf of one "Matthew Cooper," the scrutiny directed at Bolan had cooled somewhat. The soldier had seen this sort of thing play out before. Government power rolled downhill, and nobody involved wanted to get in the way of an avalanche.

"You're good at what you do," Bolan said. "You always manage to calm them down or fend them off."

"Maybe, Striker," Brognola said, "but I'm starting to wonder if I'm getting too old for this." Bolan pictured him looking out his office window in Washington, D.C. "As usual, and thanks to the authority I *do* have, I've managed to keep the TSA from throwing you in the deepest, darkest hole they've got and throwing away the key," the big Fed went on. "I had to involve the Man, Striker, and he's none too happy. A full-scale war in proximity to one of the nation's largest airfield complexes? The TSA guys are beside themselves, and I can't say I blame them."

"You know we take what comes, Hal," Bolan said. "We walked into this. And you know as well as I do that he—" the soldier paused, knowing Brognola would understand Bolan spoke of the President "—wants these people, too."

"I know." Brognola sighed. "And the sheer scope of it… If I had time to be horrified, I would be."

"About that," Bolan said. "I'm assuming you didn't call just to complain about the burden of leadership." Brognola, as head of the Sensitive Operations Group, had irons in a lot of different fires in Washington and beyond. He had been chewing antacid tablets and the ends of unlighted cigars for as long as Bolan had known him, at least in his capacity as leader of the nation's most covert antiterrorist security forces. That was a lot of weight on one man, even with the excellent team at the Farm to support him. Bolan never forgot that. He was very grateful for Hal Brognola and what the man did for the Farm, for the Executioner and for the United States of America.

"No," Brognola said. "In a moment I'm going to transfer you to Barb at the Farm. She's got information for you, including some vital data dug up based on your firefight there." Bolan had snapped digital pictures of as many of the dead as he could, sending them to the Farm for analysis. They'd had good luck so far in identifying Bolan's enemies using worldwide facial-recognition databases cross-referenced with the usual law enforcement sources, including Interpol.

"All right," Bolan said.

"Before I do," Brognola put in, "I have something you need to know. Aaron's computer taps picked it up when it hit the TSA's no-fly list, but I got direct word from Homeland Security maybe twenty minutes before, based on my previous inquiries on your behalf. For some months now, Homeland has been tracking aliases believed to cross-check to known terrorists. The alias database they've built is painstakingly compiled using an algorithm I don't pretend to understand. It compiles points of compatibility and overlap based on everything from credit-card use to traffic-camera sightings, compares these to reports of the target fugitive's whereabouts and speculation on his or her travel patterns." Bolan could almost see Brognola waving his hand dismissively. "The details aren't important. Aaron has expressed an interest in getting his hands on it, in fact, to take it apart and see if it does anything better than his own programs."

"Okay," Bolan said. "And?"

"And a man identifying himself by an alias thought to correspond to Gareth Twain boarded a commercial flight to New Orleans only hours ago," Brognola said. "Homeland alerted me, and I overrode the TSA alert. Twain will have reached his destination before you do."

"I'm going to New Orleans?" Bolan asked.

"Barb has the details. We wanted to make sure Twain got where he was going to avoid tipping him off. Chances are he's already on edge. This is a good break for us, Striker."

"If Twain surfaces," Bolan agreed, "and if I can bring him in, he could provide direct intel on Trofimov's operation, from the inside."

"You think he'll talk?"

"There's no reason he wouldn't," Bolan said. "You've read the same profile I have. The man has no loyalty to anything or anyone. If I make him an offer, promise him some deal, he'll roll over."

"I've got a lot of pull," Brognola said, "but Twain's wanted by multiple foreign and domestic agencies, or he will be. Once word gets out that he's in the bag, they'll be coming out of the woodwork to lay claim and try to extradite. I don't know what offer you can make him that I'll be able to back up."

"It doesn't matter," Bolan said. "He'll agree knowing it isn't likely we'll be able to do much. Once he's caught he'll have no better option. His type will cut whatever bargain can be had, on the hope of breaking custody later. He's tough, and he's slippery. He won't fall to pieces out of fear even once he's in custody."

"You may not be able to bring him in," Brognola pointed out.

"I know," Bolan said. "And you know I do. If it was that easy, you wouldn't need me."

"True," Brognola said. "But if Twain dies, you lose your in to Trofimov."

"There are other inroads to Trofimov," Bolan said. "I'll take one of those. If I can get to the bottom of what he's doing that much sooner, fine. If I can't, we'll keep shaking the tree until he falls out of it. Either way, Twain will be out of the picture, and that's a worthy goal. Once I'm finished with him, I intend to give Delaney first call on his disposition, if we do take him alive."

"That will make the Bureau happy," Brognola admitted, "as that was why they bought into this in the first place."

"'You pays your money,'" Bolan quoted.

"'And you takes your chances,'" Brognola finished. "All right, Striker, I'm transferring you to Barb."

"Got it."

Price came on the line a moment later. "Striker," she said. "Still in one piece?"

"Yes," Bolan said, looking around at what was left of the hangar, "but not for lack of trying. Hal's had a rough time of it, I gather."

"I think we can shed some light on this," Price said. "We've identified several of the dead men. All are employees of SCAR, this Security Consultants and Researchers company we've managed to trace back to Twain. All of them have histories as soldiers for hire, too. They're a pretty rough bunch. I'll transmit the various rap sheets to you if you'd like some light reading for Jack's plane."

"Probably unnecessary," Bolan said. "I'll take the highlights."

"It was the VIN numbers on the trucks that gave us our lead," Price said. "Each of those trucks, including the Humvees, is registered to, of all things, an outfit in Dallas that provides prop guns and heavy equipment to the movie industry. They have offices in Nevada and on the East Coast, but their main headquarters is in Dallas. The owner is a local boy and a military buff. Fellow named Ed O'Donnell. I talked to him this morning."

"What did you learn?"

"I e-mailed him some of the photos," Price said, "and he was able to pick out a pair of them who paid for the trucks and arranged for their delivery in Houston. He said they told him it was for a huge military picture, an epic that was to film overseas in Tunisia. He said they ordered all kinds of military gear."

"The M-16s they were firing weren't props," Bolan said.

"No," Price said, "we've traced those to a shipment stolen from a military armory in New York last June. They've apparently been circulating ever since. The volume you've recovered accounts for almost the entire shipment, so that's something."

"Yeah."

"The other equipment comes from a variety of sources. We're still working on tracing the heavy weapons, like the LAW rockets you found. I won't be surprised when we find out they're stolen, too, or maybe imported from a foreign export target."

"Hooray for the international arms market," Bolan said. "The gift that keeps on giving."

Price didn't comment on that. "We did in-depth background checks on both men who talked to O'Donnell," she said. "We managed to turn up a common-law wife for one of them, a woman living outside of Chalmette, Louisiana. The Bureau lent us a local tactical team and I had them pay her a visit. They knocked on her door an hour ago."

"Casualties?"

"None," Price said, "but she came apart easily when they made it clear she was staring down federal conspiracy charges. Rolled right over on her man, who apparently was pretty free with the pillow talk before he had the misfortune of meeting you today."

"Go on."

"She was a little hysterical," Price said, "but reading through the report just flashed to me by the head of the tac team, it looks like this sizable contingent of SCAR mercenaries was headed to Afghanistan."

"Disguised as Army troops?"

"Yes," Price said. "Striker, it's… Well, it's hard to believe. According to the woman, the plan was to impersonate a military unit and perpetrate a series of atrocities in Afghanistan. They were planning on going over and sowing discord. It's a common enough tactic. You recall the incidents of terrorists dressed as Iraqi police, hitting Iraqi civilians and law enforcement from within and using the disguises to confuse their motives."

"Yeah," Bolan said grimly. "I remember." To attack an enemy from within, disguised as one of him, was also nothing new to the Executioner, who had used the method more than once in righteous strikes against enemies both foreign and domestic. That didn't make this any easier to accept, however.

"So Twain's people were going to show up on foreign soil pretending to be U.S. troops, and further bloody the U.S. military's image," he said, his jaw clenching. "With Trofimov's news network pushing that video, they'd have a damned easy time of making it stick, too. But how can a rogue military force operate in-country? Wouldn't they be stopped before they got there, or discovered once they were there? We have a sizable force over there, but it's not *that* big. There's no way the charade could work long enough for them to do what they're trying to do. Is there?"

"There might be," Price said. "We're examining the logistics. Aaron has been pulling his hair out. The long and the short of it is that they would have to have orders.

Forged orders, or orders procured under illegitimate circumstances. We're looking into that now, but we don't have anything yet. It doesn't seem likely that a blatant forgery would hold up for long, especially not as word was passed up the chain of command."

"Who could procure the orders behind the scenes?"

"Officially, it's a relatively limited number of people," Price said. "Realistically, any government or military official with the right connections could manage it."

"Which means..." Bolan began.

"Which means," Price stated, "our list of possible traitors runs the gamut from senators to congressmen to anyone with an office at the Pentagon, and then some."

"Wonderful," Bolan said. "Whoever's in on it is also party to smuggling large quantities of illegal drugs. The DEA estimates the street value of the meth and heroin stockpiled here to be in the millions, for whatever that estimate is worth."

"That's if they intend to sell it on the other end of the pipeline," Price said.

"I'm guessing a good chunk of it will find its way to markets that serve our troops," Bolan said. "No doubt a lot of it is a profit center used to finance Trofimov and SCAR's operations, but given what we've seen of him so far, I'm willing to bet he's looking to addict as many of our people as he can. More harm, more death and more problems for the military. This is a serious operation, Barb, just the drugs by themselves. It's got to be coming from somewhere. I'd like to find it and plug the hole, if I can. If Bear's team can sleuth out anything that will help me, I'd appreciate it."

"We'll stay on it," Price promised. "Let me know if you uncover anything else. You're good to go for now, at any rate. We've got Jack staged on the closest available runway."

"I can probably hitch a ride to him with one of the locals," Bolan said, surveying the various law-enforcement officers moving around him. "There are enough cruisers and blacked-out sport utility vehicles here to ferry an army. Hal says I should feel strongly motivated to head to New Orleans to intercept Twain."

"Yes," Price said. "It's not publicized, given SCAR's only semilegitimate status, but we've found what we believe is Twain's main office."

"That raises a question," Bolan said. "The SCAR personnel I've encountered have been only too happy to shoot first. How can Twain be running this outfit on American soil? They'd be guilty of mass murder time and time again."

"The same way Twain's managed to steer clear of government operatives and stay out of custody," Price said. "He's very smart. The company itself has been very low-profile until recently. We've managed to trace some of SCAR's clients, and they run the gamut. Basically, anyone with enough money to afford hired muscle, and enough enemies to need a private army, has used SCAR from time to time, but they've managed to stay free of incidents. The company itself has no overt ties to Twain, of course. We had to dig that up, and some of the things Aaron did to bring it to light are pretty far from legal."

"So there would have been no reason in particular to go after SCAR before now," Bolan said. "What's changed? All of a sudden they're operating on a slash-and-burn policy, staging fully armed groups of paramilitary soldiers to engage in violent acts of treason abroad. That's no small change."

"No," Price said. "Which means something big is happening."

"Trofimov," Bolan said. "The link is there. Twain is working for Trofimov, who in turn is following his agenda toward whatever his ultimate goal is supposed to be. It makes sense. If he's behind the military murders, and the protests, and the assassinations hiding *behind* the protests, it all comes together. He's ramping up his activities, taking bigger risks, going for bigger body counts. It can't just be coincidence that this supposed massacre has fallen into his lap, upping his ratings while it hurts U.S. military interests."

"Exactly."

"I'm tempted to go straight for Trofimov's throat," Bolan said, "but Twain's just as big a piece of the puzzle, and if I don't try to take him where we know he'll be, I may not get another chance. Trofimov can wait a bit longer."

"Hal and the Man would appreciate it if you found whatever there was to find before you cut a path through him," Price said.

"I know," Bolan said, "and I intend to. The roots of this conspiracy go deeper than we thought. Trofimov is a violent sociopath who hates America. He's got a private army working for him, and it looks very much like he's tried to send that force in active opposition to the military interests of this nation. That alone earns him a bullet. But there's more here. I can feel it. I have to know, so I can stamp this out for good, every part of it."

"Understood, Striker," Price said. "Are you ready for the rest of the bad news?"

Bolan paused. "There's more?"

"We have an analysis on the tech you recovered from

Cedar Rapids," she said. "Striker, have you heard of Warlock?"

"It's an IED protection system, isn't it?"

"Exactly," Price said. "Warlock is a jamming system that blocks nonmilitary frequencies. It's used to protect vehicles from roadside bombs. As you know, the typical improvised explosive device is detonated by a wireless signal, often generated by a wireless phone. Warlock prevents those signals from getting through, creating a safe zone around the device. Mounted in a vehicle, it generates this jamming field and protects the personnel in that vehicle. Since the implementation of Warlock in Iraq, there has been a significant decrease in casualties caused by IEDs targeting our convoys and patrols."

"The transmitters in Cedar Rapids were for use in roadside bombs?" Bolan said.

"They're radio-frequency triggers," Price said, "which could be used to detonate any explosive device, yes. But these are special. Unlike the types of explosive devices that Warlock and similar systems protect against, these modulated-frequency triggers cannot be blocked through conventional means. Striker, these are tailor-made terrorist devices. Imagine what would happen if these made it into the hands of insurgents in, say, Baghdad. Convoys we thought were protected would start to get hit again, and there would be little we could do about it."

"It would be a major blow to our military interests, in other words," Bolan said. "Not to mention making us look helpless."

"Sounds familiar, doesn't it?"

"Trofimov's goals are becoming very clear to me," Bolan said. "The metal samples?"

"Still under analysis," Price said.

"Let me know when you get confirmation," Bolan said. "I have a theory."

"Will do," Price said.

"All right," Bolan said, reaching down to shoulder his duffel bag with one hand. "I'll pick up Agent Delaney."

"Good hunting, Striker," Price said.

"Thanks. Striker out."

CHAPTER ELEVEN

The trip from Louis Armstrong International Airport had been the usual mess, but Gareth Twain didn't care. He pulled his slouch cap down low over his eyes and did his best to ignore the noise and the chatter of the taxi driver. He'd have enough crap to deal with once he got to the office. There was no point borrowing trouble until then.

He'd caught hell from Trofimov, of course, for leaving. Bad enough that the Russian's hobby of knocking over funerals had taken a turn for the worse, with the death of one of the Kwoks. But then word had reached him that the Cedar Rapids plant had been knocked over, and with it several of his erstwhile employees.

That was bad.

This bad news was followed by an urgent call from Little Rock. The training center had been raided, and he'd lost a fair number of men—both the veterans running the place and the new class of trainees.

That was worse.

It was as he'd feared. The operation was compromised, and the people working them over seemed to know just where to find them, just where to hit them.

He was at a loss to explain it. They'd always been so careful; their computer networks were certified hacker-proof, and there were multiple levels of redundancy protecting the true identity of SCAR's ownership. There was no direct connection between the assembly plant and the training center, except for the fact that SCAR operatives worked in or protected both sites. Even that fact was protected by a few companies-within-companies on the books. Still, Gareth Twain had never believed in coincidence or luck. It was time to put out the cat and lock the doors, as his mom used to say.

Trofimov had given him hell over that, too. First the Russian hadn't wanted to meet; he'd considered it a waste of his precious time to have to stop and confer with the hired help. Of course, only Twain was, technically, a hireling. Mak Wei was another sort of fellow entirely. Twain understood the broad strokes of the link between Mak and Trofimov, of course. You'd have to be deaf, dumb and blind not to get it. Still, something about Mak made him nervous. He accepted the "security personnel" Mak sent him because Trofimov ordered him to do so, and paid a premium for Twain's cooperation in the matter. That didn't mean Twain trusted those fishes any further than he could throw the inscrutable lot of them, however. He was happy to use them to bolster his guns, yeah, but he wasn't about to put any of them in positions of authority. They were all expendable, as far as he was concerned.

There were a damned lot of them, though, and it had made possible the sheer enormity of the SCAR-backed operations Trofimov was paying Twain for.

No, what worried Twain about Mak Wei was that he hadn't invited Mak to the meeting, and to his knowledge, Trofimov hadn't called the Chinese operative, either. Mak had simply shown up when Twain did. That meant the Chinese were monitoring Twain, or Trofimov, or both of them, and the Irishman simply didn't like the idea of being under that magnifying lens. It made him think he was about to be burned.

His headquarters in New Orleans was the last line of defense for his organization, which was scattered throughout the country for good reason. There was no specific need for some of the facilities to be located where they were, rather than centralized, except that keeping them so far apart and operating them remotely gave Twain yet another level of plausible deniability. It also meant that, if something went wrong—as was only too clearly the case now—he could be hundreds of miles away, in a position to deny everything should it ever come to actual questioning, and poised to flee the country if it came down to that.

His false identities weren't likely to hold up to much in the way of direct interrogation. So far they had held. He'd had a near moment there, at the airport, when he thought he'd finally made a mistake in flying commercially. There had been some looks exchanged among the screeners he hadn't liked, staring at their terminal and then at him. It had been nothing after all, though, and they'd let him pass. Still, that had worried him quite a bit. It might be time to retire the name under which he currently traveled, pay his usual source for a new passport and a new lease on life.

He dropped his gear bag inside the doorway to his private office, sighed and made his way to the washroom through the small access corridor behind his desk. There, he gave himself a long, hard look in the mirror, splashed water on his face and shook himself like a dog.

Something was wrong and he couldn't get the sense

of it. He couldn't shake a sense of foreboding. Someone just walked over your grave, he thought. That's what Mom used to say. And that was the feeling he had now. It was a bone-deep dread, a cold uneasiness that had coiled in his chest and wouldn't let go. He kept thinking about all the times he'd faced death and survived, all the lives he'd taken without a second thought. It wasn't that he felt guilt, now. Not Gareth Twain, not ever. But there were times when he wondered if it wasn't all a big game, and he was bound to end up owing somebody, somewhere, somehow, for all those dead. Usually he pushed the thought away, on those rare times when he got to thinking too much about it. Took a woman or a drink, or a job in which to lose himself.

But just now, he couldn't see it working. He couldn't see it helping. He just couldn't shake the feeling, and it was making him uneasy. He splashed more water on his face, sliding his fingers from his scalp to his chin. Maybe he should get out. Maybe he should run. Maybe the clock, for him, was running a bit tight. Yeah?

Bollocks, all of it.

He'd worked hard to get where he was. He'd be damned if he'd let the bastards get the better of him now. Maybe, just maybe, he thought to himself, rubbing his face with one hand as he looked in the mirror, I should get some plastic surgery, change my face completely.

It was an option. He knew a doctor, someone he used for discreet repair of gunshot wounds and other reportable injuries, who might be able to recommend someone equally discreet. That translated to a doctor with license problems, or some other issue hanging over him. It was hard, Twain thought, to get quality medical care when you were an internationally wanted fugitive.

He laughed out loud at his own joke, the sound a harsh bark that echoed off the tiles of the small washroom.

He flicked off the light switch and walked out into the office. This six-story building in New Orleans, within a long walk of Bourbon Street, was his last bolt-hole. With things coming apart, it was necessary to retreat here, to take stock, to figure out what actions he'd need to take. He'd resigned himself to the fact that he would need to blow his cover, and that SCAR's carefully protected veneer of legality would be blown to hell. That would have happened eventually as part of the plan. He'd put the company together as part of Trofimov's long-term scheme, with Trofimov's financing and with Mak Wei's troops to get the ranks up to snuff. They'd had to get American equipment for the big dodge he was to run in-country in Afghanistan, yeah, but until then most of his gear was provided by the Chinese. Some of *that* was of varying national origin, probably because Mak Wei still believed he was hiding his country's involvement in all this. Twain thought that laughable.

He'd overheard enough between Trofimov and Mak Wei to know that Mak's people had, more than once, tried to run covert military operations on American soil. That was the source of Mak's hesitation, and the reason the man had gone all fearful when Twain had described the gun-down at the funeral. He'd fed them that line of pox about the mob just to see if they'd bite, to draw out Mak. The Chinese could never resist proving he was right, even at the expense of tipping his hand, and Twain hadn't been disappointed by his reaction during the meeting.

No, Twain thought, it was all snowballing faster than originally planned, and that meant he was going to have to pull up stakes and get the hell out of North America sooner than he'd thought. That, too, had always been part of the plan. He'd figured to spend a little time in South Africa, see if there was still some security work to be done there. Maybe take a bit of a rest in Capetown, where he knew a fine young thing. He wondered if Linda was still single and, if she wasn't, if she'd sleep with him anyway. It was likely. He'd managed to blow through town every couple of years for a while now. She had always made it worth his while.

He smiled at the thought. His office was Spartan, boasting only a plain wooden desk, a liquor cabinet, a television mounted on the wall and a laptop plugged in and charging on a side table. Ignoring the computer, Twain went to the liquor cabinet, took out a glass and a bottle of gin and poured himself a healthy swallow.

Nasty stuff, gin, but he'd developed the taste a decade ago while hiding out in a squalid London flat. He hadn't been able to shake it since.

Swishing the liquor around in his mouth, Twain sat behind the desk. From the top right-hand drawer he withdrew his .44 Magnum Desert Eagle. He'd left it in the office rather than trusting it to check through his luggage when he'd first left to see Trofimov. While it was still theoretically possible to travel by plane in the company of a firearm, there were too many things that could go wrong, and bringing attention to himself was the most basic of them.

Being separated from the weapon gave him the sweats. Its weight was comforting in his hand. He popped the magazine and pulled the slide back to verify that the chamber was empty. Then he reinserted the magazine and chambered a round.

"Good to have you back, baby," he said out loud. He took another long gulp from his glass of gin.

The remote control for the television was on his desk. He switched the set on, chuckling when he realized he'd left it tuned to Trofimov's network. The blond "anchor," pretty enough he wouldn't mind having a go, was reading some report or other while text crawled on the screen in a few different lines below her. Twain turned up the sound just as the report cut to the video footage of the massacre in Afghanistan.

Too right. They were buying it. Buying it by the truckload, too, from the look of it. That, at least, would keep the Russian happy. Trofimov had wailed that Twain was abandoning him just as things were getting sticky; the man just didn't have a sense of priorities. When the heat came down, you went home and dug in. The Russian could do that in *his* office; he had plenty of armed men on hand, both Twain's trained mercenaries and Mak Wei's Chinese thugs. And it wasn't so bad that the Russian was calling off the operation, Twain had pointed out—much to Trofimov's ire. Leaving the man sputtering, Twain had caught the first available flight back to the Big Easy.

Little as he cared about anything, Twain had always liked New Orleans. He'd been in Egypt, briefly, when news of the hurricane came down, and he'd actually been sad to think the city had suffered so badly. The plucky Americans were rebuilding, though, and as it turned out, with the state in turmoil and the city itself still waterlogged, nobody'd given him a second thought when he bought his office building at a cut rate and started staging his operations from within. Hell, law enforcement in the city was so notoriously and famously corrupt, they'd practically called *him* to arrange for the appropriate bribes. That's why he stayed, and that's why his secret headquarters in New Orleans was the perfect spot in which to ride out the coming storm. Once he had some idea who was hitting them, and why, and how, he'd stick his head out and tend to business. Until then, Trofimov's operation was under way and far enough along that it no longer needed Twain's direct involvement. That meant Twain could focus on the important business of survival—not that he wouldn't have, anyway. The Russian was dreaming if he thought his money bought Twain's self-sacrifice for Trofimov's causes, ridiculous as they seemed to Twain.

There had always been an endgame. When the Russian had outlined just how extensively he intended to hit the United States military, and on as many fronts as he desired, Twain had thought him mad. Then the madman had thrown so much money at Twain that the Irishman had *known* him to be mad. Still the money poured in, and as Twain organized SCAR to support the extensive op, it had started to look truly possible. Of course, none of that would have been possible had the United States government itself not been corrupt. At least, certain parts of it.

As if prompted by his thoughts, the satellite phone on his desk began to buzz. The device was connected to an auxiliary antenna just outside his window. There were only a handful of people who would be calling him on that line. Trofimov was one, but unless his high-rise was burning down around his ears, he'd still be too annoyed to lower himself to calling his employee. Mak Wei was another, in theory, who had the number, but the man hadn't spoken a word to Twain save for once: he'd arranged for a small private army of Chinese operatives to show up on Twain's doorstep in New Orleans, told him they were assigned to him for the duration of Trofimov's scheme and turned the phone off in Twain's ear. Not even Twain's dear old mother had this number, which meant it could be only one other person.

"Congressman," he said, answering the phone. "It's nice to be getting a call from you."

"I told you, don't call me that on an open line!" The man on the other end's voice gritted.

"Heller," Twain said, his voice hardening, "if you think this is an 'open line,' you're stupider than ever I thought. The phone is untraceable. Unless you're dumb enough to be calling me from your office?"

"Of course not," Heller responded, managing to sound hurt, indignant and arrogant all at the same time. The Virginia congressman was a piece of work, that much was certain. He was, to Twain's understanding, in Trofimov's hip pocket—his wallet pocket, to be specific—and had been on the payroll for quite some time. David Heller held key spots on certain appropriations committees, but he also had contacts within the United States military. He was also rumored to have financial interests in certain manufacturers who made military equipment, such as trucks and Humvee parts, though that wasn't something that could be proved. Twain imagined it was perfectly true. He and Trofimov had made a fine art of hiding their assets using nested holding companies and false identities. There was no reason the Virginia congressman couldn't do the same, using his considerable government influence to line his own pockets over time.

"Well, then," Twain said, "let's talk like civilized men. What do you want?"

"There's a…problem," Heller said.

"Well? Spit it out, man."

"The, uh, travel plans that I, that is, my office, uh, helped arrange," Heller said hesitantly. Twain felt a sinking sensation in his gut. He had a sudden, awful premonition of what Heller was about to tell him.

"Dallas," Twain blurted.

There was a pause. "You knew?" He said it accusingly, as if Twain were conspiring against him.

"I didn't *know*," Twain snapped. "I'm capable of putting two and two to make four! Now tell me what happened and stop wasting time."

"There's been some kind of raid on the Houston hangar," Heller said. "I got wind of it through my Pentagon connections. They've initiated several investigations that have to do with stolen military weapons. Houston was mentioned as the recovery point. I…" Heller paused again. When he continued, there was a bit more steel in his voice. "I *put two and two together*," he said. "So I checked with my friend at the TSA, the one who arranged for certain activities in Houston to remain unnoticed for as long as possible. He confirmed that there was some sort of big dust-up there earlier today. They've locked down parts of the Houston Airport System. The BATF is involved in cooperation with the military. They've issued several bulletins about explosive devices. And the DEA is reporting recovery of massive amounts of heroin and meth amphetamine, also related to a raid in Houston."

"Jumping Jesus," Twain blurted. "That's the entire shooting match blown, the way you've described it."

"The body count is impressive," Heller said. He sounded like a lost little boy. "Twain, I need your guarantee you'll cover my back on this. If I'm found out, it's not just me that's in danger. I'll have no choice but to cut a deal, tell what I know."

"Now you listen to *me,* you gutless wanker," Twain yelled into the phone. "Do you have any idea how many men I've lost? How much time and equipment? Trucks, weapons, personnel…even a goddamned *helicopter,* more than likely impounded, and do ye have any idea at all how much one of *those* bleedin' things costs?" As he shouted, Twain's brogue asserted itself. He could feel himself losing composure, talking to this spineless weasel of a politician. "Now, you just sit tight, sonny boy, and keep yer bleedin' mouth shut. They'll be damage enough to deal with, without yer whinin' about it all!"

"Twain—"

"Shut up!" The Irishman shouted him down. "We'll be needing you, no doubt, when Trofimov decides his next move. In the meantime, it's my job to clean up the mess. You just make sure you funnel any information you can to me, you hear? Whatever you find out, yeah? And don't call me again. I'll call you." He closed the connection and fought the rising impulse to throw the sat phone through the glass of the window.

Mashing the buttons on the face of the desktop intercom, he waited until Toby Jones, his field commander in New Orleans, came on the line. "Yeah, boss?"

"Toby!" Twain shouted. "Get your ass in here. Why do I have to hear about Houston secondhand?"

Jones almost fell over himself hurrying into the office. He was one of Twain's people from the early days in the IRA, a fellow Irishman who shared Twain's lack of scruples and love of money. He was one of the few people Twain felt he could truly trust.

"Gareth, we've only just—"

"Don't you 'Gareth' me!" Twain stormed. "Why is bleedin' Congressman Heller the one to tell me Houston's been shot to hell?"

"We only got word while you were on the plane," Jones said. "All our men were lost."

"All?" Twain blinked. "No survivors?"

"Not a one," Jones said. "If not for the people we have planted at TSA, monitoring the runways and such, we'd never have known."

"What have you done since you heard?"

"I activated backup in Houston," Jones said. "They got as close as they dared. I've just heard back."

"And?"

"Total loss." Jones shook his head. "Weapons, equipment, the chopper, Stilson, all gone."

"Stilson?"

"Chopper pilot."

"Ah," Twain said, nodding absently. "Then Houston is dead to us, and the outbound shipment compromised."

"The drugs themselves, the processing, the distribution, that's all still up and running," Jones offered.

Twain turned from the desk to his laptop, which sat on standby. He opened it and waited for it to come to life, then tapped in a series of passwords. There was data here that wasn't found on SCAR's mainframes, data that pertained specifically to the drug-smuggling operations. Nasty business, drugs. Twain understood the purpose was to addict as many U.S. servicemen as possible, thus reducing their efficiency and increasing their suffering. The drugs were a high-liability item, however, and in Twain's mind, sometimes more trouble than they were worth. He checked on the status of several distribution points, looking up at Jones as he did so.

"Did you confirm with Mak Wei's people?"

"Aye," Jones said. "They claim all's running as it should be in their areas of responsibility, was how they put it."

"Fair enough," Twain said. "Contact the backup team. Tell them to get out. Pull them back, reassign them to Trofimov in Orlando."

"Why there?"

"They'll be needed sooner or later," Twain said. "Is Kwok downstairs?"

"He's in the building somewhere."

"Put him on the third floor," Twain said. "And tell him that whoever it was killed his brother is likely on the way here."

"Are you sure, Gareth?"

"Sure as hell," Twain said. "Make no mistake, Toby. We're all in for it now. We need to be ready here, and we need to fortify that bleedin' idiot Trofimov."

"For what?"

"For when it finally comes down to whoever the bastards are who're hitting us, and the Russian himself. We'll need to put as many men in place as we can. Contact the men already in Orlando. Have them stage Mak Wei's men so they absorb the worst of it. Put our men behind Mak's. They're spread among our boys here, and there's not much we can do about that now. But we can see to it they take the worst of it defending Trofimov. Mak and his men may as well make themselves useful when the worst comes down."

"What do y'mean, Gareth?"

"Toby, my boy," Twain said, turning from the computer and nervously fidgeting with the Desert Eagle as he sat behind his desk, "I don't like how this looks. I don't like it at all."

"We've faced worse odds," Jones said hopefully. "The Royals, even those gutless bastards in the IRA wouldn't do what needed doing. Dodged the government here… Then there was that dictator in South

America, wanted payback for us blowing up the ambassador, you remember? We've done it all, Gareth. We can handle this."

"Aye," Twain said. "But something about this just feels off. I don't like it. I can feel it in my—"

Twain stopped abruptly. His desk was vibrating. The glass decanters on the liquor cabinet began to rattle in their wooden holders.

"What the bloody hell?"

Then the rumble of the explosions reached them.

"Bloody hell!" Jones said, pulling a 9 mm Beretta from his waistband. "What do you suppose that was, now?"

"It's here," Twain said.

"Who's here?"

"Death," Twain said.

CHAPTER TWELVE

The grenade made a deep, hollow thump as it flew from the launcher mounted under Bolan's Tavor assault rifle. The double glass doors of the main entrance of Gareth Twain's SCAR headquarters disintegrated, whipping tiny shards of glass and pieces of metal through the foyer. The blast ripped apart the armed men who had been standing in front of the doors, heavily accessorized M-4 rifles at the ready. They died suddenly, their screams cut short by the hail of razor shards, propelled by the concussive force of the 40 mm grenade.

Bolan and Delaney had made a cursory recon of the site, using binoculars and communicating via their earbud transceivers. It had been quickly obvious that men with automatic weapons were crawling all over the building. Bolan had checked the front, while Delaney, from the rear parking lot, had spotted a sentry in the lot and several more armed men visible through windows on upper floors. After calling in to the Farm to verify the address, Bolan had gotten the all clear: the target was indeed SCAR headquarters as determined by the Stony Man cyberteam's investigation.

Still, Bolan wasn't one to take chances with innocent lives. He had found a small piece of asphalt in the front parking lot and thrown it at the glass doors. Two SCAR mercenaries had responded; they wore nondescript battle dress utilities with SCAR patches on the shoulders, which Bolan had seen clearly through his binoculars. Apparently, Twain was determined to keep up the appearance of semilegitimacy to the very end. Perhaps the uniforms impressed those local law-enforcement officials who weren't on what Bolan assumed was likely an extensive bribery payroll.

The mercenaries had taken one look at Bolan, standing there, and raised their weapons. "Take him!" one of them had shouted.

Bolan had whipped the Tavor from the duffel bag at his side, crouching on one knee as he triggered the grenade launcher.

Now the battle was on.

"Cover the rear," Bolan said into his transceiver. "I don't want anyone, especially Twain, escaping out the back while I come in the front."

"You and me both, Cooper," Delaney's voice said in his ear. She sounded calm, and before the transceiver screened the worst of it, he heard her MP-5 chatter.

"Delaney?" he asked.

"Under control," she responded. "They made me. A couple of shooters tried to rush me, but I've got them pinned in the doorway."

"Good," Bolan said. "Keep it that way. I'll meet you in a little while."

"They'll leave through the front if you cut around," Delaney said.

"I'm not coming around," Bolan said. "I'm going up and through."

"What?"

Bolan ignored that. He loaded and fired another grenade, which exploded to deadly and spectacular effect in what was left of the SCAR headquarters foyer. Spraying out a 30-round magazine, Bolan followed the weapon in. These were tried and true tactics for the Executioner. In the earliest days of his war against society's predators, this had been known to friends and enemies alike as the Bolan Blitz. Overwhelm the enemy, take the initiative and never let it go. Never let your foe recover; never give him time to regroup. Keep him on the defensive, always. These were the watchwords by which Mack Samuel Bolan lived and fought.

He stalked through the ruined foyer, his combat boots crunching on pieces of broken glass and splintered wooden furniture. Shedding his field jacket, the Executioner had ready access both to his slung canvas war bag and to the weapons he wore on his body and that he carried in the pockets and pouches of his combat blacksuit.

There was an elevator facing him, and the fire door of a stairway to the right. Stepping back a few paces, Bolan put a 40 mm grenade through the doors of the elevator, ducking back before the shock wave and debris blew over him. When the dust cleared, the elevator doors and the shaft beyond were a twisted, smoking ruin. Somewhere deep in the building, a fire alarm rang, the incessant ringing muted by intervening floors. Bolan looked up and spotted a bell on the wall nearby, bent out of shape and obviously rendered inoperable by the explosions in the foyer. He was a little surprised that the building had no sprinkler system; the blasts he had triggered would doubtless have set off such a system.

He paused at the fire door to the stairwell. There were doubtless quite a few mercenaries in the building, all of them armed and more than willing to respond with deadly force. Whatever had held them back until recently was no longer in effect; the troops at the Houston hangar had shown SCAR's willingness to kill, and to do so without regard to civil and legal consequences. If Twain and SCAR were backing Trofimov's plan, and Trofimov was becoming increasingly bold in sponsoring and coordinating his hits on military personnel and their funerals, it meant that everything Trofimov, Twain and those helping them hoped to accomplish was ramping up, hurtling toward a conclusion. The Afghanistan massacre video played into it, too, and had to be more than just a coincidence. But everything he'd managed to learn about Trofimov thus far felt like a prelude to some bigger endgame. If that was the case, and he truly believed it was, it made sense that Trofimov and all those around him were willing to go for broke and opt for open, naked, bloody violence.

Bolan could understand that, and in fact preferred it. He would take a stand-up fight any day to a lot of subterfuge and confused rules of engagement.

But it meant he had no idea how many guns waited on the other side of that fire door, and there was every chance that there were many.

He pressed himself against the wall to the side of the fire door, reached out with one hand and opened the door halfway.

Gunfire ricocheted off the inner surface of the door. Bolan let it go, narrowly avoiding a few bouncing pieces of hot lead. He removed a phosphorous canister grenade from his war bag, pulled the pin with his thumb and let the handle pop free. Then he ripped the fire door open again and threw the grenade into the stairwell.

The almost immediate blast of the phosphorous

grenade bursting cast long shadows through the opening in the doorway. Screams erupted inside the stairwell. Pulling the Tavor in close against his body, bracing it so he could fire it one-handed, Bolan threw himself through the doorway and immediately triggered a blast into first one, then a second writhing mercenary, putting them out of their misery as they danced in the agony of the phosphorous flames.

Changing magazines on the run, Bolan took the stairs two at a time. At the next landing, which was marked with a large 2, he paused to set a miniature Claymore mine connected to an electronic proximity fuse. The small explosive device was one of John "Cowboy" Kissinger's passive denial specials. The Farm's armorer had supplied Bolan with several of these, which would now come in handy in guarding his backtrail. He might or might not be able to contain all of the building's occupants, but taking down each individual mercenary in Twain's employ was not his concern. He wanted Twain—perhaps not as badly as Delaney did, but the Irishman was his best inroad to Trofimov and the Russian's apparently extensive domestic and foreign terrorist operations.

He entered the second floor, the Tavor leading. The level was divided by inexpensive cloth partitions. The cubicles held desks and computers; this was some sort of administrative or training area. There were no personal effects in the cubicles, which was consistent with temporary, recycled workspace.

Movement from the back of the level caught Bolan's eye. He heard men speaking urgently in Chinese. Then the unmistakable hollow, metallic chatter of Kalashnikov assault rifles cut loose, and bullets began to rake the air just above Bolan's head.

The Executioner dropped to one knee, leveled the Tavor and held back the trigger, firing on full-auto through the flimsy fabric of the cubicle walls, his bullets streaming just above the level of the desks. The enemy wailed as they were hit. There was no way to know just how many of the shooters Bolan had tagged, so he kept moving, triggering several bursts from the Israeli weapon as he moved around the perimeter of the cubicle divisions.

There were three Asian men, all wearing SCAR uniforms, all of them holding AK-47 variants. Two appeared to be down for the count, but the third caught sight of Bolan and dived for cover, firing his weapon. Bright red tracer fire took Bolan by surprise as the man hosed the air between them, narrowly missing the soldier; Bolan reversed course and began half crouching, half running to cut him off.

It worked as the soldier thought it would. He met the Asian gunner on the opposite end of the cubicle corridor and put a single 5.56 mm bullet between the man's eyes.

He checked the floor for more enemies, but found none. There was very little time, but he snapped a couple of photos of the dead men with his secure phone, transmitting the shots to the Farm.

As he moved toward the stairwell door, the miniature Claymore he'd set detonated.

Each mine carried a payload of small ball bearings, about the size of the ammunition for a BB gun. When it exploded, the mine would send a directed spray of those ball bearings in a tight cone that would devastate anyone within two yards of that kill zone. He checked the fire door and then opened it cautiously. The results of the explosion weren't pretty. The dead man was another Asian. Bolan took his picture, too.

The Executioner removed another Claymore and set the proximity timer, moving out of the way before the device could arm itself.

He encountered no resistance as he moved to the third floor. The fire door stood ajar. Beyond, he saw movement. This level of the building was one large, open space, with a projection screen on one wall. It was obviously some kind of briefing room. Three men dressed in civilian clothing were on their knees in the center of the room. Standing off to one side of them were half a dozen men, all holding Kalashnikovs on the apparent civilians.

"You out there!" one of the gunmen called. "We see you! Come on out or the hostages get it!"

Bolan didn't answer.

"I mean it!" the man called again. "Drop your guns and come out or we wax these poor bastards!"

Still, the soldier didn't answer.

"Oh, shit, man," a second voice said more quietly but still audible. "I told you, man. They ain't the police. They couldn't be, the way they're shooting up the place. I'll bet Gareth was right! I'll bet it's the Mob and they don't care who they shoot!"

"Or who *we* shoot!" said another voice.

"Shut your mouths," another of the men said forcefully in accented English. "You will maintain discipline."

"Up yours, Kwok!" came the first voice. "I've had about enough of your—"

There was a gunshot, followed by the sound of a body hitting the floor.

"Holy shit! He shot—"

There was another gunshot, and another. A burst of automatic-weapons fire was followed by several more single shots. Bolan risked a glance around the corner of the doorway. He saw a single Asian man in a SCAR uniform, holding a 1911-pattern .45, standing over the bodies of the other SCAR mercenaries and the supposed hostages.

"Come out," Kwok said. "Face me. I will not fire. These…fools…had no business in this line of work. I grew tired of their prattle."

There was a raw edge to the man's voice. He was walking the line or over it, flirting with madness.

Bolan took a gamble. Tavor in hand, he stepped into the doorway, ready to trigger a full-auto burst if the Asian made a move.

"I am Kwok Sun," said the Asian.

"Brother to Kwok Jin," Bolan supplied.

The Asian man's eyes widened. "You," he said. "Your people killed my brother."

"I killed your brother," Bolan said.

"You…" Kwok looked confused. He appeared to be looking beyond Bolan. "You are alone."

"More or less," the soldier admitted. "Why? Were you expecting an army?"

"I am surprised," Kwok said. "For what you have done to be the work of one man is not something to take lightly." He gestured with his pistol, but didn't bring it up. "If I were to put this down, you would fight me man to man? For the honor of my brother?"

"No," Bolan said.

Kwok looked at him curiously.

"Put it down if you want," Bolan said. "I'll shoot you where you stand."

"I do not understand. Why tell me this?"

"Because I'm not you," Bolan said. "Because I remove people like you so that innocent men, women and children may go about their lives in peace."

Kwok snorted. "That is laughable. You are righteous on the one hand, yet on the other you tell me you would kill me rather than face me honorably."

"You shot your own men," Bolan pointed out.

Kwok shrugged. "It was a stupid plan," he said, "and they deserved to die for their stupidity. Whether your bullets or mine, the result is the same. Any fool could see that a group…or a man…who can do what you have done would not be deterred by the presence of hostages. You are obviously ruthless." Kwok Sun's fingers were flexing around the grip of the .45, which was pointed at the floor.

Bolan saw no reason to dissuade the Korean. Had there been genuine hostages, he would have been duty bound to save them. Something about this setup had smelled, however, and Kwok had confirmed it was a trick.

"You're ruthless yourself," Bolan said, keeping him talking, mindful of any trick the Korean might try during the conversation. "You shot your own people. Even among paid mercenaries, that's not exactly done."

"What do I care?" Kwok said. "I died when my brother died."

"Your brother had a choice," Bolan said. "So do you."

"Then I make it," Kwok said. "For my brother."

The .45 whipped up. Bolan was faster. He threw the Tavor in his hands at the Korean, who reflexively ducked. His shot went wide. That was all the opening Bolan needed. He ripped the .44 Magnum Desert Eagle from its holster and fired a single round, punching a hole in Kwok's forehead. The Korean fell into the pile of dead men he had created.

"Now you can be with him," Bolan told the dead man. He retrieved the Tavor and moved on.

He encountered no resistance on the fourth floor,

which consisted of storage. He found several munitions lockers, which were empty, and several Pelican cases that bore rifles similar to the Remington 700 that waited with Grimaldi back at the plane. On the fifth floor the stairwell ended. He tried the fire door, but it was dogged shut from the other side.

When he and Delaney had reconnoitered the building, he'd counted the floors from the outside. There was another floor, which meant that it was accessible only by going through the fifth floor to some other access point. The other doors had not been locked. There was a surprise waiting for him on the other side; that much was certain.

"Cooper." Delaney's voice sounded in his ear. "I've just taken down two more sneaking out the back. You okay up there? I heard an explosion a little while ago."

"Okay so far," Bolan told her. "Hold it together. I'm nearing the top, about to breach the fifth floor. The top floor can't be reached through the stairwell, so I'm going to check for access on five."

"Be careful, Cooper."

"I'll do my best. Stay alert down there."

"Any sign of Twain?"

"Not so far. Don't worry. If we get him, you've got first call on him."

"God, I hope we do," Delaney said. Her voice held real hatred. Bolan ignored that and concentrated on the task at hand.

The space was too close to use the Tavor's grenade launcher. He had a few tricks left in his war bag, however. Removing a small C-4 charge from the bag, he placed the plastic explosive over the door handle and inserted a timed detonator. The detonator was another of Kissinger's little toys.

He pressed the firing stud on the detonator and backed up as far as he could, the muzzle of the Tavor aimed at the doorway.

When the charge blew, it made his ears ring. He ignored that. The blast was enough to rock the fire door off its hinges. It fell toward the interior of the fifth floor.

Bolan processed the fleeting glimpse of the floor beyond, counting at least a dozen armed men waiting for him.

"Now!" someone shouted

Bolan fired a grenade through the doorway.

Even as the deadly 40 mm payload was flying through the air, Bolan was reloading the Tavor's attached grenade launcher. He punched the second grenade through the opening as the first one exploded. The follow-up blast created even more havoc, as those who hadn't been felled by the first grenade tried to fire back and were slaughtered by the second shock wave.

Firing the Tavor on full-auto, the Executioner stepped into their midst. He pumped burst after burst into the enemy who stilled moved, dropping first one man, then another, his ruthless justice the only force in the universe at that moment.

He stopped when there were none left to oppose him.

The wrecked area was some sort of combination common room and mess hall. There was a large-screen television mounted on one wall, its screen spiderwebbed with bullet holes. A shot-up kitchenette occupied one corner. Several of the dead men had met their fates sprawled across what was left of the couches and loungers on the opposite wall.

There was a doorway in the facing wall. Bolan tried the door and found it unlocked. The corridor beyond,

The Reader Service — Here's how it works:

Accepting your 2 free books and free gift (gift valued at approximately $5.00) places you under no obligation to buy anything. You may keep the books and gift and return the shipping statement marked "cancel." If you do not cancel, about a month later we'll send you 6 additional books and bill you just $31.94* — that's a savings of 24% off the cover price of all 6 books! And there's no extra charge for shipping! You may cancel at any time, but if you choose to continue, every other month we'll send you 6 more books, which you may either purchase at the discount price or return to us and cancel your subscription.

*Terms and prices subject to change without notice. Price does not include applicable taxes. Sales tax applicable in N.Y. Canadian residents will be charged applicable provincial taxes and GST. Offer not vaid in Quebec. Credit or debit balances in a customer's account(s) may be offset by any other outstanding balance owed by or to the customer. Offer available while quantities last.

If offer card is missing write to: The Reader Service, P.O. Box 1867, Buffalo NY 14240-1867

NO POSTAGE
NECESSARY
IF MAILED
IN THE
UNITED STATES

BUSINESS REPLY MAIL

FIRST-CLASS MAIL   PERMIT NO. 717   BUFFALO, NY

POSTAGE WILL BE PAID BY ADDRESSEE

THE READER SERVICE
PO BOX 1867
BUFFALO NY 14240-9952

Get FREE BOOKS and a FREE GIFT when you play the...

LAS VEGAS GAME

Just scratch off the gold box with a coin. Then check below to see the gifts you get!

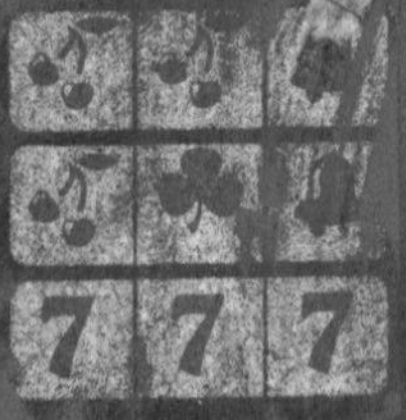

YES! I have scratched off the gold box. Please send me my **2 FREE BOOKS** and **gift for which I qualify.** I understand that I am under no obligation to purchase any books as explained on the back of this card.

366 ADL E4CE **166 ADL E4CE**

FIRST NAME

LAST NAME

ADDRESS

APT.#

CITY

STATE/PROV.

ZIP/POSTAL CODE

Worth TWO FREE BOOKS plus a BONUS Mystery Gift!

Worth TWO FREE BOOKS!

TRY AGAIN!

Offer limited to one per household and not valid to current subscribers of Gold Eagle® books. All orders subject to approval. Please allow 4 to 6 weeks for delivery.

Your Privacy—Worldwide Library is committed to protecting your privacy. Our privacy policy is available online at www.ReaderService.com or upon request from the Reader Service. From time to time we make our lists of customers available to reputable third parties who may have a product or service of interest to you. If you would prefer for us not to share your name and address, please check here ☐. **Help us get it right**—We strive for accurate, respectful and relevant communications. To clarify or modify your communication preferences, visit us at www.ReaderService.com/consumerschoice.

▼ DETACH AND MAIL CARD TODAY! ▼

© 2009 WORLDWIDE LIBRARY. Printed in Canada.
® and TM are trademarks owned and used by the trademark owner and/or its licensee.

which he checked equally carefully, was empty. At its end, a spiral staircase led upward.

The Executioner moved slowly up the stairs, an avenging angel ascending to hell.

The sixth floor contained a waiting room and, beyond that, an office. Bolan stepped inside the open door. A man sat in the chair behind the desk, his back turned to the Executioner.

"Turn around," Bolan ordered.

The chair swiveled slowly. "I surrender," the man said. It wasn't Gareth Twain.

"Who are you?"

"Toby," the man said. "Toby Jones."

"Why are you here?"

"To kill you!" Jones shouted. He wasn't fast enough. As his finger tightened on the trigger of the shotgun mounted underneath the desk, Bolan was diving to the left. Both barrels of double-aught buckshot splintered the doorway where the soldier had been standing. He had time to trigger a single shot from the Tavor as he ducked to the side. The round took Toby Jones in the head, killing him where he sat.

The sudden silence engulfed him. There was no more resistance, no more enemies.

Gareth Twain was nowhere to be found.

Bolan stood for a moment. When no other threat presented itself, he surveyed the room. Besides the dead man, there was a laptop, which sat abandoned and running on a side table. Only when he stepped closer to it did he realize that, despite losing Twain, he and Delaney had caught a break.

The laptop's password had been entered. It was unlocked.

CHAPTER THIRTEEN

Grimaldi had landed them at Midway rather than O'Hare International, saying something about traffic patterns and muttering a few choice profanities in conjunction with whatever authorities governed the local airspace. The Farm had arranged for yet another rental vehicle to be available to them. Delaney and Bolan had found the Ford F-150 waiting for them, and in the truck bed Bolan found a care package that included ammunition, grenades and a few other gems from Stony Man's armorer. He was grateful for the field resupply.

Delaney had been sullen since discovering that Twain had slipped their grasp somehow. They couldn't have missed him by much. Toby Jones's identity had come back from the Farm after Price had Kurtzman and the team run his photo. The man was one of Twain's top operatives, having served under the Irish mercenary for longer than almost any of his other known associates. Jones's presence indicated that Twain had likely been close by. How he had gotten away was still a mystery. Delaney hadn't wanted to talk about it, and Bolan didn't blame her. Probably she was wondering if she'd missed something, if she'd somehow failed to stop the killer she had sought for so long.

The Farm had produced identity matches for several of the dead SCAR operatives. Most of them came back with military histories, criminal rap sheets, or both. Most of the Asians were as yet unidentified, but Kurtzman had managed to dig up a dossier on one of them. He was another Chinese special forces operator, also declared dead about a year previously, Price had informed Bolan in her call to him.

"It's very likely," she had said, "that the Chinese are involved with Trofimov. How deep we don't yet know, but it looks damning."

"Can we do anything about it?" Bolan asked.

"Not officially," Price said, "though Hal said there are a couple of angles he can work. We may yet get buy-in from the Man. You know how delicate things are with the Chinese right now. There are a lot of apple carts Hal can't afford to upset. He's hoping to find a way anyway, though."

"Tell him I wish him luck," Bolan had said. He'd closed the connection not long after, thinking that he didn't envy Brognola the byzantine world of international politics.

Twain's laptop had proved to be a gold mine of information. Specifically, it detailed the production quantities and laboratory locations for an extensive illegal drug operation. Notes appended to these indicated projected dispositions abroad. It was obvious the drug shipments were, for the most part, intended for dissemination among military bases and thus military personnel. The hub of the drug distribution, and the location of the heroin production, was just outside Chicago, Illinois. There were cryptic references to the manufacture of the meth amphetamine being brought in and distributed alongside the heroin, but there were no clues to the location of the meth lab or labs. While it would have been nice to have complete information, Bolan was satisfied with what they'd managed to get: a solid lead to the next step in Trofimov's terrorist chain, namely the distribution center for his drug operation.

Now they were rolling to the GPS coordinates provided in Twain's computer. The truck's GPS system was taking them to a destination just outside Chicago, in a suburban neighborhood that wasn't as congested as some. Delaney, who had been very somber for most of the trip, talking quietly now and then on her cell phone, finally broke her silence with Bolan.

"Do you think Twain will surface again?" she asked.

"I don't know," Bolan told her truthfully. "Now that he knows he's being targeted directly, there is a very good chance he'll go to ground and stay there until he thinks the heat has blown over. I know that's exactly what you don't want to hear, but it's the truth."

"Thank you for your honesty, Cooper," Delaney said, then sighed. "I just wish I knew how the bastard got past us!"

"Don't beat yourself up over it," he said. "If we had time to search the building more thoroughly, we may well have found a secret exit, something leading out that we couldn't have detected. It's common enough, and someone like Twain would be cagey enough to have an exit route planned in case he was trapped."

"It does fit his profile," Delaney agreed. "Cooper, I just... I have to get him."

"I know," Bolan said. "Believe me, I do."

She looked over at him as he drove. "When I took this assignment," she said, "I didn't realize I would be heading into a war zone."

"Didn't we have this conversation?"

"I mean it, Cooper," she said. "Do you realize just how much I would have to answer for if not for whoever it is that's covering for you out of Washington? My boss at the Bureau tells me some serious pressure is being brought to bear from D.C., and whatever isn't being used to keep the Bureau or a dozen other agencies off *you* is being used to keep me out of the fray. He was, frankly, amazed."

"You're welcome."

"Seriously, Cooper," she said. "Who are you? Who do you work for, really? Don't hand me that Justice Department line. It's deeper than that. I spotted you for a military man from the first moment I saw you. Level with me."

Bolan looked at her, then returned his eyes to the road. "There's a lot I can't and won't tell you," he finally said. "But yes, I'm former military. And right now, I fight a war. Every day. I fight a war against those who are chipping away at our nation and at our Constitution, at those who seek to destroy this country from within and from without. The Trofimovs and the Twains of the world, and countless others like them."

"You do work for the government, don't you?"

"I have an arm's-length relationship with the government," Bolan admitted. "But I do what I do under government auspices, yes. Most of my assignments are provided by the government."

"Most?"

"Delaney," Bolan said. "Jennifer. I'm a patriot. I fight for this nation, and for all those citizens of it who can't or won't, for whatever reason, fight for themselves. The enemy doesn't play by the rules. The enemy will gladly commit murder and a hundred other crimes. The enemy won't stop, doesn't feel pity and never feels shame. The enemy has to be met and overwhelmed with superior force. That's where I come in. That's what I do."

Delaney thought about that for a long time. As they were nearing their destination, she said, "All right, Cooper. I'm in."

"You always were," Bolan told her. "You just didn't know to admit it to yourself."

They stopped a few blocks from the target address.

"Déjà vu," Delaney said.

"Sound tactics are sound tactics." He shouldered his duffel bag. His war bag was again in place across his shoulder, with his field jacket covering his weapons and disguising his blacksuit.

"So now what?" She fidgeted, making sure her MP-5 K was hidden under her jacket.

"The target is a house," Bolan said. "We'll just do a little house cleaning."

The house was a dilapidated ranch, with entrances front and rear, the rear a fenced-in yard sheltered on three sides by similarly enclosed yards overgrown with trees and scrub. A wide driveway at the side of the house led to an attached two-car garage. Bolan imagined that would make a suitable improvised loading dock for the distribution of the large quantities of drugs.

He had Delaney wait and walk down the opposite side of the street, looking as casual as possible, while he did a quick recon around the target house.

"All right," he said, rejoining Delaney. He reached down with his free hand and held hers. She looked up at him, startled.

"What...?"

"Just relax," Bolan said, smiling and not looking

directly at her, "and pretend we're out for a nice, romantic stroll."

She got what he was driving at and did her best to look like she meant to be right where she was. The two of them walked past the front of the target house, still on the opposite side of the street.

"What next?" she asked.

"I don't see any sentries," Bolan said. "The windows are all blacked out behind the closed blinds. I don't see any evidence of surveillance cameras, though they could be so small we'd never detect them. I think you should go around front and simply ring the bell. I'll go around the back and see if I can't make my own way while you distract them."

"I've seen what happens when *you* go in the front door," she said. "I'm fresh out of rocket-propelled grenades."

"Don't worry," Bolan said. "You'll do fine."

"I'll try to keep my head down," she said.

They split up. Bolan looked left, then right, making sure no one was watching him. Then he vaulted first one, then a second fence, finally moving up and behind the target house. He was careful in walking across the small, enclosed yard. It was possible, though not likely, that the property was booby trapped. He didn't think the chances were good. Anything that would stop him from sneaking up on the house would also detonate if it encountered a stray dog or a curious kid, and that sort of thing would blow the cover of those inside in short order. No, he figured they would keep a low profile, and that meant their defenses would all be inside the house itself, beyond prying eyes and at a lower risk for false alarms.

"Comm check," he said.

"I hear you," Delaney said, speaking softly. He waited as she got into position. His transceiver picked up the sound of her knocking.

"Hello?" she said finally.

There was the sound of a chain being rattled. The door creaked open. Bolan pictured a face peering out beyond the barrier of the door chain, eyeing the attractive Delaney with what would probably be both suspicion and interest.

"What do you want?" The voice was low and full of gravel.

"I was wondering if I could borrow your phone," Delaney said.

"No," the voice said, low but audible over the transceiver link. "Go away."

"I'm afraid I'm going to have to insist," Delaney said.

Uh-oh. That tone could only mean one thing. Delaney had pulled either her badge or her gun.

"Cops! Cops! Cops!" screamed the voice.

It was on.

Bolan wasted no time. He put down his duffel bag, removed the Tavor, and loaded a lock-breaking shotshell round into the 40 mm grenade launcher. Then he triggered the blast, vaporizing the lock and door handle on the rear door of the target house.

Gunfire sounded from within. It was too far away to be directed at him.

Bolan kicked in what was left of the door, his Tavor's lethal snout leading the way. He was in the kitchen. He hadn't gone more than a few steps when the first of several armed men burst into the room, shotguns in their hands. He burned down first one, then another, with precisely aimed bursts from the Tavor. A third managed to get off a blast that shattered the dirty dishes on top of a round kitchen table in the corner. Bolan punched a single round through his head, dropping him where he stood.

"Delaney!" he said.

"On my way in," Delaney confirmed. He heard her MP-5 K stutter, heard screams both over the transceiver and a few rooms away in the house.

He left the kitchen and made his way down a hallway facing a set of stairs. A man wearing only a pair of pants ran down the steps, carrying a revolver. Bolan tracked him from the side of the stairs and, when the man finally realized what was happening and swiveled to target the soldier, the soldier shot him down. He tumbled down the steps in an undignified heap.

"Delaney, take the upper floor," he said. "Be careful. I just shot one coming down."

"Got it," she said. "And you?"

"I'll take the basement."

"Roger."

The door leading into the basement was opposite the stairwell, in a fairly conventional configuration for a home of the building's size. Bolan put one combat boot sole against the wooden door in a brutal kick. The wood splintered, but something beyond would not give. The jarring impact traveled up Bolan's leg.

He'd thought that might be the case. The door was reinforced with steel. He took another one of Kissinger's timed C-4 charges from his war bag, planted it on the splintered wood casing of the steel door and pressed the arming stud before ducking up and out of the way.

The explosion didn't unseat the door, but it blew the lock. Bolan was able to push the door aside. An open staircase led down. He fished out a pair of flash-bang grenades from his canvas war bag, pulled the pins, let the spoons pop free, then bounced the grenades down the stairs.

He covered his ears as the blasts reverberated up the stairway. Then he was rushing down the stairs, taking them two at a time, reloading his Tavor and bringing it on target. The armed men down there covered their eyes or their heads, some of them bleeding from the ears. Bolan took in the scene in one quick flash, searching for active hostiles.

The smell was what hit him first. There were metal garage shelves down here, and each bore several cans and bottles of varying chemicals. Bolan recognized a few of them as being used to cut heroin. A few others were associated with the manufacture of crystal meth, though there was no meth lab here and no indication of one nearby. He'd seen meth labs before. They were a lot messier than this and a lot harder to hide. Inside, the defenses taken against the outside world were more obvious. There was an acetylene torch rig in one corner of the basement. Metal bars had been welded in place over the head-height basement windows. The door reinforcement also appeared to be a homemade welding job. The fumes in the basement were thick enough to make Bolan light-headed, and he wondered just how toxic the atmosphere really was.

Also in the basement were a series of folding tables. On these were plastic bag after plastic bag stuffed full of what looked to be heroin or cocaine, as well as crystal meth. The tables were divided by product, and each one had several wooden crates stacked nearby, which had been labeled with a thick black marker.

They bore the names of cities and towns in Iraq and Afghanistan.

A few also bore domestic locations. Bolan saw several cities across the United States, as well as a few marked for local delivery in Chicago. He had to admit, it was an impressive display. Here, in a single, large basement, a drug distribution ring that serviced a great deal of this country and portions of two others was busily preparing to poison thousands, if not tens of thousands, of American citizens and soldiers. That wasn't counting anyone else along the way who got mixed up in the vile traffic.

All of this ran through Bolan's mind in the split second it took him to evaluate the scene. The men here were apparently both bodyguards and manual laborers. They were positioned in a way that indicated they were working at the tables, sorting, measuring out, packaging and stacking individual portions of the drugs. Some of these portions were large enough for resale. Others were small, individual doses, clustered in large groups that would probably be sold and delivered to regional pushers and dealers.

One of the men recovered from the effects of the flash-bang grenade to point a 9 mm automatic pistol in Bolan's direction. The Executioner shot him through the heart. He died on his feet and fell without a sound.

"Everybody on the floor," Bolan yelled, louder than normally would be necessary. The workers, or guards, or both, if that was what they were, complied with this order begrudgingly. When the Executioner was satisfied that they were all on the floor and there were no other enemies lurking to take a shot at him, he called to Delaney.

"Delaney," he said, "what have you got?"

"I shot two on the upper floor," she said. "Enforcer types. They didn't take kindly to being interrupted and tried to take me out. One of them had a woman with him. She's probably a prostitute."

"Anyone left alive?"

"Just the hooker," Delaney said.

"See if she knows anything," Bolan said. "It's unlikely, but you never know."

"I might be able to do better than that," Delaney said. "There are some cardboard cartons up here. If I'm not wrong, they're full of crystal meth."

"Got plenty of that down here, too," Bolan said.

"Have yours got mailing labels on them?" Delaney asked.

"No," Bolan said. "Why, what do yours say?"

"There are several boxes here," she said, "that have been reused. They have shipping labels that show an address in Scranton."

"Pennsylvania?"

"Yeah," Delaney said. "It's a mess up here," she said. "But I've got some envelopes that appear to have the same address. They look like coded shipping manifests."

"Of what?"

"Shipments of meth, I think," Delaney said. "At least, there are references by number here, and a couple of the cardboard cartons have numbers written on them that match."

"All right," Bolan said. "Let the girl go, if she is indeed just local talent. She won't know anything and we don't need her."

"She's scampering off as we speak."

Movement in the corner of his eye caught Bolan's attention. He brought the barrel of the Tavor on target just in time to see one of the men on the floor produce a grenade of his own. The red canister rolled across the floor, the pin pulled and the spoon nowhere in sight.

"Oh, Jesus!" one of the other men on the floor said. "Manny, you didn't—"

Bolan realized it then. The grenade was an incendiary.

He broke for the stairs, dropping the Tavor as he vaulted the steps, using both hands to claw his way up the staircase.

"Delaney!" he shouted. "Out the nearest window! Go! Go! Now!"

He had just enough time to make the bay window off the living room when the basement erupted and the whole world exploded.

CHAPTER FOURTEEN

The fire trucks were parked three deep around what had been the target house. Bolan stood against one of them, talking on his secure sat phone. Nearby, Delaney, slightly singed but none the worse for wear, was talking to a pair of uniformed police officers and the fire chief. Things hadn't gone too badly, all things considered. As it turned out, local law enforcement had been suspicious of the activity in the house, and a drug raid had been discussed if not yet brought to the planning stages. All in all, they could have been a lot less understanding than they were being.

Firemen were spraying down the blazing house as Bolan talked. The fumes were fairly poisonous, and most of the firemen were wearing breathing gear. Some spectators had gathered but were being kept far back behind police barricades. It was the most excitement the neighborhood had seen in some time, apparently, at least as far as those living in the area were aware.

"Hal asked me to pass on the question," Price said, "and I quote, 'Was it necessary to blow up an entire house in a suburban neighborhood?' Unquote."

"It wasn't my idea," Bolan said. "Somebody with more guts than sense used the only weapon he had in a room full of volatile chemical fumes. Turns out that weapon was an incendiary grenade."

"Not the brightest move," Price acknowledged. "But then, running heroin and meth was never the most brilliant of career choices."

"These weren't SCAR troops," Bolan said. "At least, not most of them. There may have been a few mixed in, but we caught them flat-footed and made quick work of them. Twain's people are brutal, but not stupid. They wouldn't have pulled a maneuver like that."

"But the drug house was specifically mentioned in Twain's records."

"Hired help," Bolan said simply. "Twain was using this site as his distribution point. It's accessible to O'Hare and Midway, and in a good location geographically for serving most of this part of the country, if not the nation."

"Have you considered a next step?" Price asked.

"I was going to consult the list of prioritized Trofimov sites again," Bolan said. "Delaney saw some materials bearing an address in Scranton, Pennsylvania." He recited the address as Delaney had reported it.

"I'll have it checked," Price said. "I can tell you it's not on the priority list we already produced. I do have a suggestion for you, however, that I think supersedes Pennsylvania."

"Shoot."

"The analysis has come back on the metal samples you found," Price told him. "You remember the political flap over the availability of up-armored Humvees and other trucks in Iraq?"

"Yeah," Bolan said. "The enhanced armor is used to

protect military vehicles from—" he paused, realizing the significance as he said it "—roadside bombs."

"The metal you found," Price said, "turns out to be the same alloy used in the up-armor kits."

"But those samples came apart like chalk."

"Exactly," Price told him. "The armor samples were treated with a chemical the intelligence community has encountered before. It has no name, only a numerical designation. Prolonged exposure to the chemical weakens the molecular bonds in metal, such as steel, turning it into the brittle, useless stuff you found."

"When and where was this encountered?" Bolan asked.

"The formula was first devised by the Soviets during the Cold War," Price said. "We know the Communist Chinese picked it up, at some point, and tried to make it work, but we figured they hit the same wall the Soviets did. It wouldn't have made sense to keep trying, not with this particular formula."

"What do you mean?"

"It's never seen widespread use," Price said, "because it's fairly useless. Oh, sure, it has its applications, but they're limited, and for good reason. The chemical simply can't be weaponized, because to do its work, the target metal has to be fairly saturated over a period of hours. If you were to spray this on enemy tanks, for example, the battle would be over long before any damage could be done, and the enemy could dilute the chemical with ordinary water to rob it of its potency."

"But if the enemy were working within, rather than without..." Bolan speculated.

"Exactly, Striker," Price said. "One of the targets on the priority list is a Kirillov Motors import parts and servicing plant in Detroit. Some of Kirillov's manufacturing capacity is devoted to production of parts for the military, as a subcontractor. They make truck parts, some jet-engine components…and they subcontract up-armor kits for Humvees in the field."

"So Trofimov is arranging for the sabotage of the armor kits," Bolan said, "leaving our troops more vulnerable in-theater. And he probably got the formula from his friends the Chinese, who have been providing him with special forces operatives and, unless I miss my guess, weapons and equipment, too."

"There's more," Price said. "We've traced delivery of the antijam IED transmitters to the same plant in Detroit."

"Why send the transmitters there?" Bolan asked. "Unless they're—"

"Unless they're building roadside bombs or other explosive devices for delivery overseas," Price supplied. "Incorporating the antijam triggers."

"All right," Bolan said. "You've sold me. Does Jack have our travel details?"

"He does," Price said. "I've got him warming up the engines as we speak."

"Then I'll grab Delaney and we'll get a move on," Bolan said. "Tell Cowboy I'm afraid I've lost one of his toys. I'll need to replace that TAR-21."

"I'll let him know," Price promised.

"I don't suppose Twain has turned up anywhere."

"No," Price said. "He's dropped off the radar. None of his known aliases have popped up on the grid since his flight to New Orleans."

"I was afraid of that," Bolan said. "But it makes sense. All right, Barb. We're on our way to Detroit. Striker out."

As they drove to the airport, Delaney didn't ask about Twain, and Bolan didn't volunteer the bad news. She'd know as well as he did that if he had nothing to tell her, that meant there was nothing to tell. She was doing a better job of hiding her disappointment, but he didn't blame her. She'd fought hard only to have her quarry slip past her. That was never easy.

The Farm and Jack Grimaldi had some more surprises up their sleeves. Grimaldi taxied the jet to small hangar assigned for the purpose, once they reached Detroit. Then a shuttle truck arrived, taking Bolan, Delaney and Grimaldi to a nearby helipad. There, a Huey bearing Red Cross markings waited for them, the rotors turning and ready to go.

"Haven't seen one of these in a while, eh, Sarge?" Grimaldi shouted over the rotor noise. "Bring back any memories?"

Bolan smiled grimly.

Grimaldi explained as they flew that the Detroit manufacturing facility was too far out from the airport for a fast drive-by via truck or car. There was no time to waste. Bolan had done enough damage to Twain's operations, and thus to Trofimov's plans, that the Russian might feel compelled to accelerate whatever timetable he was working against. That meant the ride from the airport to the Detroit facility would be accomplished by chopper, with the Farm's own Jack Grimaldi in the pilot's seat.

"There's no way," Bolan said over the intercom headset Grimaldi had given him, "that we're going to make an unobtrusive insertion in this."

"Don't have to, Sarge," Grimaldi said. "Figured it was hit 'em hard time, you know?"

"Meaning?"

"Meaning we've got a door gun!" He laughed, gesturing, and Bolan found, in a crate dogged to the floor at the rear of the chopper, an M-60 machine gun. He dragged it into place in its mount in the open door of the chopper, securing the ammo belt and cocking the weapon.

Delaney's eyes were wide. No doubt she thought she'd just woken up in a Vietnam War movie.

"All right, Jack," Bolan said. "Let's give them something to think about."

Grimaldi brought the chopper in low and slow over the target facility, an industrial factory-warehouse surrounded by similar properties in a gray, heavily paved, congested suburb of Detroit. Smokestacks in the distance spewed black plumes into the sky. The entire landscape looked and felt bleak. Grimaldi, experienced pilot that he was, skimmed the roof of the target warehouse, the skids nearly touching the corrugated metal.

"Jack," Bolan said, "do you think this will work?"

"You tell me, Sarge!" Grimaldi smiled. "Looks like we've got somebody's attention already!"

"You never explained why we're sporting red crosses," Bolan put in.

"Isn't it obvious?" Grimaldi said. "If they shoot at us, you *know* they're bad guys!"

The chopper made another low pass, buzzing the warehouse again.

A bullet whined off the skin of the chopper, startling Delaney in her seat harness.

"There they are!" Grimaldi pointed.

There were men on the ground. Several of them had emerged from doorways on two sides of the warehouse. They were aiming M-16 rifles at the chopper and firing at will, in some cases on full auto. The shots were going wide. Bolan was thankful that in this industrial district, there would be little in the way of pedestrians or homes.

When those bullets came back down, they'd likely fall on yet more industrial property, endangering as few people as possible.

Bolan pulled the door gun in tight and aimed.

The big M-60 bucked as he pulled the trigger, its ear-splitting racket deafening up close. Delaney put her hands against the sides of her head, watching Bolan with intense interest and more than a little fear. The machine gun spewed empty cases and separated metal links, delivering 7.62 mm judgment. Every few rounds, a red tracer lighted the sky. Bolan burned down the men on the ground on one side, then strafed the gunners on the other side of the building. He and Grimaldi made a good team. It wasn't the first time they'd fought together as pilot and gunner, and wouldn't be the last.

They made a few more passes. Bolan softened up the doorway on the east side by spraying several feet of his ammo belt into it. "Down there, Jack!" he said. "Put us down there if you can!"

Grimaldi nodded and brought them in and down. The skids barely touched the asphalt as Bolan and Delaney jumped for it.

They hit the shattered doorway at a run and came under fire as soon as they entered the building. Bolan, his 93-R set for 3-round bursts, began to acquire and drop targets on the move, his finely honed sniper's reflexes kicking in. Delaney followed him in close support, her MP-5 K stuttering here and there, taking first one, then another, then a third gunner.

The interior of the factory was a maze of assembly lines, worktables, fork trucks and tracked cranes used for transporting skids from one section of the ware-house to the other. Light came from banks of fluorescent tubes high in the ceiling. There were a few windows, some of which were painted over, while others were dusty and cracked. Several had been blown out by Grimaldi's fast passes or, more often than not, Bolan's 7.62 mm fire. Outside, Grimaldi continued to circle the building, apparently hoping to add to the confusion of the gunmen inside the warehouse.

Bolan gunned down a man trying to get a bead on him, sending the shooter tumbling over a conveyor belt. Next to him, Delaney shot a man on the catwalk above, which connected the tracked cranes.

"Keep an eye on the upper deck," Bolan said. "I'll aim low."

"Got it," Delaney said calmly.

They began working their way from one end of the warehouse to the other. There were plenty of armed guards here, some wearing SCAR uniforms, some in plainclothes. They were all armed with automatic weapons, handguns or shotguns. The automatic weapons were a telltale sign that something about the facility wasn't right. No private security firm operating in the States regularly equipped its people with full-auto weaponry.

"Go, go," Bolan said. He shot yet another man in the head as they worked toward the back of the warehouse space. There were offices partitioned here. It was possible, if there was any information to be had about this site, that it would be kept there.

They didn't have much time to examine the items being assembled, under fire as they were, but Bolan noted several devices that appeared to be the same components he had seen in Cedar Rapids. He also saw explosives. One worktable was laden with what could only be Semtex, the plastic explosive so popular with terrorist groups the world over. As he fought, he felt his righteous anger rising. These bastards were, it seemed, indeed producing explosives that were most likely intended for use against American troops.

They were taking fire from several directions at once, but it was confused, not focused. Grimaldi's improvised fly-by had apparently done its job, rattling the gunmen and making them feel they were under attack from all sides. The chopper circling rapidly helped keep up that impression, and every so often a shooter's head would turn toward the windows and the silhouette of the passing chopper, giving Bolan the distraction he needed to gun down yet another would-be murderer.

"Make for the offices," he told Delaney. "I'll hold here. I want to know what's back there."

"Will do," Delaney said.

"And be careful," Bolan said. "No telling what's back there."

Still shooting, he backed up following her, placing himself between Delaney and the remaining gunners. His surgical gunfire was taking a toll on the SCAR operatives and those helping them. Resistance was fading fast in the face of the Executioner's superior abilities and tactics.

Bolan positioned himself by the entrance to the office, reloading a fresh 20-round magazine into his Beretta 93-R. He tagged two more enemy operatives, then moved, circling, gliding heel to toe as he maintained a steady shooting platform. Here and there enemy shooters broke from cover to take shots at him, but the Executioner was ready for them. He burned them down as fast as they appeared, circling their position and always on the move. He was a wraith, a ghost, a wisp of smoke among them, and he made sure none of the enemy gunners would be in any condition to present a lethal threat while he and Delaney were present.

As if a switch had been thrown, the gunfire ceased. Bolan looked around, the barrel of the 93-R hot from the extended gunplay. There were no more enemy gunners moving. Had they gotten them all? He thought perhaps they had. Not one to take unnecessary chances, he made another circuit of the warehouse floor, checking each downed man, kicking away the weapons they held and occasionally searching the bodies for more. It seemed almost a moot point, by now, but he also took some pictures of the dead to send to Stony Man Farm.

"Cooper." Delaney's voice sounded in his transceiver. "You'd better get back here."

Careful to watch his back, Bolan approached the offices. He found Delaney standing over a desk in the last segmented area.

She held a gun on a man Bolan had seen before.

"He looks familiar," he said.

"He should." Delaney nodded, gesturing with the MP-5 K. "This is James Thomas Winston, formerly of MIT, and currently number eight on the FBI's Ten Most Wanted List."

The round-faced Winston looked up at them. He was a paunchy, jowly man, wearing a sloppy white button-down shirt. His black tie was at half-mast, and his wire-framed spectacles were crooked on his nose. His hair fell in wisps around his ears but ended just above them, leaving the rest of his freckled scalp bald.

"Winston, the Green Bomber?" Bolan asked.

"The very same," Delaney said. "Made a hobby of mailing bombs to factories, before graduating to corporate coffeehouse chain stores. He's an electronics expert with a minor in chemistry."

"In other words," Bolan said, "exactly the sort of person you'd have on your payroll to build bombs for you."

"Yes," Delaney said.

"Look, whoever you are," Winston started, "whatever they're paying you, I'll double it."

"Who's 'they'?"

"Whomever," Winston said. "Look, we can work this out."

Bolan took the Beretta 93-R and shoved the barrel of the machine pistol under Winston's chin. "Now, you listen to me, and you listen good," he said. "I've got no time for you. You're going to answer my questions and answer them truthfully. Lie and you get a bullet."

"Cooper!" Delaney said. "The man's a wanted fugitive. You can't just—"

"I can and will," Bolan said. Unseen by Winston, he winked at her. "This piece of trash is putting together bombs. Tell me he's not. Tell me he's not building explosives here."

"I can explain," Winston said feebly.

"Do it, then," Bolan said. "One lie and the last thing that goes through your mind will be a 124-grain jacketed hollowpoint round."

"Trofimov!" Winston blurted. "I work for Yuri Trofimov!"

"I thought as much," Bolan said. "What are you doing here?"

"Building bombs, like you said," Winston said hurriedly. "He made me do it! Said he'd kill me if I didn't! It's not my fault!"

Bolan cocked the hammer of the Beretta. "What did I tell you?"

Winston went suddenly quiet.

"Cooper," Delaney said, "remember that Pennsylvania address? If I remember the Wanted sheets, Winston was last seen in Pennsylvania."

"Well?" Bolan said. "What of it?"

"I was...I was there," Winston stammered. "Please don't kill me. I'll tell you whatever you want to know."

"Then spill it," Bolan said. "And give me the short version. We don't have time for your life's story."

"They brought me out to oversee the final designs for the devices," Winston said. "I didn't want to come out here. I wanted to stay in Scranton."

Bolan and Delaney exchanged looks. "You have an address there. Give it to me."

Winston recited the address. It was the same as the one Delaney had found.

"So what do you do in Scranton?"

"They pay me to design the devices," Winston said, "and anything else I can come up with. I'm very good at what I do."

Bolan resisted the urge to pistol-whip the terrorist. That wasn't how he operated, but the man was the lowest form of traitorous scum. Being in close proximity to such people reminded Bolan of the need for his war.

"What do you know about drugs being produced at the same address?"

"There's a lab there, sure," Winston said. "But they don't bother me, so I don't bother them."

"'They'?"

"The Brothers of Blood," Winston said. "It's a biker gang. Trofimov pays them to protect me and to cook the meth he ships from Scranton. It's a really efficient operation."

"Spare me the glowing praise," Bolan said. "How long have you been working with Trofimov?"

"A few years now," Winston said. "When the government found me out and wanted to put me in prison, I ran. I network among other Green and peace-loving groups, and they hid me for a time. We have some connections in common, and he found me and put me to work for a good cause."

"What cause is that?"

"Why, striking a blow against the imperialist American war machine, of course," Winston said, as if that explained everything. He looked down at the gun Bolan still held under his chin. "I don't suppose you'd understand."

"I don't suppose I would." The Executioner holstered his Beretta.

"Call in the police and the closest branch of the FBI," Bolan told Delaney, motioning to the cell phone on her hip. "The sooner this piece of work is out of my sight, the better."

"What's next, Cooper?"

Bolan looked at Winston, who cowered under his direct gaze.

"Scranton," Bolan said.

CHAPTER FIFTEEN

Bolan, positioned on a hill overlooking the location Winston had confirmed, peered through the scope of his Remington 700. He could see several bikers moving in and around the house, which was really just a double-wide trailer set in the middle of a field. A prefabricated metal storage building had been erected some distance to the rear of the house. Pipes jutted from it, spewing acrid smoke into the air. That was the meth amphetamine cookhouse, without doubt.

The trailer was where Winston had spent most of his time working, apparently. The Brothers of Blood seemed to be circulating between the trailer and a series of tents set up in the field around a large bonfire pit. There was no fire right now, but the pit was smoldering as if there had been one the previous night.

There was nothing about this operation that the local authorities and perhaps the Wilkes-Barre SWAT team couldn't have handled, but Bolan wanted to keep the pressure on. Blitzing this outpost, letting Trofimov know that no part of his operation was safe, would go a long way toward further destabilizing things from his point of view. The more upset Trofimov was, the more nervous he became, the more likely he was to make a mistake. Those mistakes were what would help expose his terrorist operations, and the more exposure, the better. Brognola was going to have his work cut out for him explaining why an American citizen and wealthy businessman had his world blown out from under him. If it became obvious that the man was a traitor and a murderer, the questions would slow or stop altogether.

Bolan cared less about that than about stopping Trofimov altogether, and keeping pressure on the Russian was part of *that* plan, too. Still, he saw no reason to make Brognola's job any harder than it needed to be.

Even with all the information backing his play, Bolan needed confirmation of the righteousness of this hit, just as he always demanded for his operations. Delaney, increasingly bold, had offered to provide that verification. As Bolan watched, Delaney, far below him, rolled up in her rented GMC Yukon, raising a cloud of dust on the dirt road that led to the trailer and ran past the circle of biker tents.

"Excuse me." Her voice was clear in Bolan's transceiver, and he could even hear her window rolling down automatically. "Could you help me? I'm lost, and my cell phone's gone dead. Is there a phone around here I could use? None of my family knows where I am, and I don't want them to be worried."

It was a fairly transparent play, and Bolan wouldn't have expected it to work had he been dealing with the Chinese special forces operatives or Twain's SCAR personnel. These Brothers of Blood, however—the colors and logo they all sported was read easily enough through the scope of Bolan's Remington—were far from paid professional soldiers. They were hired muscle, and that was all, local "talent" that was the best rural Pennsylvania had to offer.

Through the scope, Bolan saw the two bikers closest to Delaney's vehicle exchange glances. They were cookie-cutter similar: leather jackets, shaved heads, some visible tattoos, a clear lack of personal hygiene. He could hear one of them say, "Oh, missy, I think they're gonna be worried. I think maybe we're just gonna give them something to worry about. What's say you come on over and meet the boys? Don't worry. They'll all get a turn before we're through with you." He reached into the truck, grabbing Delaney through the window.

Delaney slammed the Yukon into Reverse and flattened the accelerator.

That was the signal, and verification that the Brothers of Blood were anything but upstanding citizens.

The biker who'd grabbed Delaney was pulling a large hunting knife from under his leather jacket. Bolan tightened the Remington against his shoulder, sighted carefully and squeezed the trigger.

The 146-grain, .308-caliber bullet bore a hole through the man's skull and dropped him where he stood.

The biker standing next to the dead man hesitated for a moment. Then the rolling thunder of the shot reached him, and his brain lurched into gear. He was running for the tents when Bolan's second round caught him in the center of the back of his head, dumping him on the ground. The revolver he had been pulling from his belt went flying, landing somewhere in the bonfire pit.

Per the plan, Delaney was pulling the Yukon back. The dirt road narrowed farther up, and the truck would be sufficient to block vehicle access into and out of the property. Bolan wasn't so worried about being interrupted from the outside as he was allowing any of the bikers below to escape. He wanted to make a clean sweep of this, bring them all in or down, to intensify the effect that hitting the lab would have on Trofimov. As always, the purpose was to keep the pressure on, and Bolan was an expert at gaining and keeping the initiative in an engagement.

Bikers began scrambling from the tents and from within the trailer, though Bolan noticed that no one emerged from the cookhouse. He calmly worked the bolt of the Remington, took careful aim and dropped a biker. Then he shot another one, and another one, each time working the bolt with icy calm. Mack Bolan was a master sniper, and the men below still hadn't found his range.

The bikers were attempting to mount resistance, however. They were firing up the hill. At least a few of them were smart enough to realize that sniper fire was likely to come from the nearest point of elevation. They were responding accordingly, and their less intelligent brethren were following suit. Bolan dropped three more bikers before it became obvious he would have to move in closer. The bikers retreated into the trailer and began to fire from the windows, shooting blindly at nothing. He might be able to tag one or two through a window that way, but Bolan saw no reason to wait them out. He packed the Remington back in its hard case and began to work his way around, flanking the trailer, getting ready for a house call.

So fixated on the hilltop were the bikers that they never noticed Bolan work his way down the opposite side of the hill and around the side of the trailer. Desert Eagle and Beretta 93-R in hand, Bolan stopped outside the trailer, stepped to the side and rapped on the door with the barrel of the Desert Eagle.

"Who the fuck is it?" came the nervous voice from inside.

"Special delivery," Bolan said.

"We didn't order no special delivery," the biker snarled. "Now clear outta here, man, there's somebody shooting from up in the hills! Ain't you seen the bodies, man?"

"Special delivery," Bolan said evenly.

The door was ripped open. "I'm gonna stab you through the neck and watch you twitch," the biker said, switchblade in hand. "What the fuck are you special delivering, you idiot—"

"Bullets," Bolan said, and shot him in the face.

A well-placed combat-boot sole smashed the door inward, and Bolan stepped over the dead biker on the front step. He rolled as he hit the carpeted floor, avoiding a shotgun blast that passed over his head. Another shot from the Desert Eagle put a .44 slug through the brain of the shotgun-toting biker. Then Bolan was up and through.

A man with a sawed-off shotgun tried to shoot Bolan's legs out from under him. The soldier side-stepped the clumsy attack, and when both barrels were empty and the man was clawing for the release to break the gun and reload, Bolan shot him dead, center of mass. Another biker leaped up and swung a heavy motorcycle chain at Bolan, scoring a glancing blow against the soldier's left wrist. Bolan reached out, grabbed the chain on the next swing and pulled the man into him left-handed. Off balance, the biker slammed into Bolan.

With his gun pressed against his side, the Executioner fired, punching a bullet through the man's heart.

He looked around.

"All of you, on the floor!" he ordered.

No one complied. It never hurt to try. There were

several other bikers falling over themselves to run from him, stumbling through the confines of the trailer and realizing that, unless they wanted to throw themselves out the windows, there was nowhere to go. Bolan shot one man just as he attempted to do just that. He shot a second wielding an Uzi. The subgun chattered and stitched the wall to Bolan's left, but the soldier avoided the enemy fire and put the subgunner down.

At the end of the corridor the soldier found the largest bedroom in the trailer. He stepped into the doorway, gun ready, and triggered two rounds into the chest of a man who came at him with a machete. The machete-wielding biker went down, but Bolan was tackled from behind by another man. The two of them rolled and wrestled for control of the Executioner's gun, which was lost in the melee.

Bolan kneed his opponent in the stomach, hard. The biker gasped but managed to pull free and stumble to his feet. The switchblade appeared in his hand as if by magic.

"You bastard," he wheezed. "I'm going to cut you so bad your family won't know you."

"I doubt it."

"You got a knife there." The biker nodded to Bolan's belt line. "Come on, dude. We'll blade it out, man to man. You look like a tough bastard. What do you say?"

Bolan said nothing. He drew the Beretta 93-R and pulled the trigger.

The man with the switchblade toppled forward, a shocked look on his face.

The Executioner's fingers brushed the hilt of the Boker combat dagger sheathed inside his waistband. He could have gone for the knife, certainly, but this was not meant to be a fair fight. He bent to retrieve the Desert Eagle when something exploded from the bedroom closet.

The biker was small, but incredibly densely muscled, built like a fire hydrant. He rammed into Bolan's mid-section, driving the air from the Executioner's lungs, tearing the Beretta from his grasp. Then the man had his huge arms around the soldier's middle and was squeezing for all he was worth.

Bolan felt his vision begin to gray out around the edges. Spots swam before his eyes. He thought he could feel his ribs cracking; the pain was incredible. The biker laughed as he literally tried to squeeze the life from his opponent.

The soldier managed to drop his hand to the knife he had refused to draw a moment before. The keen, wide, double-edged blade came free as his fingers tightened around the weapon's handle. Then the blade was slicing into one of the biker's arms, causing the man to shriek in pain and horror.

Bolan kicked off the wounded biker and stumbled backward, gasping for breath. Still clutching the knife in his right hand, he found the butt of the Beretta with his left, leveled it and fired a 3-round burst into his attacker. The biker fell and died, the look on his face one of complete astonishment.

It always seemed to be a shock to them when they died violently, Bolan reflected, despite their willingness to do violence to others.

"Cooper?" Delaney's voice sounded in his ear. "Are you all right? You sound like you're breathing funny."

"I'll live," Bolan said. "Just a slight…disagreement…with one of the paid goons."

"You sure?"

"Yeah," Bolan said. "Stay put. Just a few loose ends to tie up."

He swept the trailer again after finding and holstering his Desert Eagle. There were no more bikers to be found. Then he emerged from the trailer and checked the tents. There was nothing in those except for a lot of dirty clothes, empty beer bottles and other debris.

The cookhouse was next. Bolan, weapons ready, made his way to the doorway of the metal shed. It was padlocked. He stepped back, aimed the Desert Eagle and shattered the lock with a single .44 slug. Then he ripped open the plywood door.

The meth lab was empty.

Pulling an incendiary grenade from his war bag, Bolan moved well back, armed the grenade and tossed it into the open door of the metal outbuilding. Just to be on the safe side, he put the trailer between himself and the meth lab. The explosion shattered the windows of the trailer and rattled the entire building in its frame. The cloud of black smoke that erupted would probably be visible for miles once it spread.

"God*damn*, Cooper," Delaney said. "What was that?"

"A loose end being tied up," Bolan replied. "Come on in."

With Delaney's help, Bolan searched the trailer. The larger bedroom was apparently the room Winston had used. They found several notebooks with hand-drawn designs and painfully small, incredibly detailed commentary filling page after page. Each was signed by Winston himself, so there was no doubt as to the origin of the material. They threw all of these into a large trash bag to be taken with them. The notebooks would eventually make their way to the Farm to be used as evidence. Winston himself had been dropped into the system and was probably still being processed by whatever federal agency eventually laid the strongest claim to him. He may have been on the FBI's Ten Most

Wanted List, but he was also a wanted by half a dozen other agencies and municipalities.

Bolan didn't care, as long as the man was off the streets, unable to help people like Trofimov. If it were up to Bolan, he would see all of Winston's work burned, to prevent even the possibility of its use by others.

They were packing the Yukon when first Delaney, then Bolan heard the sound of motorcycle engines coming up the dirt road.

"Looks like there were a few unaccounted for," Bolan said. He drew the Desert Eagle and used the engine block of the truck for cover. Delaney skirted the truck and took up a position around the side of the trailer, which afforded her a better angle.

The bikers roared in and stopped when they saw Bolan behind the truck. They cut their engines. There were five in all, riding four machines, one of which had a sidecar.

"Who the hell are you," the lead biker said, "and why are you pointing a gun at us?"

"Drop to your knees," Bolan ordered. "Lace your hands behind your head. You are all being taken into government custody."

"Like hell," the biker said. He grabbed for the butt of a MAC-11 shoved in his waistband. The illegal full-auto weapon blazed away as he held the trigger down, spraying the area.

Bolan shot him.

The other bikers went for their guns, but Bolan put .44 slugs into two of them, while Delaney triggered a burst from the MP-5 K that dropped the rest.

Suddenly it was quiet again, except for the crackle of the flames coming from the wreckage of the cookhouse.

"That's that," Bolan said. "Let's get moving."

"Uh-oh," Delaney said. "Problem."

Bolan followed her gaze. The wild full-auto fire had left a trail down the flank of the Yukon, flattening both tires on the driver's side.

"Not the first time that's happened," Bolan said.

"Now what?" Delaney asked.

"You ride at all?"

"No," Delaney said.

Bolan looked at the motorcycle with the sidecar, then back at her.

"I think I see a solution."

"Oh, hell," Delaney said.

THE RIDE BACK to the airport and Grimaldi, with the materials recovered from the trailer stuffed in the sidecar with Delaney, was rough, but they managed. Grimaldi laughed when he saw them roll up but didn't comment. He waited for Bolan to give him the story, then got on his cell phone to start making arrangements with the rental company.

"So much for the security deposit," Bolan said to Delaney.

She laughed, then groaned as she tried to stretch out the soreness in her muscles.

Bolan next contacted the Farm, checking in with Barbara Price.

"Striker," Price said, "we have more developments."

"Give me what you've got," Bolan said.

"We've traced the orders for your phony Army unit," Price said. "Hal's keeping it very hush-hush for now, to give you time to deal with the situation in your own way."

"Who is it?"

"A Congressman David Heller," Price said. "He has an office in Richmond, and our sources tell us he's there now. You're finished in Pennsylvania?"

"At least for now," Bolan said. "The meth lab Trofimov's people were running is history. We found confirmation of the bomb-designing activities. I've got quite a bit of material to ship back to you for use as evidence or in analyzing any IE devices we might uncover."

"All right," Price said. "I think the good congressman should be your next visit, then," she said. "At least, Hal strongly suggests it. As it turns out, we're not the first government agency to take an interest in Heller. He's been under scrutiny for a while, and it seems he's due for a talking-to."

"I can think of two people I'd like to talk to more," Bolan said, "and their names are Twain and Trofimov. I think Heller should make a good stop along the way."

"I've got a complete dossier on him," Price said. "It includes surveillance data gathered to date. There's nothing remarkable so far, other than suspicious undertones, but it will set the table for your arrival. I'll upload it to your phone."

"Thanks, Barb. Any news on the 'massacre' video?"

"It's getting worse, Striker," Price said. "Several of our allies, or at least nations that permit us to operate military bases on their soil, are screaming that we can't be trusted. There's talk of pulling permission for several strategically important bases. We can't afford that. This goes beyond the nation's image. Some of those sites are vital to the wars in Iraq and Afghanistan, and others have critical strategic importance for different reasons."

"There's still no ID on the soldiers involved?"

"None at all," Price said. "It's turned into a real media circus, too. Trofimov has been on his cable news network half a dozen times in recent memory. Now he's promoting a phone 'tip line' that he hopes will 'bring these heinous murderers to justice,' if I remember the phrasing exactly. He's actively soliciting informers to provide the names of the soldiers, and he keeps publicly running the names he receives even if they're from obvious cranks."

"How's that legal?" Bolan said. "He can't just accuse specific soldiers of participating in the massacre without evidence."

"There are some loopholes," Price said. "He's claiming not that they've actually done the crime, but that he's simply reporting, unedited, what comes in on the tip line, in case one of those tipsters stumbles onto something. The intent is clear, but the legal dodge protects him. Plus, most of our people serving in the military don't have the money to hire lawyers that could compete with Trofimov's crew of relentless, highly paid sharks. Wealth has its privileges, and among them is insulation from lawsuits."

"There must be something we can do," Bolan said. "I'm convinced that the video is fake. That's the only reason I can see that we can't seem to identify the men in it."

"You're not keeping up on your conspiracy theories," Price told him. "The buzz on the Web is that the men in the video were spirited away by the U.S. government, either for quick deaths or for covert lives in the lap of luxury. I guess it depends on how cynical you are, in terms of which you're more likely to believe."

"We can't continue to let this go unchecked."

"I can't see that we can do anything about it, Striker," Price said, sounding frustrated. "I wish we could."

"But we *know* Trofimov is dirty. I know that doesn't mean anything in a court of law at the moment, but we can fight him at his own game. Put Bear and his people on producing some kind of counterpropaganda relevant to this."

"You'd be surprised just how many pro-American bloggers and other Internet pundits are willing to spend their time doing just that," Price said, "including analyzing the tape from every conceivable angle, cataloging its appearances and those who received money for sharing it, etc. In the end, though, it doesn't really change the minds of those who think this nation is hurting its allies. We are all suffering as a result."

"All right, Barb," Bolan said. "We're headed to Richmond. I'll go have a word with the congressman."

"Good luck, Striker."

"He's a politician. I'm going to need it. Striker out."

CHAPTER SIXTEEN

Mak Wei sat sphinxlike in his customary chair, smoking and saying nothing, while Trofimov paced.

"I cannot believe this!" Trofimov exclaimed. "The entire operation is falling around our ears! Have you seen these reports?" He waved a handful of faxed sheets under Mak's nose. The man looked up him disdainfully.

"I have seen them," he said simply. "I am not impressed by your operation thus far."

"My operation?" Trofimov said indignantly. "It's *your* operation, too!"

"I think you miscalculate," Mak Wei said. "The People's Republic of China has no direct involvement in your schemes. And I have no official standing with my government."

"We both know that's a lie!" Trofimov said.

"Need I remind you," Mak said, smiling faintly, "that it was you who first approached us?"

"But you've lost men, too!" Trofimov said.

"We have lost no one." Mak Wei shook his head. "No one who is not already dead, or whose ties to our government cannot be substantiated. There are many individuals who turn to lives of crime. We cannot keep track of all of them, but we certainly do not bear responsibility for their continued misdeeds."

Trofimov stopped, wiped his face with his hand and looked at Mak Wei. "Mak, I need your help. You must *do* something! The operation, one in which you have said you believe, is in danger!"

"I? Why must I do something?" Mak said. "You would shame me, force me to take responsibility for that which I bear no blame? I do not think so."

"Be reasonable. We need each other. Your nation needs my help. My plan can work. But I need the support of your resources. I need more troops."

"You have many troops," Mak said. "A substantial number of which guard this very building, and your person. You tell me now these are not enough?"

"Enough to protect our hides," Trofimov said. Mak noticed he was careful to say "our" and not "my."

"But not enough for the remainder of your plan," Mak offered.

"No," Trofimov admitted. "Not now. Not with the loss of the unit in Houston, and Gareth Twain's training center and headquarters. And just this morning I've had word that the meth laboratory in Pennsylvania's been hit, as well as my bomb plant in Detroit. All of these were cornerstones of the plan!"

"It was an ambitious plan," Mak said. "Perhaps too ambitious. Perhaps you sought to fight your war on too many fronts at once. Sun Tzu teaches us—"

"To hell with Sun Tzu!" Trofimov interrupted. "Can't you see we're past that?"

"I think it is time you stopped shrieking at me like a spoiled child," Mak said evenly, "and assess your resources. It is time to cut your losses, evaluate the situation and formulate a new plan, one that adapts to the reality of your situation now. Stop whining over what might have been. I have seen enough undertakings by my government fail in this way. I do not need to hear you wail about your own."

Trofimov took a deep breath. Mak regarded him for a moment. The man was very obviously vain, and overmuch concerned with symbolism rather than substance, but he wasn't stupid. And though Mak wouldn't now admit it to the man, Trofimov's ambitious plan had showed every sign of working. Portions of it still worked; portions of it still *could* work. First, however, the Russian would have to get over his temper tantrum and deal with reality, rather than cry over it. Mak detested the man when he behaved in this way. He had seen it a few times before, though not often, for Trofimov was usually on the winning side of things. Faced with a defeat, even a salvageable one, he was truly insufferable.

Trofimov had phoned him urgently that morning, screaming for help, and Mak had decided he had best leave his hotel and visit Trofimov in his office, lest the frantic Russian do something inadvisable that they would all regret. Mak's handlers had warned him that this was one aspect of the job he couldn't overlook. He was to manage Trofimov as much as he was to attempt to profit from the scheme his government chose to support, however indirectly.

The irony was, of course, that Trofimov thought he was using Mak and the People's Republic of China. The fool actually believed he could outsmart Mak, that Mak and those working with him were nothing more than tools Trofimov could use, break and throw away. That was the sort of arrogance that would eventually earn Trofimov a bullet in the brain. The Chinese agent allowed himself few illusions and fewer fantasies, but that was one fantasy he entertained: he hoped he would be the one to put that bullet in Trofimov, shutting up the loud-mouthed Russian forever. The blessed silence that resulted would be a gift to humankind.

"What do you want me to do?" Trofimov asked. It was a mystery to Mak that this man who considered himself a titan of industry would allow himself to appear so vulnerable. Clearly he felt entitled to his position, so much so that he dared appear vulnerable to an ally. Either that, or he truly was unstable. His obsession with harming the military forces of his own adopted nation certainly pointed to a fair amount of irrationality. While intellectually Mak could understand why the Russian hated the West and hoped to harm it from within, the pragmatic Mak simply could not grasp the need for that type of revenge. The past was the past; the world was the world; there was no point fretting over political regimes come and gone, or nation-states that had collapsed under their own weight. Even anger over a war since resolved struck Mak as pointless. When hostilities ceased, there was only who gained and who lost.

"Assess your losses," Mak instructed. "Dispassionately. Realistically."

"We've lost a large portion of Gareth Twain's SCAR personnel," Trofimov said. "We've lost most of the drug distribution operation, including the Chicago hub and the meth laboratory in Pennsylvania. We've lost the services of Winston, and we've lost the bomb assembly plant, as well as the components used to make the special transmitters. We've lost the disguised unit that was to travel abroad and impersonate U.S. soldiers, and we've lost all the resources staged to support them."

"Very well," Mak said. "And what do you still have?"

"We finished with the chemical plant," Trofimov said, "though Heller is now pulling back from his promise to help us distribute the armor through channels. My financial assets are heavily guarded and remain extensive. This facility itself, and those within it, are equally heavily guarded. And we have the means to create more videos, perhaps even to discover further atrocities committed by the same soldiers."

"And Heller?"

"Heller puzzles me," Trofimov said. "He was willing enough to help before. Then we lost the disguised soldier unit. Now he will not return my calls. I do not know what to make of it."

"Forget Heller," Mak said. "Corrupt U.S. politicians are never hard to find. You can always buy another."

"I suppose," Trofimov said dubiously. He continued pacing.

Mak, of course, knew the real reason Trofimov couldn't reach Heller. It has been decided that such a resource—a congressman so willing to be cooperative, no matter the request, as long as the price was right—was too good to be squandered on Trofimov's schemes, promising as they were. Mak's people were in negotiations with Heller directly, attempting to work out an agreement whereby Heller's connections in Congress and in the U.S. military could benefit China and China's own military might. Mak had received the coded information just that morning, in fact. The notion had pleased him.

Trofimov's intercom buzzed.

"Yes?"

"Gareth Twain is here to see you, sir," the receptionist reported.

"Show him in at once."

"Yes, sir."

Twain walked in, looking considerably less arrogant than he had when last Mak had seen him.

How the mighty have fallen, he thought. It would have been amusing had it not been so familiar. It had happened to his own people enough times, engaged in similar operations among the Americans.

"Twain," Trofimov said, "we know what has happened. Sit down."

Twain sank into a chair, looking nervous and pale. Mak didn't feel like waiting for Trofimov to get around to asking, so he asked himself. "What," he said, "happened to you?"

Twain looked at him for a moment as if he had two heads. Obviously the Irishman was unaccustomed to a direct question coming from Mak Wei; Mak had seldom deigned speak to him in such a manner. That didn't matter now; issues of status and hierarchy were unimportant. What Mak wanted now was information.

"They hit us," Twain said. "Hit us hard in the Big Easy, right where we live. I was lucky to get out at all. I have—had—a hidden exit built into my office. And damned if I didn't see her!"

"See who?"

"The girly-girl what chased me down with the FBI not so long ago," Twain said. "She was there. She didn't see me, but I saw her."

"Are you saying," Mak said, taking a drag from his cigarette, "that the American FBI is behind these assaults on your people?"

"Not hardly," Twain said. "She was there, yeah, but these weren't no FBI raids that knocked over my people and his things." Twain jerked his chin toward Trofimov. "Death on the hoof, that big bastard is. Caught a glimpse of him as I was fleeing. Not one I'd care to see again. But I guess I got no choice, yeah?"

"What do you mean?" Trofimov asked.

"Well, put it together, why don't you," Twain said to him. "You don't think you're just going to sit up here nice as you please, without a care in the world, do you?"

"I will have you know—"

"Oh, shut your piehole," Twain interrupted the Russian. "They hit me, and they'll be coming for you. The whole thing's blown, boy-o! The whole thing! All your schemes, all your plans, you think you can hide any of them? If they found me, they can find you."

"Your job," Trofimov said, "is to protect me. That is your primary function. All other military actions are secondary to this."

"Don't I know it, boy-o. Don't I know it. And I'm here to do just that. I've pulled in my troops and they're massing here. I've got people in Charlotte and Jacksonville, too, because, and here's the bulletin, my boy, that's all you've got left."

Hearing it like that gave Trofimov pause, obviously. He stared first at Twain, then at Mak, then back at Twain.

"Can you do it? Can you protect me and what I have remaining?"

"Frankly, I doubt it," Twain said. "But I aim to try, don't I? Now, quit your blustering and show me where you keep the booze. I need a drink."

Trofimov, so distracted he didn't even react to Twain's presumptions, pointed him in the direction of the liquor cabinet.

"There must be something more I can do," he said to Mak.

"You have taken all the steps you can take." He stubbed out his cigarette in the ashtray nearby. He would light another momentarily, but for now he was sated. "Did you really think, Trofimov, that one man, no matter how rich and no matter how powerful, could take on the combined military might of an entire nation and succeed without the slightest setbacks or delays? Did you really think it would be so easy?"

"But I'm not fighting the entire military," Trofimov complained. "I don't know *who* I'm fighting!" He pointed at Twain, who was sucking whiskey directly from a decanter. "*He* tells me it is the Mob, and then he tells me it is the FBI. He doesn't know. You speak of military failures, of past operations on American soil, of vague defeats about which you can offer no details. You speak of it as an old woman speaks of the bogey-man. Do you know nothing about what we face? Can you offer no insight?"

"Are you really so foolish?" Mak asked.

"I did not ask for your insults!"

"Listen to me anyway," Mak said. He paused to light another cigarette from the silver lighter he kept in his pocket. "The government of the United States is vast and powerful. In that way it is no different than the government of my nation, or the government of the Soviet Union that once was."

"So?"

"Of all the resources available to that government," Mak said, "do you truly believe there exist no men willing to take direct and violent action to secure your nation's aims? You would be foolishly naive to think otherwise."

"You are saying that we are the victims of some unknown government force, some ruthless group of government killers?"

"Perhaps," Mak said. "Perhaps. It is at least possible, is it not?"

"So what can I *do?*" Trofimov said.

"Carry a weapon," Mak said simply. "Be prepared to use it."

"That's not a solution!"

"Isn't it? Who was it that said something about all political power stemming from the barrel of a gun?"

Trofimov had nothing to say to that. He was an educated man, or reasonably so. He would know what Mak Wei meant.

Twain finished his drink and pulled a sat phone from his pocket. He went to the window and angled the device for the best signal he was likely to obtain, then started to make calls. Trofimov ignored him, but Mak listened to see what he could learn.

It quickly became obvious that Twain wasn't shamming. He really was running scared, and he firmly believed that they would come under attack in Orlando, inevitably. As Mak listened, Twain continued to shore up the defenses in Charlotte and Jacksonville. The Chinese agent knew that Jacksonville, in particular, was very important to Trofimov. It was there that he stored hard, liquid assets, such as gold coins, to maintain his wealth should an economic collapse occur. And surely it was economic collapse with which Trofimov flirted, for in his desire to see the United States harmed, he set forces in motion that couldn't be contained once released. If the United States lost so much standing in the world that it became weak, and its weakness created a power vacuum, such an act would be very dangerous indeed. Yes, China stood to benefit by stepping in to claim that power vacuum, but only a fool failed to recognize an enemy for what it was. The United States economy drove the economies of the rest of the world. Hurt the United States, and you hurt that world economy.

China, which traded extensively with the United States, couldn't lose so vast a market for its manufacturing capacity—not without suffering consequences.

Mak believed that the consequences, though negative, were far outweighed by the gains to be had in supplanting the United States as the world's dominant superpower. This was the motivation behind China's willingness to support Trofimov in the first place. That support had to come indirectly, for China still required plausible deniability, but come it had.

"Twain," Mak said, "I would speak with you at greater length. Come with me."

"Fine."

The two men left Trofimov to fret and pace in his office. Mak walked the corridors of Trofimov's high-rise with brisk, military precision. Twain slouched along beside him, clearly distracted.

"I have a business proposition for you," Mak said without preamble.

"Yeah?"

"You are a man who understands certain pragmatic realities," Mak said. "This is so?"

"Sure and it is, then."

"Very well. Do you believe that Trofimov's plans can be salvaged? Do you have faith in your role in them?"

"Beats the hell out of me."

"An honest enough answer," Mak said. "I make for you a contingency, then."

"How so?"

"My government has an interest in the success of Trofimov's efforts. Those efforts can take place without him as easily as they can with him, provided there is *someone* to drive them."

"What are you saying?"

"I am saying that Trofimov, for all the brilliance of his schemes, is clearly coming unraveled now that he faces adversity."

"True, yeah," Twain said. He smoothed his coat a bit; perhaps Mak's statement had hit a bit close to the mark.

"I do not wish all of my nation's time and effort to be wasted," Mak said, "and in truth much of the resources I have diverted to Trofimov found their way into your hands anyway. My men, the weapons, certain funding…we both know that you are the driving force behind this plan. Without the men and matériel you bring to bear, there can be no plan, can be no scheme by Trofimov."

"True enough, yeah."

"I offer you twenty percent."

"Of what?"

"Twenty percent again of your fee from Trofimov. That much over what you now earn, to turn to my side. You are a man who fights for money and nothing else, yes?"

"Yeah," Twain said. He was a bit uneasy. He'd never liked Mak Wei; he had considered approaching the man himself with just such an offer, and discarded it several times previously for that reason. He wasn't sure he wanted to be any more under the man's thumb than he now found himself, with Mak's security personnel spread out amid his own forces.

"Give me some time to consider your offer," Twain said.

"Very well. Do not take too much time. I am a patient man, but my government is not so patient. You know I must answer to others. Do not keep those others waiting too long."

"All right, yeah. Yeah, right. Just give me a bit."

Mak Wei said nothing. Eventually, Twain looked up

at him. "I have to go to Jacksonville," he said finally, "to make sure the golden goose don't get cooked, yeah?"

"Very well. Have your answer for me when you return."

Twain muttered something and hurried off. Mak watched him go, shaking his head.

Mak checked the Chinese-made Makarov copy he kept in a shoulder holster. The pistol was loaded and a round chambered. He snapped the safety on and re-placed the weapon, then returned to Trofimov's office.

The Russian was on his phone, making calls to those who maintained his financial stockpiles. He made no secret of it; he had boasted to Mak Wei several times that he had enough gold and precious stones to sustain him if the economy collapsed. Such a vast physical quantity of wealth required a high-security repository. Mak gathered that this was in Jacksonville. He was more privy to the details of Trofimov's other financial data than the Russian suspected, for the firm that handled Trofimov's monetary dealings—both legal and otherwise—was itself owned by the Chinese government, indirectly.

"You are prepared to do what must be done?" Mak asked when Trofimov hung up the phone.

"I have goals," Trofimov said. "I would achieve them."

"Good. Then let us not have a repeat of the unfortu-nate conversation of some moments ago. You are above such hysteria."

"You're right, of course." Trofimov's lips made the ap-propriate movements, but his eyes still spoke of his fear.

"Twain is preparing your defenses," Mak said. "Fear not. We shall meet this challenge and overcome it."

"I just need to know I can count on you, Mak," Trofimov said. "I need to know your government's support is not wavering."

"My dear friend," Mak said, "China is nothing if not ever devoted to those who ally with it. You need not worry."

"I hope not." He turned away, looking out his window once more.

Mak smiled, and it wasn't pleasant.

It was the smile of a man who realized he had made a very significant mistake.

CHAPTER SEVENTEEN

On the monitor in the panel van parked outside the Richmond, Virginia, offices of Congressman David Heller, Mack Bolan and Agent Jennifer Delaney watched the congressman meet with Ambassador Wu Lok. The feed came courtesy of fiber-optic bugs installed by the NSA some weeks previously. Apparently, Heller had been under investigation for a while. Brognola and Price, working together to trace the orders for the Houston military unit, had uncovered both Heller's involvement and the fact that he already had a questionable NSA dossier. Some quick string-pulling had resulted in cooperation from "No Such Agency," and now Bolan and Delaney had access to a van full of NSA surveillance equipment, left for them by a taciturn man in a dark suit who hadn't said two words while handing over the keys.

On the screen, the tall, wrinkled Wu Lok sat like a praying mantis with his hands folded in his lap. A pair of his guards stood at the ready behind him.

"You can understand the delicacy of the situation," Wu said in lightly accented English. His voice was a low rasp, almost a death rattle low in his throat. "You are aware of the…arrangement…on behalf of certain elements sponsored by my government, and this Trofimov."

"Yes," Heller drawled. "I surely am. I've worked with Mr. Trofimov to good effect, until recently."

"Yes, well," Wu said, nodding, "that brings us to the reason for this direct visit. Understand, Congressman Heller, that once I leave here today, it would be very much inadvisable for us to meet in person soon, if ever again."

"I understand." Heller nodded eagerly.

"We can count on your discretion in these matters?"

"Oh, of course, Ambassador," Heller said. "I think you'll find I'm nothing if not discreet."

"And I believe in being direct," Wu said, inclining his head in a slight nod of his own. "Perhaps more so than my countrymen are known to be. You will forgive me if I state my business plainly?"

"Of course, Ambassador."

"Very good." Wu smiled faintly. "You had an arrangement with Trofimov. In exchange for his financial support, you provided to him certain government services. These services were rendered on the basis of your extensive contacts within your government and, especially, within the military. We know you have interests in multiple military industries, most of which are not known to the public."

Heller fidgeted a bit in response to that, clearly uncomfortable. "Yes, well, I mean, that is—"

"Please." Wu held up a hand. "I wish only that we understand each other. You can imagine the embarrassment my government might experience were my activities on its behalf to become public knowledge, just as you would feel embarrassed if your own less-public activities came to light."

"Of course, Ambassador."

"Good, good," Wu said. "My government wishes to establish certain channels to yours. We wish you to be the liaison."

"Well, of course." Heller nodded again. "Anything the United States can do for its friend and partner in trade, the People's Republic of China."

"Yes, of course," Wu said. "But I had something a bit less direct in mind. We wish for you to provide us, as I said, the same services you provided to Trofimov. But we want you to be prepared to do more."

"More?"

"There will be, for example," Wu said, "a variety of military interests into which we would like insight. This is insight you are positioned to provide."

"You want military secrets."

"That is a blunt way to put it, yes."

"I could get in serious trouble for providing you that information," Heller pointed out.

"You could," Wu said. "My government, in turn, could ill afford the public-relations complications that would result should our acquisition of the data come to light. As you know, those to whom I answer are sometimes overzealous in their pursuit of Chinese advantage on the world stage."

"You could say that." Heller nodded.

"We would, of course, offer you significant financial compensation."

"How significant?" Heller asked.

Wu recited a figure. Even on the video screens, the widening of Heller's eyes was noticeable.

"Well," Heller said, coughing slightly before he sipped

from a glass of water he kept next to a decanter on his desk, "I—I think we can come to an agreement, yes."

"Good, good," Wu said. "I am told you have certain account numbers you will need to provide us."

"Yes, I have those right here," Heller said. On the screen, he held up a small leather portfolio, which he handed to Wu.

"I'm not sure if I should feel relieved or cynical, Cooper," Delaney said, watching all of this unfold.

"What do you mean?" Bolan asked from his seat.

"Relieved that the government was already investigating Heller, who is apparently not just corrupt, but also a traitor, or cynical that this is true but the man is still active in the Congress, still walking around free."

"Justice takes time, sometimes," Bolan said.

"Yes." Delaney smiled. "You strike me as the real 'wait around and see' type."

They watched intently as the meeting between Heller and Wu Lok concluded. Wu signaled his security personnel, all of them heavily armed under diplomatic immunity. The man typically traveled, Price had warned Bolan over his secure phone, with a couple of vans' worth of security guards. No one man needed quite that much security, but the Chinese did it to play up Wu's importance. Having so many guards implied that everything Wu did was so weighty, he might be assassinated at any moment by any of a legion of enemies.

Bolan wasn't sure how much was symbolism and how much was just plain force. From their vantage point in the NSA surveillance van, they'd had a couple of different views of Wu and his security contingent arriving at Heller's office. Wu's people were no honor guard, no exhibition. They appeared to be hardened, trained soldiers. That was likely to be a problem.

Still, that was no reason to turn back now.

"All right," Bolan said. "I think I've heard enough. Time to go acquaint Congressman Heller with the facts."

Heller's office was on the third floor of a stately brick building in downtown Richmond. The structure housed a number of other government offices, as well as some municipal services. Bolan made sure his weapons were properly concealed and climbed down out of the van.

"You sure about this?" Delaney asked.

"He's a representative of the people," Bolan said. "I would think he'd be glad to hear from a constituent." He shut the van door and made his way across the street.

There were metal detectors at ground level. Bolan flashed his Justice Department credentials, bypassing these, though the act earned him an angry glare from the armed security guard stationed there. He was from a private company Bolan didn't immediately recognize, but it wasn't SCAR. Chances were good it was a perfectly legitimate service. He just hoped the man would have the good sense to keep his head down and stay out of the way when the fireworks started.

He took the nearest stairwell, avoiding the elevators. At the third floor, he checked the hallway. The corridors were long and wide, with expensive marble floors. A quick glance at the directory revealed that Heller's local offices were the only ones on this floor. That was good; it meant there would be few, if any, extraneous personnel to wander into the cross fire.

The soldier stalked down the hallway. The door to Heller's office opened, and Wu's security personnel began to file out. When the first man caught sight of Bolan, his features hardened. He pointed and said something in Chinese. The Executioner didn't understand the language, but the intent was clear. He was being ordered off.

Bolan spread his hands, feigning a lack of understanding.

"He said," one of the Chinese security guards translated in accented English, "to leave this floor." The man's hand disappeared into his black suit jacket.

"I don't know about you," Bolan said, "but the last I knew, I was an American citizen in the hallway of a building in an American city on an American street. I don't think I'll be leaving."

The closest guard pulled a Glock from a shoulder holster, pointing it at Bolan's face from a distance of only inches.

"Now do you feel like moving, *American?*" the guard who had already spoken said arrogantly.

"That," Bolan said, "was a mistake."

"I will kill you where you stand!" the guard with the gun threatened. His finger tightened on the trigger.

Bolan had seen enough. Wu's diplomatic immunity didn't extend to death threats to private citizens, as far as the Executioner was concerned.

He moved like a rattlesnake, whipping his head to the side, snapping his hand up and shooting the web of his free hand into the guard's throat. As the Chinese guard went down, Bolan peeled the Glock from his grip, reversed it and aimed it at the other security operatives.

"All of you," he said, "get on the floor."

"You cannot do that!" one of the guards said. "We have diplomatic—"

Bolan clubbed him in the head with the Glock. He dropped like a sack of wet cement.

All hell broke loose.

The guards pulled submachine guns and pistols of their own. Bolan threw himself back against the side of the corridor, his appropriated Glock barking. He brought down first one, then a second, then a third security guard, shooting into the target-rich environment with carefully placed shots. Then, because they wouldn't expect it, he threw himself toward the knot of enemy, into their midst.

There were shouts of confusion. One guard managed to shoot another, trying and failing to track Bolan. The soldier pistoned a kick into a knee here, a vicious edge-of-hand blow into a throat there, smashing first one and then another man in the head with the Glock. He scattered the guards, leaped over the last of them, and then rolled into Heller's office, slamming the door shut behind him.

Congressman Heller and Ambassador Wu stood there, both frozen in panic.

"Congressman," Bolan said. "Ambassador. Get on the floor. Now." He leveled the Glock.

The two men did as they were told, and none too soon. Wu's security people began firing through the doorway. The fusillade of bullets struck the wall opposite where the two men had been standing only moments previously. Bolan flattened himself against the wall, covering the two men and waiting for the security guards to realize the blind fire wasn't helping them.

There was a lull in the firing. The door was kicked in. Bolan simply waited patiently for the first of the security guards to come rushing in. As he did so, Bolan shot him from behind.

The next man blundered in after the first, and Bolan put a bullet in him, too. Considerations of fairness never entered into it; these men were trying to kill him, and

Bolan would take every advantage available to him until they were neutralized.

A third man followed the first two. Some combat instinct alerted him, and he twisted his body at the last moment, trying to bring his gun up and into play. Bolan shot him through the neck, the only angle available to him. The man went down gurgling.

The remainder of the security guards were now hanging back, firing through the open doorway. Heller and Wu had managed to move themselves out of the direct line of fire and were crouched at the opposite side of the room, trying to avoid the bullets that pocked the walls and ricocheted around the space. Bolan, wondering how many times in one operation he could expect the same tactic to work, popped the pin on a flash-bang grenade from his war bag. He let the spoon fly, counted and tossed the bomb through the doorway, squeezing his eyes shut and covering his ears.

The grenade detonated. There were afterimages still dancing in his vision, the glare having penetrated through his eyelids, as he broke cover and brought the Beretta up and in line with the enemy. The Chinese guards were stunned, but still struggling and still very much able to fight. They fired their guns at him, missing him by wide margins, struggling to overcome the disorientation of the grenade.

Bolan methodically worked his way from left to right, firing single shots, the 124-grain jacketed hollowpoint rounds taking each man in the head.

Then it was quiet.

He stepped over the dead security operatives. Grabbing Ambassador Wu by the shirt, he pulled the man upright and put him against the wall.

"Stay there," he said. He took a plastic riot cuff from a pocket of his blacksuit and secured Wu's hands.

"You cannot do this to me!" Wu said. "I am a duly appointed ambassador of the People's Republic of China! I will have your head for this!"

"Get in line," Bolan said evenly. When he was satisfied Wu was secure, he pushed him into a sitting position in the corner. Already, he could hear sirens in the distance. The gunfire had prompted someone to call the police, and they were responding with all the speed they could manage.

Bolan grabbed Heller, pulled him upright and secured his wrists behind his back. Then he pushed the man against the wall, placing the Beretta under the man's chin.

"Congressman Heller," Bolan said, "you don't know me. I'm with the Justice Department."

"Justice?" Heller was very pale.

"The ride is over, Congressman," Bolan said. "I suggest you cooperate fully."

Heller looked down at the gun, then back to Bolan's eyes. "You...you wouldn't shoot me."

"Wouldn't I?" Bolan said. He jerked his chin toward the pile of dead Chinese security guards.

"Tell him nothing!" Wu spat from his position on the floor.

"You," Bolan said, not turning, "shut up. Or I'll club you until you lose consciousness." That was a bluff, but Wu didn't know that, and Bolan was counting on the showdown with the guards to buy him some instant credibility in the ambassador's eyes.

"Please," Heller said. "I'll cut a deal. Just give me immunity and I'll testify."

"Testify to what?" Bolan said.

"Trofimov," Heller blurted. "Yuri Trofimov. Head of TBT! He's running a terrorist operation."

"A terrorist operation with which you helped him," Bolan said.

"He tricked me!" Heller said lamely. "I didn't know. I didn't understand. Please, you've got to believe me. I'm a good American! I serve the people!"

Bolan motioned as if he would pistol-whip the congressman. Heller flinched and was quiet for a moment. "As it happens," he told Heller, "I'm conducting an investigation, of sorts, into Trofimov's activities." That wasn't true, technically. Bolan was no detective, and his blitz of Trofimov's holdings wasn't an investigation so much as it was a search-and-destroy mission. But Heller wouldn't understand that. All Bolan needed was whatever information Heller might hold.

"I'll cooperate!" Heller said.

"You fool," Wu said. "Can you not see he will kill you when he is finished with you? Look at him! Look at his eyes! He is a killer!"

Bolan cast a hard look at Wu. "One more outburst," he said, "and I'll gag you."

The police sirens were growing louder. Someone on a bullhorn was broadcasting orders at the front of the building.

"We're almost out of time," he told Heller. "Give me what I need, and I'll dump you somewhere to work out whatever deal you can."

"SCFI!" Heller said. "SCFI!"

"What's that?"

"It's…it's, uh, Shanghai Corporate," Heller said. "Shanghai Corporate Financing International. They're in bed with the Chinese. All of Trofimov's funds go through them. He admitted as much to me, and said the entire operation was a laundering front for the Chinese operating in this country. Warned me not to invest, if you can believe it!" Heller was on the fine edge of hysteria now.

"Fool!" Wu snapped.

Bolan planted a combat boot in the ambassador's midsection, knocking the air from him but not hurting him seriously. "Quiet," he said.

"All my payments through Trofimov came from SCFI," Heller said. "If anyone has the goods, the money trail, it would be them."

"Now that," Bolan said, "is actually helpful. Do you know anything else?"

Heller actually appeared to consider that. Finally, reluctantly, he shook his head. "I'm just a public servant."

"If you're a public servant," Bolan said, indicating Wu with a jerk of his head, "then *he's* a humanitarian."

The local police began flooding the building. Delaney was with them, waving her FBI credentials and making sure everyone present knew Bolan was on the right side. When the cops in the lead realized who was being held prisoner, they stopped and stared.

"Is there a problem, Officers?" Bolan asked. He began herding Wu and Heller down the corridor.

"Uh, wait," one of the cops said. "Uh, Agent…"

"Cooper," Bolan said. "Justice Department."

"Look, Agent Cooper," the officer said, "We can't… I mean, we can't just let you… Well, look, that's Congressman Heller, and he's the Chinese ambassador!"

"That is an accurate assessment," Bolan told him. He continued herding the two men toward the exit.

"Holy God," one of the other cops said. He had found the carnage farther up the corridor. "There's…there's a pile of bodies here!"

"You'll find them all armed," Bolan advised the cop

who was trailing him. "Self-defense. Contact the Justice Department if you need clarification." He breathed a silent apology to Hal Brognola, hoping the big Fed's stress level wouldn't rise to stratospheric levels before this was all over.

"But, sir," the cop said. "This is highly unusual...."

Bolan stopped. He eyed the cop, meeting his gaze man to man. "Officer," he said, "Congressman Heller is wanted on charges of corruption, conspiracy and treason."

"He is?"

"Yes." Bolan nodded. "Ambassador Wu here has his own problems. Now, please, move out of my way."

"I'll need to see some identification, sir," the cop insisted. "She vouched for you—" he indicated Agent Delaney "—but that's not enough."

"All right," Bolan said. He showed the officer his Justice Department ID. "Now, step aside."

"Yes, sir."

Once outside the building, Bolan headed for the NSA van, the only vehicle they had handy. He opened his secure phone and speed-dialed the Farm. Barbara Price answered on the first ring.

"Barb," Bolan said, "I've got a real mess here. Hal's going to be up late dealing with it."

"Let me guess," Price ventured.

Bolan explained to her what had happened. "I need you to put a bag over Wu and Heller," he said, "until someone can figure out what to do with them."

"All right," Price said. "I'll have our friends at the NSA take them into custody."

"Get me everything you can on Shanghai Corporate Financing International," Bolan said. "Heller indicated that's where Trofimov does all his extralegal banking."

Delaney caught up with him, helping him maneuver

the two prisoners to the van. Heller looked shell-shocked. Wu was openly hostile, but seemed content to be led, for the time being.

"What now, Cooper?" Delaney asked.

"Now," Bolan said, "I've got to look into my investment portfolio."

CHAPTER EIGHTEEN

Bolan ran his finger along the edge of the small electronic device that had been brought by fast courier from one of the Farm's local assets. He was talking on his phone to Barbara Price yet again. Delaney was driving the rented SUV that carried them through the streets of Charlotte, North Carolina, toward downtown and the gleaming One Wachovia Center. At forty-two stories, the building was the tallest in the city, and was their landmark. The SCFI building sat in the shadow of that taller edifice, and had until now escaped real scrutiny.

"Aaron says you just have to find network access," Price was telling him, "and that little gadget will do the rest. It's something Akira whipped up originally."

"What does it do?"

"It will crawl the SCFI network," Price said, "looking for profiles that fit what we've programmed into it. In this case, it will turn up anything linked to Trofimov, Heller or the Chinese government as it relates to those two. It will also keep an eye out for any major scandals it thinks we might find of interest."

"Sounds almost alive."

"No," Price said, "just very, very clever. Aaron and Akira have been practically giddy over it. Well, Akira has been giddy. Aaron has been mildly enthusiastic, which for him is almost mad with glee."

"Understood," Bolan said. "What am I up against in there?"

"That's the bad news," Price said. "We've done some checking. On the surface, the operation is entirely legitimate, just another Chinese banking operation. Their network couldn't stand up to our cyberteam, however."

"If we hacked their network," Bolan asked, "why do I need to connect Akira's gadget to their computers directly?"

"The truly sensitive data will be partitioned on-site there, available to local access only," Price said. "It's a firewall measure taken for utmost data security. It makes sense. They're hiding a lot of skeletons that they don't want to see the light of day, if what we've uncovered thus far is any indication."

"Like what?"

"It looks like SCFI is, in fact, a wholly owned subsidiary of the Chinese government. We've also got some data on personnel disposition in and around the SCFI headquarters."

"What does that mean?"

"It means you're going to face a sizable security force on-site," Price warned him. "SCAR is contracted to provide security, specifically. If what you've faced till now is any indication, they'll probably be armed to the teeth, too."

"Doesn't matter," Bolan warned her. "I'm going in."

"I know," Price said. "Be careful, Striker."

"Striker out." Bolan closed the connection.

"Going to leave me behind again?" Delaney asked.

"You're welcome to tag along," Bolan told her. "Just don't get shot."

"You're all heart, Cooper."

Bolan parked the SUV in a paid lot not far from One Wachovia Center. He had a new rifle, also couriered by way of the Farm, to replace his lost Tavor. The M-16/M-203 over-and-under combination was an old standby, capable of launching 40 mm grenades and using the same magazines and ammunition that his Tavor had used. This particular specimen had the marks of Cowboy Kissinger's action tuning.

"I don't suppose you're going to do something sneaky," Delaney said. "You know, stealth? Subterfuge? Something other than walking up to the front door with a rifle and shouting 'Trick or Treat'?"

"I hadn't planned on it," Bolan said. He got out of the SUV and went around to the back. There, he loaded and cocked the M-16, placed it in its open duffel and hefted the bag.

"I'm coming with you," Delaney said.

"You don't want to take the back?"

"Crazy as I must be to walk in a front door with you, Cooper," she said, loading and cocking her MP-5 K, "no, I don't want to take the back." She made sure the weapon was secure on its sling under her arm.

"Suit yourself," Bolan said.

They marched directly to the front of the SCFI building. No sooner did they enter the foyer than they were challenged by a pair of uniformed SCAR security operatives.

"No one is allowed beyond this point," one of the guards said.

"I have an appointment," Bolan said.

"No one has appointments," the other guard said.

They exchanged glances. They moved for their slung rifles.

Bolan was faster. He yanked the M-16 out of the duffel bag, dropping the bag, and snapped off the safety. He raked the two men as their Kalashnikovs came up, bowling them over and ending their lives.

"Come on," Bolan said. "We've got to find a computer terminal."

Price had been able to provide only the most basic floorplan and HVAC layouts for the building. There had been no online or networked data regarding the positions of network terminals within the building. They would have no choice but to check floor by floor. Bolan was reminded of the bloody slog through Twain's headquarters, but there was nothing that could be done. They would simply have to work with what they had.

Alarms began to ring. A metal security shutter slammed down over the foyer exit.

"Cooper!" Delaney pointed. "We're trapped!"

"Good," Bolan said.

"Good?"

"That means they're trapped in here with us," Bolan said, "and there's no chance an innocent can wander into the battle."

"You know, Cooper," Delaney said, "you make a lot of sense, but you're also completely insane."

Bolan said nothing. He paused at the elevator and planted a pair of the miniature proximity Claymores.

"Move away, quickly," Bolan said. "Don't get within two yards of those devices unless you do it from the back." Each miniature Claymore was clearly labeled Front Toward Enemy.

Delaney covered him as he pushed through the fire door into the stairwell. The stairs were very wide, and each landing was huge. Bolan moved cautiously up to the next level.

Gunfire greeted him.

The floor beyond the stairwell door was divided into office space around the perimeter, with a common area dotted by couches, tables and comfortable chairs in the center. Bolan poked the snout of the M-16 through the partially opened doorway and triggered a grenade, blowing apart the nearest of the offices and scoring some fairly significant damage among the couches.

"Losing proposition," he said, ducking back. "I didn't see anything that looked like a network terminal, just office space."

"If we keep moving up with them in there," Delaney said, "we'll be caught between them once they start to move.

"Exactly," Bolan told her. "Time to go for broke."

"What?"

Bolan shed his field jacket, then pulled the war bag from his shoulder. He dumped several grenades onto the floor of the stairwell. They were a mixed bag: phosphorous, incendiary, frag and flash-bang. He replaced the much-lighter bag on his shoulder.

"Grab a handful," Bolan said.

"You have got to be kidding."

"No," Bolan said. "Pull the pins and get ready. We've going to throw them all in."

"This is insane," Delaney muttered.

"Ready…" Bolan said, whipping the door open again. "Now!"

They hurled armed bomb after bomb into the office space beyond, then Bolan slammed the door shut.

"Brace yourself!"

The explosions came, one after another, the relatively dull thumps of the more conventional ammo drowned by the deafening roar of the flash-bangs. The walls vibrated. Bolan motioned to the door, and Delaney ripped it open once more. A huge plume of smoke rushed out.

Bolan fought back the urge to cough and plunged into the smoke. Here and there he caught movement, and when he saw an enemy with a weapon, he triggered a 3-round burst from the M-16, putting the man down. Working methodically from one side of the ruined, scorched floor to the other, he cleared the area as efficiently as possible.

Gunfire began to rain down on Delaney from the landing above her.

"Cooper!" she called. "Help!"

The Executioner was already moving. He had expected the SCAR personnel on the upper floors to take the initiative at some point; the explosions on this level had been enough to convince them of the need. It might have been his imagination, but he thought he'd felt the entire building shake. That would be enough for the SCAR operatives to realize the severity of the threat.

Bolan joined Delaney. He angled the M-16 up and triggered a burst, then another, then a long stream of full-auto fire. The last was enough to drive the enemy back. "Come on," he said. "While there's time."

They worked their way up the stairs. A dead man was sprawled on the next landing, where Bolan's blind cover fire had caught him purely by bad luck. The soldier checked the corpse to make sure the man was truly dead, then advanced on the open doorway to the next floor. It was wedged open; someone had shoved an empty M-16 magazine into the gap between the hinges.

The invitation was an obvious one, and Bolan didn't intend to fall for it. He had used his supply of grenades, so he took out one of Kissinger's proximity mines, armed it and tossed it through the opening.

"What the…" someone said. "That's not a—"

"Put it down!" another voice screamed.

The explosion brought shrieks of pain. Bolan rushed the doorway, with Delaney close behind.

They emerged in a computer work farm. Row after row of terminals were arranged in a semicircular pattern, radiating from a central hub that boasted a large projection screen. The two wounded men had dropped their Kalashnikovs. One was no longer moving. The other was struggling to claw a revolver from a shoulder holster.

Bolan put a single mercy round through his forehead. He checked the other man; the proximity mine had killed him.

"Jackpot," Delaney said. "Something tells me your network access can be had here."

"Except it will take time," Bolan said. Price had warned him that Akira's data device needed time to operate, during which it couldn't be removed from the network. "Guard the door," he said. "If anybody comes down or up, fill that stairwell with lead. The only people likely to be in this building are us and SCAR's operatives. They'll be playing for keeps."

"I understand, Cooper," Delaney said, nodding.

Bolan found an appropriate USB port and jacked the little device into it. Lights on the casing began to blink. The LED indicators were first red, then yellow, and then green, followed by a blinking amber that indicated data transfer. The machine was doing its job.

Bolan removed his phone and speed-dialed the Farm.

"Barb," he said when she answered, "it's in place."

"We're getting the transmitted feed now," Price said. "I'm transferring you to Akira."

"Akira here," Tokaido said. Bolan could hear the faint echo of the heavy-metal music pumped into Akira's ears through the headphones of his MP3 player. The young Asian was the Farm cyberteam's talented computer hacker. Bolan could hear the younger man's fingers flying over his keyboard as he kept pace with whatever his device was doing.

"Cooper!" Delaney called from the doorway. "They're coming down!"

"We're about to come under fire here," Bolan said calmly.

"Understood, Striker," Tokaido acknowledged. "My little black box is opening a port in their network's firewall. It will stream all relevant data to us, using a special algorithm that moves the data around, makes it untraceable. They'll never know where it went, or even that it was copied."

"All right," Bolan said. "Call me when the transfer is complete." Gunshots rang out in the stairwell beyond the door Delaney guarded. "I've got work to do."

With the M-16 in hand, Bolan took the left side of the doorway, while Delaney, firing left-handed with her MP-5 K detached from its sling, took the right. They traded burst after burst with the enemy beyond.

"Running low here," Delaney said, just loud enough for Bolan to hear over the earbud transceiver.

Bolan produced some loaded magazines for the MP-5 K from his war bag.

"We can't keep this up forever," Delaney said.

"We won't have to," Bolan promised. He glanced back at Tokaido's device, still blinking away, hopefully out of the direct line of fire.

The shooting from the stairwell stopped.

"You in there!" one of the mercenaries shouted. "We

have you pinned down. It's suicide to keep fighting. Throw out your weapons, put your hands behind your heads and come out quietly."

Buying time could only help them now, Bolan reasoned. "I'm listening," he called.

"That was it!" the voice shouted back. "Those were the terms! Now stop dicking around and come out of there."

"How do I know you won't just shoot us when we come out?"

"Look—" the voice sounded exasperated "—I'm giving you the only chance you're going to get. Surrender and make this easy on yourself."

"There's an awful lot of very heavily armed security here for a bank," Bolan countered. "Maybe you're doing something here that isn't entirely legal. Maybe that means you're less than trustworthy."

"Screw this!" someone else yelled. A new wave of gunfire hit the doorway. Bolan threw himself back to avoid being tagged by a ricochet or a lucky shot. Delaney crouched where she was, then triggered an answering burst from her MP-5 K.

"I guess that answers that," she muttered.

Bolan's secure phone began to vibrate in his pocket.

"Cooper," he answered.

"We have it," Tokaido said. "Analyzing now. I am transmitting a self-destruct code to the device. It will be rendered inert."

At Tokaido's words, the electronic device began blinking red furiously. Then it emitted a plume of smoke and its LEDs went dark.

"Have Barb get me a synopsis as soon as you can," Bolan said.

"Are you all right?" Tokaido asked.

"Nothing I can't handle," Bolan said. He closed the connection.

Bolan considered the situation, then looked back at the computer stations arrayed behind him. Individually, none of them would stop a bullet. Taken in a line, however, there were quite a few metal casings full of circuit boards and other guts to consider. It wasn't great cover, but it just might do.

"Delaney," he whispered, watching her, "can you hear me?"

Delaney nodded.

"Good," he said. "Now, listen to me. I want you to work your way around the outside of the room, then duck behind the last row of workstations. Don't let them get a clear line on you from the doorway. I'm going to do the same. Go now."

She obeyed, moving quietly and gracefully. Bolan mirrored her movements. The gunners outside fired a few more times, but the shots were sporadic. They were no longer certain of their tactics. That was good; it was just the sort of doubt that Bolan was counting on.

He made the far end of the room and settled himself in behind one of the rows of workstations, next to where Delaney lay prone. She had her MP-5 K out in front of her in both hands, trained on the door through the gaps in the rows.

"Okay," she said. "Now what?"

"Now we wait."

They didn't have to wait long. The SCAR gunners began moving closer and closer toward the open doorway. Delaney motioned as if to shoot.

"Don't," he whispered. "Let them get closer."

"I don't see them!" one of the men called to his fellow mercs.

"Shout it to the world, why don't you, you frigging moron," another mercenary snapped. "There's no exit through there. They must be in there."

"What if they went out a window?"

"Do you see any windows in that room, stupid?"

"Jeez, lighten up, man."

The mercenaries stalked into the room, moving among the terminals in what they obviously thought was stealth. They weren't bad, but they weren't good. Bolan wasn't impressed.

Delaney looked at him anxiously. The nearest gunner was getting closer to her position. In a few moments he would be able to see over the terminal desk, and he would spot her.

Bolan shook his head.

Delaney grimaced, but she held her fire. Then, at the very last minute, Bolan nodded.

The mercenary closest to Delaney took a half step. He saw her.

"Wha—" he started. "Here! They're here—"

Bolan shot to his feet and triggered a 3-round burst through the man's chest.

Delaney did the same, taking the men behind Bolan, firing past him and to either side, careful to avoid hitting him. The computer terminals erupted in a shower of sparks. Dead men danced and jerked as the automatic fire did its deadly work, sending them to forever in a hailstorm of metal jackets. Bolan swiveled, fired, turned and fired again, making short work of the remaining troops.

There were several men who had stayed in reserve beyond the doorway. They bunched up, trying to rush in to help their comrades, and Bolan made them pay for it. He switched the M-16 to single fire and began picking off the gunners one by one, dropping each of them with precise head shots as they scrambled through the doorway on top of one another.

It was over almost as quickly as it had begun.

Bolan checked the hallway. "Clear!" he said. "At least for now. You all right?"

"Clear here," Delaney said. She looked around at the dead men and the damaged computers, MP-5 K still clutched in both hands. "Looks like we did it again, Cooper."

"Yeah, we did," Bolan said.

They made a cursory check of the floors above the terminal floor, but they found no other mercenaries. The rest of the building was deserted. The Farm presumably had all the computer files it needed, so they checked quickly for hard copies. When nothing presented itself, Bolan took Delaney by the arm.

"Come on," he said. "Let's get out of here before the police arrive."

"Aren't you used to them by now?"

"Let's say I don't want to push my luck." They took the stairwell down to ground level and picked their way through the wreckage toward the exit. Bolan removed the small pry bar from his war bag and wedged it into the metal barrier. He grunted and dislodged the shutter, moving it aside just enough so the two of them could crawl out.

In the distance, the first sirens were audible.

CHAPTER NINETEEN

"Let's get moving," Bolan said.

He and Delaney climbed into the SUV. It would be a reasonably quick drive back to the airport. Bolan put the vehicle in gear and stepped on the gas.

The truck rocked forward when a speeding panel van plowed into it.

"Hold on!" Bolan shouted. He slammed the accelerator to the floor. The SUV shot forward. In the rearview mirror, Bolan could see a pair of cargo vans in pursuit.

"Who are they?" Delaney asked, slipping on her seat belt, watching in the side mirror.

"Has to be SCAR operatives," Bolan said. "They must have been waiting in reserve. Most likely followed us out. They may think we have data that must be recovered, or they'd just be looking for payback. It doesn't matter." The SUV's engine roared as Bolan whipped the truck through a tight turn, almost bringing it up on two wheels. "We need to lose them or stop them, but we can't do this forever." For one thing, they were outnumbered, and their SUV wasn't built for speed. To their advantage was the fact that the vans pursuing them weren't particularly fast, either, but they were fast enough. Bolan tried every trick he could think of to lose them, but the SCAR drivers hung in.

Delaney rolled down her window. "I'm going to see if I can take out their tires," she said.

"Don't," Bolan said. He jerked his chin at her MP-5 K. "You'll never get them without nailing a lot of the landscape at this distance," he said, "and I can't slow down, or they'll start to take shots at us."

"I'm open to suggestions!" she shouted over the noise of the engine and the rushing wind from her open window.

"Here!" he said. "Take this!" He handed her the .44 Magnum Desert Eagle. She took it as if it were something dead, holding it with distaste.

"Use it," he insisted.

Nodding grimly, she forced herself to take a secure grip on the weapon. As they rode, swerving this way and that, Delaney took off her seat belt and climbed up using the support handle inside the door. She perched half in and half out of the open window, aiming the Desert Eagle with both hands on the gun. She wrapped her legs around the seat to keep her steady and stop her from being thrown from the window.

Shooters in the vans began to fire at the fleeing SUV. Bolan's side mirror took a round dead-center and spun away in a sudden flurry of plastic shards.

"Hurry!" Bolan called.

"I'm doing my best," she shouted back.

"Hang on!"

The turn ahead was almost a ninety-degree angle. Bolan slammed the brake and whipped the wheel around, praying they didn't manage to roll the SUV. An accident now would leave them at the mercy of their pursuers but, more important, rolling the SUV would be instant death for Delaney in her precarious position.

The tires were burning and smoking as Bolan negotiated the angle. He managed to smash a mailbox on the corner. Parcels and letters flew everywhere as the mangled metal box came to rest on the side of the street.

"Do it now!" Bolan said as they hit a straightaway. "Do it while there's time!" He put his foot flat on the floor, urging as much speed as possible from the SUV, trying to give Delaney distance in which to work. The intervening space had to be just right. Too far, and she wouldn't be able to tag the tires. Too close, and she would be in range of the enemy's guns, an easy target despite the movement of both vehicles.

Delaney started to fire. The recoil of the hand cannon seemed to startle her at first, but she hung in there gamely, aiming carefully with one eye closed and doing her best to steady each shot.

Finally she scored a hit.

The van behind them swerved and slammed into a light pole as the driver lost control. Bolan slammed on the SUV's brakes, drawing a curse from Delaney as she was slammed around in the door frame. He heeled the SUV over and brought it around in a cloud of smoking tires. The surviving van was attempting to slow down and stop, but Delaney didn't give the driver a chance. She started to fire and kept shooting until the Desert Eagle ran empty.

The second van slowed, then crashed into the first, coming to a stop. The driver inside slumped over the wheel. The windshield was starred with a series of .44 Magnum holes, where Delaney had walked her shots in and tagged the driver.

The sliding doors on the sides of the vans moved

back. Uniformed SCAR mercenaries piled out, automatic weapons in their hands.

"Get down!" Bolan yelled.

Delaney did as he instructed, snaking back into the SUV and crouching behind the dash. Bolan half crouched, staying upright enough to steer, and jammed on the accelerator again. The SUV shot forward.

Bullets pocked the hood and spiderwebbed the windshield as the SUV absorbed bullet after bullet. The engine block protected the pair as the soldier and the FBI agent played out the only hand available to them.

One of the mercenaries waited a moment too long in the face of the speeding SUV. While his comrades jumped aside, he stood, firing into the windshield. He was still shooting as the grille of the SUV slammed him back into the metal sidewall of the first wrecked van.

He slumped over the hood of the truck and was still.

Bolan and Delaney jumped out of the vehicle, Bolan wielding his Beretta 93-R, Delaney holding her MP-5 K in both fists.

Bolan circled the SUV, using it for cover. Delaney went in the opposite direction. The SCAR gunners backtracked, using the van for cover.

Then Bolan heard it.

The sound of a bicycle bell.

The kid came out of nowhere, riding a purple bicycle. She shot from the alleyway between two buildings, apparently taking a shortcut. Bolan thought this was a school day, and this little girl definitely belonged in class if it was. She was maybe twelve and blonde, looking for all the world like the quintessential innocent bystander. Bolan silently cursed the luck that had brought her here.

One of the SCAR mercenaries saw his chance. As the

girl rode up the sidewalk on the side of the street, marveling at the wrecked vans and the debris strewed about them, he leaped out and grabbed her, whirling to put her between himself and his opponents. The remaining SCAR gunners fell in behind him, arrayed to either side in support. They pointed their guns in every direction. Bolan had to admit that their training was good. Seeing the terrified look in the girl's eyes, though, he was anything but okay with their tactics. To use an innocent like that was wrong. He was going to make them pay for it.

"Ease down!" the lead mercenary called. "Just ease down, and nobody gets hurt!"

Bolan took up a position behind the engine block of the SUV, aiming the Beretta over the hood. Delaney angled over behind the van, using the space between her and the mercenaries to her advantage.

"We just want whatever you took," the mercenary said.

"There isn't anything to give you," Bolan said. "You're out of luck."

"We know you were in the network!" the mercenary said. "The security station lit up like a Christmas tree when you were in there. Just give us the data you took and nobody has to die!"

"You don't think I'm going to let you walk out of here, do you?" Bolan said.

"Cooper!" Delaney rasped, audible over the transceiver. "What are you doing? You'll set him off."

"Trust me," Bolan said quietly.

The little girl began to cry.

"Don't worry, honey," Bolan said to her. "I'm a policeman. Everything's going to be all right."

"Shut up!" the mercenary holding the girl shouted. "My men are going to come forward," he said. "They're going to take you in hand and they're going to search you. You are going to cooperate, and your friend behind the van is going to stand there and do nothing. Fail to obey my orders and I *will* kill this girl."

"Delaney," Bolan said quietly, "I need you to trust me."

"What are you going to do?"

"Just trust me. Promise me."

"Okay."

The mercenaries moved out, flanking their leader and the girl. They brought up their guns.

Bolan broke cover. Moving forward, gliding as he stepped from heel to toe, he triggered a single shot. The first of the mercenaries went down.

"Son of a—" one of them shouted.

The bullet in his forehead cut off the rest of his words.

Bolan turned, fired, turned incrementally and fired again. He kept firing until all of the mercenaries, believing their hostage gave them an advantage over the enemy, fell to the asphalt. They had learned the hard way that no hostage could stop a foe who was determined not to play by the enemy's rules.

"You stupid bastard!" the mercenary yelled. He pressed his Glock 17 pistol to the girl's temple. "You stupid son of a bitch! Do you realize what you're going to make me do? Do you?"

"Go ahead," Bolan said calmly. He advanced on the mercenary, his machine pistol held in both hands. "Go ahead. Kill her."

"Cooper!" Delaney whispered hotly. "What the *hell* are you doing? Do you want him to murder her?"

Bolan didn't try to respond. He moved closer, his weapon still on topic. The girl squirmed in the mercenary's grip. He held her more tightly, sweat streaming down his face.

"I'll do it!"

"No," Bolan said, "you won't. Not because you have any decency, of course. If you did, you'd never have grabbed a child in a the first place."

"What the fuck are you talking about?" the mercenary demanded.

"You're going to let her go," Bolan said, "because you know that if you hurt her, you've lost the only leverage you have, and I will shoot you where you stand. You'll be staring into the black pit of forever, and you'll find out just what it means not to exist anymore. You're not sure how you feel about that. In fact, you're scared to death of it. You don't want to know what's on the other side."

"Stop talking! Stop talking right now!"

"We're going to come to an understanding," Bolan said, still moving closer, "that starts with the sure and certain knowledge that if you harm that little girl, I will make you *hurt* before I put you down."

"Stop! Just stop!" the mercenary screamed. He was near hysterics.

Bolan judged he had pushed it as far as he dared.

"Now," he said, "I'm going to lower my weapon. I'm not going to put it down. I'm not going to let you out of this quite that easily. But I'm going to lower it. And you are going to lower your own weapon and let that girl go. If you do, you just might live past the next thirty seconds."

"I want assurances," the mercenary ventured. "I want to know you're going to keep your word."

"I've given you no word to keep," Bolan said. "You have no options."

"Back off, then," the mercenary said. "Back off and I'll let her go."

"No," Bolan said. "Not good enough."

"Step back, I said!"

"I'm going to count to three," Bolan said. "When I get to three, I'm going to take very careful aim, and I'm going to shoot you through the head. Hiding behind the girl won't save you. I'm a very good shot. You are much larger than she is. You can't hide behind her, not completely."

"Stop talking!" the mercenary demanded.

"Even if you manage to shield your skull," Bolan said, relentless, "I'll find another piece of you, put a bullet in it and then shoot you through the brain when you stick your head up. You have one choice only."

"Stop!" the mercenary roared.

"Let the girl go. Now. One."

"Listen," the man started to plead. The girl in his grip began to shove against him. "We can cut a deal."

"No deals. Two."

"I said I'm willing to cooperate!"

"Do it now. Three."

"Okay! Okay! Don't shoot!" The mercenary shoved the girl away from him. She stumbled but didn't fall. Crying a little, she ran. Delaney scooped her up as she neared the sidewalk, grabbed her bicycle and walked both girl and bicycle hurriedly into the alley from which the girl had emerged. Over the transceiver, Bolan could hear the FBI agent talking to the girl, soothing her, telling her that this was all a misunderstanding and that the police would take care of the very bad man.

Bolan would take care of the very bad man himself.

"Lower your gun."

"You lower yours!"

"Do you think you're faster than me?" Bolan said. "I'll tell you what. We'll both do it, and you can face me man to man. If you win, you can go. I'll give you a head start. Look the other way."

The mercenary lowered his weapon to the ground as Bolan did the same. When both guns touched the pavement, the soldier allowed his fingers to part, leaving the gun where it was. The mercenary did the same.

They stood and regarded each other.

Bolan bent his knees slightly. His hands came up, palms open and out.

The mercenary adopted a martial-arts stance of some kind, his hands straightened into blades.

"Come on, you son of a bitch," he said. He suddenly attacked, throwing a flying kick at Bolan's midsection.

Bolan sidestepped and punched him in the chest. The mercenary went down, rolling out, coughing and shaking his head, but still mobile. Then he was up and charging in again, this time throwing a flurry of forward kicks. Bolan smashed each kick down with his forearms, battering them away as fast as they came in, stopping them from making solid contact. Then he took the initiative, driving in and forward, slamming his knee into the man's thigh and spinning him off balance. The mercenary howled as Bolan drove an uppercut elbow into his chin, then followed by hooking the back of his neck, bending him forward and driving a knee into his gut.

The man made a retching noise as the wind was driven from him. Bolan swept his legs out from under him, allowing him to land on the pavement face-first. He made a tortured sound as his nose was crushed. Bolan couldn't tell for sure from the angle at which he stood, but he thought the guy's nose was broken.

"Get up," Bolan ordered. "Come on, tough guy. Get up."

The mercenary struggled to his feet, blood streaming from his flattened nose. He made a halfhearted attempt at a reverse punch. Bolan sidestepped it easily and drove a hard fist up and under his chin. He followed that with a cross and then a horizontal elbow. The mercenary hit the pavement, hard, and stayed there. He was out cold.

Bolan searched him, relieved him of a folding knife and his wallet, and secured his wrists behind his back with a set of plastic riot cuffs. He and Delaney would drop the man with security at the airport before they left, and allow the locals to process him and question him. They probably wouldn't learn anything of value, but another of Trofimov and Twain's SCAR hirelings would be off the streets.

Delaney approached. The girl was nowhere to be seen.

"What did you do with her?" he asked.

"She told me where she lived," Delaney said. "It was very close. I just walked her over and made sure her mother knew she was okay. The mother had heard gunfire. I gave her my contact information and showed her my FBI identification, just in case. She'll be fine. Probably have a story to tell her friends that none of them will believe." She shrugged.

"Good," he said. "Thanks for taking care of that."

"Cooper," Delaney said, "you had me scared witless there. I thought for sure you'd lost it. I thought maybe you were really some sort of mindless thug, deep down, finally getting a chance to play the macho game with an opponent."

"I would hope, even after so short a time, you know me better than that."

"Yeah," Delaney said. "But I was never out of range, Cooper. I heard every word. And I saw most of the fight. Does it come easily to you, to do something like that?"

"The fighting?"

"Not that so much," Delaney said. "The, well, the way you mind-screwed him. That was disturbing."

They returned to the SUV. Bolan looked over the damage. The dead man slumped over the hood was where they had left him, and wouldn't be going anywhere without help ever again.

"The mind of the predator is easily enough understood," Bolan told her. "That's what this man is." He nodded to the mercenary as he opened the rear door of the SUV and dumped the man in the back.

"You're not really going to drive away with him like that?" Delaney asked.

"I was going to," Bolan said. He could hear sirens again. "I think we'll be able to give him directly to the police, though."

"That sound seems to follow everywhere you go, Cooper," Delaney said. She surveyed the wreckage around them. "And scenes like this."

"It goes with the job," Bolan said. "Predators can't be reasoned with, Delaney. Those who prey on others, who hurt innocents, who take from others, they understand only force. They operate in the realm of force. They give no quarter, even if they expect it from others. They have no mercy, no pity, no remorse and no empathy...again, even if they expect it from others. The societal predator is more than a parasite, and more than a criminal. He's a taker, and he'll take whatever he can get and never feel the least bit guilty. Decent people, innocent people, don't and can't act that way. But this man—" he jerked a thumb to the unconscious mercenary "—well, that's a way of life for him."

"A philosopher, too," Delaney said. "I'm impressed, Cooper." She reached into the cab of the SUV, brushing pieces of safety glass off the seat. She came up with the empty Desert Eagle and handed it, butt first, to the Executioner.

"Like it?" he asked.

"Kicks a lot," she said.

CHAPTER TWENTY

Bolan sat behind the wheel of the Chevy Suburban, a vehicle appropriated for him by the Farm. It had been waiting for them at the airport.

"That's it, all right," Delaney said from the passenger seat, watching the other side of the street through a small pair of binoculars. "The address matches, and it matches the photo found in the files."

"Then we're ready," Bolan said.

They were facing a building on the outskirts of Jacksonville, Florida, a building referred to in the SCFI data simply as "the Vault." According to that data, the Vault was many things, but first and foremost, it was Trofimov's repository for his doomsday assets: gold, silver, diamonds and other precious goods, as well as stockpiles of weapons. There were hints that more went on in the extensive property than just the stockpiling and secure storage of Trofimov's wealth, but the Farm had been unable to determine exactly what. What Price had been able to tell Bolan, beyond the location of the structure, was that its perimeter was hardened against assault. There were guards stationed in specially designed watch-units on the outer perimeter of the long, low, wide structure, and the main entrance was a steel gate controlled from a guard hut. To the casual observer, the entire facility looked like—and was ostentatiously marked as—a repository for collectible coins. That probably wasn't too far from the truth, as Bolan stopped to consider it, but very few coin collectors employed private armies of illegally armed mercenaries.

"Ready?" Bolan repeated, this time making it a question.

"Definitely," she said.

"Strap in," he said. They both put on their seat belts. Bolan gunned the engine several times, dropped the big truck into gear and tromped the accelerator.

They hurtled across the street. They could both see the expressions on the faces of the guards as the truck rammed its way past the metal gates to the Vault property. Then they were in, the engine compartment smoking, twisted wreckage from the metal gate surrounding them. Bolan leaped from the truck with his M-16/M-203 over-and-under combo at the ready, while Delaney had her MP-5 K up and waiting.

The nearest guards scrambled from their watch enclosures, firing handguns, shotguns and submachine guns. Bolan and Delaney took cover behind the engine block of the Suburban, using the truck to thwart the enemy gunners' targeting. Bolan dropped first one man, then another with precisely aimed shots from his M-16. Delaney's stuttering MP-5 K claimed several more of the SCAR shooters.

"Go, go, stay moving," Bolan ordered.

They moved farther into the depths of the Vault. They blasted their way past a series of security doors, Bolan chewing up the locks with withering fire from his M-16.

They eventually ran out of doors but came to a much stronger, reinforced portal. "Back up, back up," Bolan instructed his partner. He would have to use the grenade launcher, and for that they would need more space.

Several of the SCAR gunners had regrouped and were now trying to tag them from behind. Delaney kept them back with furious bursts from her machine pistol, as Bolan punched a hole through the reinforced portal with a grenade from his M-203.

The blast rocked the Vault. They ran for it, heading for the cover of the rooms beyond.

The duo navigated a series of storage rooms, each bearing metal chests. Some of these were labeled, and some weren't. Each held, according to its markings, a small fortune in gold, diamonds and other precious metals and stones. Bolan and Delaney ignored these, chased on as they were by the determined ranks of the SCAR gunners.

They fought their way around an L-shaped hallway, dropping mercenaries left and right. Bolan kept dispensing loaded magazines to Delaney from the supply he kept in his war bag.

"There!" Bolan pointed. A reinforced fire door divided the section in which they fought from the next level of the Vault. Bolan pushed Delaney through the doorway, paused to fire the M-16 and almost made the cover of the fire door before he caught a shotgun blast.

The soldier hit the floor, hard. Delaney slammed the fire door shut, throwing the heavy bolts. The door absorbed several bullets from the other side, but none penetrated.

"Come on, Cooper," Delaney said. She pulled the damaged M-16 from his hands; the rifle had taken the brunt of the impact. A few pellets had struck him in the arms and torso, but the wounds were minor and Bolan barely noticed them through the rush of adrenaline. He would feel the pellets later, when he had time to recover, but for now there was very little blood and no impact on his performance.

There was another set of heavy doors. What Bolan had at first taken to be fire doors was clearly meant as an emergency barrier for a fight of this type—though the Vault's designers had apparently failed to consider that the same doors could stymie the Vault's defenders after an invading force slipped past the outer perimeter, as Bolan and Delaney had done.

There was yet another doorway leading farther into the center of the Vault. Bolan threw it open, with Delaney close behind.

They entered a bedroom.

The sheer incongruity of it stopped them both for a split second. Then Bolan realized what they were looking at. A large, round bed waited in the center of the room. A bathtub and shower were to one side, and a hot tub stood between the two. Studio lighting was arranged and hung from the ceiling, as did boom microphones. Digital video cameras were mounted on tripods, pointing at the bed. An adjacent changing area and dressing room boasted a mirrored table with various pieces of clothing, makeup and other accoutrements.

"Hell," Delaney said. "It's a porno studio."

"Looks like," Bolan said. "Apparently there are levels to Trofimov's illegal empire that we didn't know about."

"It does make sense," Delaney said. "He's got plenty of connections in the cable and television world. And he's got built-in distributorships, if he were to leverage his other commercial interests."

Something was tickling the back of the Executioner's mind. He looked around, examining the camera equipment.

"The only thing I don't get," Delaney said, "is why hide it here, in the middle of his most secure storage facility, where he's keeping his most valuable possessions?"

"Think about it," Bolan said. "Trofimov is a manufactured entity. He's all about image. Everything he does, everything he wears, everything he says is all calculated to enhance the image of himself that he projects. He's the elder statesman of cable news and a reluctant warrior for journalistic integrity—all because he says he is and presents himself that way."

"And porn doesn't exactly fit that image."

"Exactly," Bolan said, checking his handguns. He handed over several more loaded magazines to Delaney, who changed out the near-empty magazine in the MP-5 K. "Trofimov is happy to profit from the seediest elements of the entertainment industry—" he swept the room with one arm "—just like he runs his news network, based on sensationalism and outright lies. But if word got out how he's really doing things, what he really is, he'd be ruined. The image would be shattered."

"What's the plan, Cooper?"

"We haven't seen nearly all of this place," Bolan said. "We've passed the outer storage levels, but based on the sheer size of the site, there's got to be more. We press on."

"What about the mercs behind us?"

"They'll make their way through here in pursuit eventually," Bolan said. "We can't keep them off us indefinitely, and I see no reason to try." He removed several of Cowboy Kissinger's miniature proximity Claymore mines from his war bag.

"Put these in front of the doorway," he said. "Arm

them and get out of the way fast, before they activate. You have a delay of perhaps ten seconds."

"Got it," Delaney said, looking at the explosives.

"We'll have to keep watching our backs," Bolan said, "but that will give them something to think about."

"What about local law enforcement?" Delaney said. "We've started yet another public firefight. They'll be along soon."

"They may well be," Bolan said, "but I don't expect them to get past the outer perimeter. Those SCAR troops still active will do their best to keep them out, and they've got the advantage of what's left of their fortifications. The locals will seal off a perimeter, maybe call in SWAT, but they'll stand off for the most part, wait to see what happens. We're on our own for the duration."

"You knew that coming in?"

"I did. This is my job to do, and I'm going to do it. Anyone gets in our way, I'll drop them."

"You're a hard man, Cooper."

"I have a hard job to do."

There was a nearly hidden doorway leading out of the adult-movie studio. Bolan pushed this open and stuck his head through, Beretta 93-R in his right fist, checking for gunners. The corridor beyond was narrow and held nothing threatening. He motioned for Delaney to follow.

As the FBI agent was climbing through the narrow doorway, the proximity mines exploded. The blasts came one on top of the next, impossibly loud in the enclosed space. Bolan covered Delaney with his body, pulling her out of the doorway, and triggered several 3-round bursts from the Beretta machine pistol. SCAR mercenaries moved in from the rear, walking over their dead comrades as they hurried after the pair.

Bolan switched the Beretta to single-shot mode to conserve ammunition. He put a bullet through the forehead of one mercenary and another through the throat of a second. Still, the SCAR hard force kept coming.

"We've got to move!" he shouted to Delaney.

Bolan fired the Beretta dry, thrust the empty weapon into his war bag and drew the .44 Magnum Desert Eagle. The hand cannon bucked and thundered as he send .44-caliber death down the corridor, scattering the mercenaries and giving him and Delaney time to make the next reinforced doorway. On the other side, the soldier threw the bolts built into the door. Again, it was clear the structure had been designed with defense in mind. The designers simply hadn't considered the possibility of interlopers. Bullets pinged off the opposite side of the door, but it held. The Executioner knelt and planted another proximity mine before backing away from the doorway.

Delaney gasped.

Bolan turned around—and stopped, amazed.

The large chamber in which they found themselves was another studio, complete with lighting and an illuminated backdrop designed to simulate natural sky. What was amazing about the studio, however, was that it completely simulated the look of an Afghani village. There were sleeping goats that turned out to be stuffed, huts that looked real from the front but were skeletons of plywood and two-by-fours from the back, and even unmoving, fiberglass Humvee props painted to look like U.S. Army vehicles.

Bolan realized, then, what had been nagging at him about the porno set.

"Delaney," Bolan said, looking around. He holstered

his Desert Eagle, dropped the magazine in his Beretta 93-R, rammed home a fresh one, then holstered that weapon, too. "Does any of this look familiar to you?"

"No," Delaney said. "Should it?"

"Look closely," Bolan said.

She examined the set, clearly curious as to what he had in mind. When it hit her, it hit her hard.

"Holy shit," she said.

"Yeah." Bolan nodded.

The set was an exact reproduction of the village depicted in the "massacre" video being played over and over on Trofimov's cable news network. Or, Bolan thought to himself, it's not a reproduction at all. This is the village where the video was shot.

"Cooper, you don't think…"

"That's exactly what I think," Bolan said. "Trofimov faked it. That's why the video is so blurry, and why nobody's been able to identify the soldiers in it. They can't be found because they don't exist. They're actors or, more likely, SCAR personnel drafted for the role, play-acting the massacre right here on this set."

Bolan looked around the studio area, hunting for something that might prove useful. Then he noticed the small video-editing shack at the edge of the "village." It was clearly part of the Vault, not built into the set, and it was labeled.

"There," Bolan said. "Watch our backs. I want to see what's in there."

He took a step toward the video booth.

The door to the studio blew.

The explosion rocked the studio, cracking the plaster facades on a couple of the fake huts. The blast also caused the proximity mine to detonate, but its angle sent shrapnel back out the doorway. At least one of the

SCAR mercenaries was caught in the spray of deadly ball bearings. He dropped the M-79 grenade launcher he had used to blow the door.

There was nowhere to go. Bolan dived for one of the fake huts, knowing that its flimsy construction could provide concealment only. Bullets chased him. Delaney sprinted in the opposite direction, blazing away with her MP-5 K and doing her best to drive the enemy back.

Bolan discovered that the huts were all interconnected in the rear, and that there was nothing separating them from one another. Hiding behind the set, he worked his way up the opposite wall of the studio, unseen by the gunners who were tracking Delaney. As they tried to shoot her down, Bolan was able to get behind them.

He emerged from one of the fake huts, his Beretta in his left hand, his Desert Eagle in his right. Leveling both guns, he shouted, "Over here!"

The distraction had the desired effect. The gunners, closing in on Delaney's position, were thrown off as they turned and tried to track this renewed threat. Bolan triggered 3-round bursts from the Beretta and individual .44 Magnum slugs from the Desert Eagle. The mercenaries were mowed down, screaming their last as the avenging soldier among them took their lives and sent them to their final judgments.

The gunshots were ringing in Bolan's ears. Delaney suddenly pointed. "Cooper! There!"

Bolan followed her gesture. There was an upper balcony to the studio, set above and beyond the "sky" backdrop. Gunmen were up there, and as Bolan and Delaney dived for what scant cover there was, the shooters opened up. Rifle and handgun bullets peppered the dirt of the simulated earth.

The soldier and the FBI agent, as if by unspoken agreement, took opposite sides. Bolan wheeled left, while Delaney ran right. Splitting the fire of the men on the balcony, Bolan and his ally began firing back.

The man on the far left was hit and fell from the balcony. The man on the far right took a round through the chest and crumpled where he stood. Bolan and Delaney whittled away at the enemy's numbers, fighting from both edges to the center. When their gunfire converged on the last shooter remaining, the one closest to the center, he was riddled with bullets and fell with a scream to the fake village below.

Bolan worked his way back to Delaney. She put her back to his, and the two of them, with their guns raised, slowly rotated to assess the threat potential they now faced.

There was nothing.

They waited twenty minutes, all told, wondering if there would be further waves of soldiers. They were deep enough inside the Vault that if the police had cordoned off a perimeter around them, they wouldn't know it. Bolan decided that none of that mattered. There were more immediate needs.

"Cooper?" Delaney asked.

"Yeah."

"You all right?"

"Yeah. You?"

"Never better."

"It's not over yet," Bolan said.

"No?"

"No." Bolan pointed to one of the digital video cameras. "Can you operate that?"

"Can't be that hard," she said.

"Keep an eye out. We don't want to get caught by surprise." He surveyed the village. It had sustained some damage, but it was still very recognizable. There was, he thought, a certain irony to the fact that this place, designed to simulate a battle, had itself been the scene of a real one.

Bolan judged the angle as best he could based on his memory of the "massacre" video. He positioned himself in the center of the frame.

"Cut my head off," Bolan said.

"What?"

"I don't want my head in the video," he said. "Get my voice, but don't record my face."

"All right," Delaney said.

"Ready?"

"Ready."

"Roll," Bolan said.

When he was certain the camera was running, Bolan began to talk.

"Hello," he said. "I am an authorized agent of the United States government. I am here in the company of an agent of the Federal Bureau of Investigation. It's very important that you be made to understand that a video you've seen, purporting to show the massacre of innocent Afghanis by American troops, is a complete hoax."

He moved aside so that the camera could get a good view of the "village."

"You will recognize this village," he said. "It is identical to the one in the video, down to the last detail, because this is the set where the video was faked." He walked slowly forward, allowing Delaney time to adjust to keep his face out of the frame. Then he grabbed a portion of the nearest hut and pulled it free. He reversed this, showing the skeleton of plywood underneath.

"As you can see," he explained, "these buildings aren't real. The men who appeared in the video, pretending to be U.S. military operatives, haven't been identified because, within the legitimate United States military, they do not exist."

He moved back into his original position. "I call on every media outlet in the United States and abroad to do whatever is necessary to spread the word of this hoax. The United States military isn't perfect, but its members are not the mindless perpetrator of atrocity you have been led to believe. Thank you."

He stopped and waited for Delaney to stop recording. Then he took the camera from her, uncoiled a USB cable from it and attached that cable to his secure phone. After transferring the video file, he transmitted it to the Farm and pressed the speed dial.

"Striker?" Barbara Price answered. "What's this?"

"Take a good look," Bolan said. He waited. He could hear, over the connection, the sound of the video he had just recorded, as Price played it on her workstation.

"Striker, is this… Are you serious?"

"As a heart attack," Bolan told her. "See what Bear's team can do with this. Maybe a side-by-side comparison with the original tape, so people can see that they match. I'm thinking we can have this all over the Internet and disseminated to the major news networks in just a few hours."

"I know we can," Price said. "Striker, this is brilliant."

"I don't know about that," Bolan said. "Someone could claim the set itself was built after the fact. But this should go a long way toward correcting the worst of it." He closed the connection.

"The worst of it?" The voice had an Irish accent. "Boy-o, you don't know the half of it."

Bolan turned. A large, bald-headed man stood there,

one arm wrapped around Delaney's throat, his free hand holding a .44 Magnum Desert Eagle pressed against Delaney's temple.

CHAPTER TWENTY-ONE

"Twain," Bolan said.

"Aye," Gareth Twain said. "Got the drop on you, didn't I? It wasn't difficult. Hard to save the world when you're too busy to watch your own backtrail, yeah?"

"Put the weapon down, Twain," Bolan said.

"And where would be the fun in that?" Twain gestured with the Desert Eagle, the triangular snout of which moved from the side of Delaney's head to behind her back. "This bitch and me, we have a history, don't we? You just keep yer guns in your holsters, boy-o."

"It's over, Twain," Bolan said. "The whole operation. Your company, SCAR, is finished. Your men are dead."

"Aye," Twain said. "Knocked my headquarters over right nice, you did, and you uncovered all of Trofimov's dirty little secrets to boot." He looked around at what was left of the "village." "You've got to admit," he said with a laugh, "that parts of all this were brilliant. Had the whole country, the whole world going, he did."

"No lie can live forever, Twain," Bolan said. "The truth will out."

"Sure," Twain said. "But what is the truth? It's what people want to believe." He smirked. "I've never understood you hero types. Never will. What do you get out of it, big man? Does it feel good, running around, trying to take in people like me? Does it get you off, yeah? Make you feel like a big shot?"

"You're a predator, Twain."

"You got that right."

"You're not fit to breathe the same air that honest citizens breathe," Bolan told him. "You're a plague. A germ. Stamping you out helps everyone. Removing you promotes everything that is good in the world."

"A bit harsh, don't you think?" Twain said, indignant. "I want to know who you are, big man."

"That's not important."

"Oh, come on," Twain said. "You know all about me. Got a folder, don't you? Gareth Twain, Irish terrorist, blah, blah, blah. Who are you, big man? What is it that gets you out of bed in the morning?"

"I'm just a man, Twain," Bolan told him. "Someone trying to do the right thing."

"The right thing, yeah?" Twain scoffed. "Well, that's me, isn't it? Mind me own business, don't I. Look after number one."

"Not the same."

"It wouldn't be, to the likes of you," Twain said. "You almost had me in New Orleans, you know."

"How did you get away?"

"Concealed fire escape," Twain said. "Built into the south face of the building. Perfect for those little emergencies."

"What are you doing here?"

"Curious George, aren't you?" Twain grinned. "No harm in telling you. Trofimov wanted to make sure his little treasure trove was well-guarded. I came to see to it personally."

"And then hid yourself until the fighting was over?"

"What am I, stupid?" Twain said. "It was obvious since you first came on the scene, wasn't it, that I was up against serious heat. You rolled over us in New Orleans. You were rolling over us here. What's one more gun? I figured, let the boys handle it, yeah, and if they don't, well, live to fight another day, or something like that."

"But you're here now."

"Can't hide forever," Twain said. "And when I saw *her,* well…here and I guess I'm just a hopeless romantic."

He leaned in close, making a show of smelling Delaney's hair. She flinched, but didn't cry out. She was, in fact, holding herself very still. That was smart. If Bolan got the chance to go for one of his guns, he would take the shot. She had seen him shoot often enough to know just how good he was. She was gambling that he'd be able to take out Twain while missing her.

"There's no point to any of this," Bolan said. "Give it up, Twain. Harm a federal agent and you'll die for it, one way or another."

"You're forgettin'," Twain said gleefully, "I'm already running me a tab where that's concerned. Now back off, boy-o, or I plug the bitch, make no mistake."

"What do you want?" Bolan said.

"Well, now, that's a good question," Twain said thoughtfully. "You've destroyed my work, my job and my employer. I may have another offer on the table, I suppose—" he shook his head "—but I don't fancy taking it. A little too much stress for a lad like me. Which means, really, whoever you might be, that the only option left to me is, well, sheer meanness."

"You can live through this."

"Assumin' I want to," Twain said. "You have got me curious, boy-o. Tell me, where are the rest of your people?" He looked left, then right.

"There are no others," Bolan said.

"You're joking," Twain said, staring at him. "You mean to tell me that all of it, everything, was just you? You and this bit of fluff here?"

Bolan shrugged.

"I don't believe it," Twain said. "One man? One? Takes down an organization the size of mine, takes Trofimov and everything the man has built with him by himself? Nah, man, nah, I ain't buyin' that. You'd have to be ten feet tall and bulletproof to begin to pull that off. And you, well, forgive me, boy-o, but you're just a man, from the look of you."

Delaney, perhaps sensing that if she was to have any chance at all, she would have to act, threw an elbow backward into Twain's face, hurting him just enough to break free of his hold. His Desert Eagle went off. Bolan was already whipping his own .44 Magnum handgun from its Kydex holster. Twain had just enough time to shove Delaney aside. She went down.

Twain, rather than try to duel Bolan, hurled himself at him, slamming into the soldier with all the force of his stocky, muscled frame. The two men went down. Bolan lost his Desert Eagle, and Twain's own weapon hit the dirt of the fake village. Bolan tried to grab for the Beretta, but his adversary snapped open an OTF automatic knife that appeared in his hand. The razor-sharp blade sliced through the leather of Bolan's shoulder harness and into the shoulder, as well, cutting deep. He gritted his teeth and twisted free, but the Beretta was lost. Twain laughed and kicked the weapon away, still wrapped in what was left of Bolan's shoulder harness. He crouched with his switchblade low in front of his body, moving around the soldier in easy, slow circles.

Bolan's hand fell to the Boker Applegate combat knife in his waistband. He drew the double-edged blade, holding it reversed in his hand.

"Well, now," Twain said, "that's more like it! Give us some sport before the end of it all, eh?" He advanced. Bolan danced back, mindful of his footwork, his eyes cutting to Delaney's body in the dirt not far away. Twain followed his gaze, tried to exploit the distraction by lunging forward. Bolan slapped the arm away but wasn't fast enough with his counter cut, missing the extended limb with the blade of his knife.

Twain tried crouching and throwing dirt at Bolan's face with his free hand, but the Executioner was waiting for that and simply turned his head aside. The Irishman tried to rush in once more, but Bolan nicked him with his counter slash.

"A scratch," Twain taunted. "You'll need more than that for the likes of me."

"No one else has to die," Bolan said. He could see in Twain's eyes that he was wasting his time. The mercenary had no compassion even at his most lucid, but he was close to hysteria now. It was different from the cold hatred that had enveloped Kwok Sun. Twain was just feeling mean and hoping to inflict some pain. After losing everything, after failing so spectacularly, he was hoping to spread some misery. He had stopped caring about the consequences. That much was clear from his manner.

Twain lunged with the knife. Bolan sidestepped, slapping the knife hand way, but the Irishman was fast, and countered before Bolan could neutralize him.

The two men danced around each other, Twain slashing and stabbing, Bolan holding back, looking for an opening.

Bolan tried for a fight-ending comma cut, but Twain was faster. He took a glancing slash to his chest, barking in pain as the blade bit into him.

"Take me a piece at a time, why don't you?" he roared. He stabbed again and again, but each time Bolan ducked back.

"Last chance," Bolan said.

"Do you know what I've learned, big man?" Twain taunted, slashing with the knife. "There's nothing worth caring about. There's nothing worth doing. There's nothing worth believing. All there is, is getting by. That and making sure you're the top dog, yeah?" He lunged again. Bolan delivered a vicious slash to the inside of the man's arm. Twain howled and clutched the wounded limb, backing off a few paces. He dropped his knife.

"I'll spare your life if you give up," Bolan told him.

"You ruddy bastard," Twain said, breaking out in a cold sweat. "Kill you dead, I will, and then I'll take that little FBI bitch right on top of your cooling corpse, and see if I don't!"

He swung with both hands, slamming his meaty fists into Bolan's ribs. The Executioner grunted under the onslaught. Twain managed to kick the soldier's leg out from under him. Bolan went down.

Twain bent and scooped up the 93-R from where it had fallen, ripping it from what was left of its holster using his left hand.

"You're better than I thought you'd be," Twain said. "So now I'm just gonna kill you."

The boom of a .44 Magnum Desert Eagle reverberated through the studio. Twain was rocked in place.

Blood began to spread from the wound that had appeared in his chest.

Bolan shifted the knife in his grip. He stepped in and drove his knife, underhand, deep into Twain's stomach, up under the rib cage.

The rush of air that escaped Twain's mouth sounded like a balloon deflating. The Irishman gasped and let out a low moan, falling to his knees. The Beretta spilled into the dirt. Both of Twain's hands went to the hilt of the knife still jutting from his belly. He seemed to be pulling on the handle, but he couldn't withdraw the knife. He looked up at Bolan plaintively.

"Here...now," he croaked. "How was that...fair...?"

"Fair doesn't enter into it," Bolan said.

Twain fell forward into the dirt and was still.

Bolan hurried to Delaney's side. She had dragged herself to one of the two Desert Eagles. He gently took the gun from her hand and set it aside, holding her upright against him.

"Doesn't kick so bad after all," she said.

"You saved my life," he told her.

"Bullshit." Delaney coughed. "You'd have managed. But I thought I would save you some time."

Bolan's hands came away soaked with blood as he held her. Twain's shot had done its deadly work.

"How bad is it?" She looked at him. "I can't feel my legs."

"It's bad." It was worse than that; it was fatal. The bullet had severed her spine, if Bolan was any judge of the shot placement.

"Anything...is there anything that can be done?"

"No," he said truthfully.

"Don't sugarcoat it, Cooper." She laughed weakly. "Give it to me straight."

"I'm sorry," Bolan said.

"Cooper." She started coughing, badly. Then she looked up at him. "I'm…I screwed up, didn't I?"

"No," he said, and he meant it. "You did just fine."

"We got him? We got Twain?" In Bolan's arms, her skin was like ice.

"We got him."

"Go and get…Trofimov," she said weakly. "I want to know…you got to the end…and made him…pay."

"I will," Bolan told her. "I will. I promise."

The cold she was experiencing was from the blood loss. There really was nothing he could do; the wound was too bad. He'd seen damage of this type before. Even if she were rushed to a hospital, even if she'd been shot in an emergency room, there was no way to undo the damage dealt her. Her life was ebbing away.

"I…want to know who you are, Cooper."

"Don't try to talk," he said.

"No, Cooper," she said. "Please. I'm… This is it for me. I want to know."

"My name is Mack Bolan."

Her eyes widened. "Mack Bolan? But you…died…"

"No," Bolan told her. "I didn't. I've been fighting for what's right. Just like you did."

"I…I did, didn't I?"

The light left Delaney's eyes. She stared up at him in death, seeing nothing more.

"Yeah, kid," Bolan said softly. "You did."

CHAPTER TWENTY-TWO

Mack Bolan closed the driver's door of the rented SUV. He left the truck parked across the street. Looking up at Trofimov's headquarters, he took off his field jacket. He checked the Beretta 93-R and placed it in the canvas war bag slung over his shoulder. Then he checked first one, then the other Desert Eagle he carried with him. The first weapon was his own; the second was the one that had belonged to Gareth Twain, the weapon Agent Delaney had used to save his life. He thrust the second Desert Eagle into his waistband, forward of the Kydex holster that carried his own.

His phone began to vibrate in his pocket. He flipped it open and put it to his ear.

"Striker here," he said.

"Striker," Barbara Price said, "I thought you'd want to know that the cleanup operations in Jacksonville are complete. Our people on scene have recovered an impressive amount of evidence against Trofimov. There were several boxes of financial records with the gold and jewels stockpiled there. The cleanup teams also found raw video footage. There's more than enough to damn Trofimov several times over."

"I thought as much," Bolan said.

"Also, Agent Delaney's body has been retrieved, as you requested," Price said.

"You'll see to it she makes her way back home?"

"We will," Price said. "I've contacted the Bureau to make the specific arrangements. She had specific instructions in place, should anything happen to her in the field."

"Make sure they know, Barb," Bolan said. "Make sure they understand."

"I will," Price said. "Striker, there's one thing you should know."

"Yeah?"

"It's likely they'll want to deny the specifics of the operation. When you consider just how far up the chain this goes, it's very unlikely the full truth will ever come out."

"She deserves to be remembered for what she did," Bolan said. "She was a good agent. She was a good soldier."

"I know, Striker," Price said. "I know."

"I have to go now, Barb," Bolan said.

"I can arrange for a tactical team on-site to back you up," Price told him. "Trofimov's got nowhere to go and nothing to save him. We can bring in support on this."

"No," Bolan said. "I'm doing this myself."

"Striker…"

"No. If you send a team," Bolan told her, "they'll be too late. I'm going now."

There was a pause on the other end. Finally, Price said, "All right. Be careful."

Bolan closed the connection.

It was time to put a stop to Trofimov and his evil once and for all.

He walked across the street, his weapons in full view. There weren't too many people in the area, and he was grateful for that, but most of what was about to go down would be contained to within Trofimov's building.

He pushed open one of the series of tall glass doors leading into the lobby of the TBT building.

Several armed men looked up in surprise.

The lobby was crawling with uniformed SCAR mercenaries. Two of them were stationed behind the front desk. Bolan, in the moment he had to take in the scene, saw no civilians, no TBT employees. It was even possible Trofimov had ordered them all sent home. The site was an armed camp. The Russian, or perhaps Twain operating on Trofimov's behalf before coming to Jacksonville to meet his fate, had turned the building into a fortress. No doubt Trofimov was somewhere in the building, hoping that the number of gunmen between him and the outside world would be enough to prevent justice from finding him.

Bolan would show him just how little good those troops would do.

The pregnant pause drew out, as the mercenaries staring at Bolan struggled to decide just what to do. This wasn't normal; the enemy didn't just walk into your midst and take a long, hard look at you, daring you to do something about it.

Not unless that enemy was the Executioner.

"Justice Department," Bolan announced, drawing both Desert Eagles, wielding one in each hand. "Everybody on the floor."

The mercenaries brought up their weapons.

Bolan leveled his Desert Eagles and fired. The .44 Magnum slugs cracked, thunder rolling across the lobby, as the Executioner put jacketed hollowpoint slugs through the faces of two of the nearest gunners.

Chaos broke out. Every armed mercenary in the open space began to fire his weapon. Various weapons of war sprayed the area. Empty brass clattered on the expensive, polished tiles. Men fell, dead and dying. Mack Bolan walked through the hailstorm of deadly fire, an unstoppable ballistic machine, relentlessly and inexorably exacting judgment, justice and revenge on those protecting the traitor Trofimov.

The black-clad soldier was one man, but Trofimov's guards couldn't seem to target him, couldn't seem to bring their guns to bear on him. He would fire, move, dance between them, always in motion, always firing. Where he went, .44 Magnum death preceded him, his enemies falling like dried leaves in an autumn wind.

"Take him! Take him!" a voice shouted. Bolan whirled, aimed and punched a .44 Magnum slug through the speaker.

He heard a few random shouts in Chinese and filed that fact away for later examination. Right now, in the heat of combat, he had time only to act and react, to do unto others before they did unto him.

The lobby became a slaughterhouse as Bolan continued to move and fire. The two Desert Eagles bucked in his hands, the big .44 Magnum slugs burning down gunner after gunner. They were streaming from the stairwells now, responding to the firefight. Bolan ran for and leaped behind the front desk as bullets from his enemies' Kalashnikovs chewed up the wood veneer.

He landed on top of a dead man and next to a wounded one. The mercenary still alive had lost his weapon. He threw himself at Bolan and tried to wrap his fingers around the soldier's throat. Bolan raised his arms, still holding his pistols, up and through the opening between the man's forearms. He broke the hold and then pressed the muzzle of one of the Desert Eagles to the man's chest, pulling the trigger.

A grenade bounced over the edge of the front desk and very nearly into his lap.

Bolan didn't think. He grabbed the bomb and whipped it with all his strength up and out, into the lobby proper, where it exploded in midair. Shrapnel blasted into a pair of gunners, eliciting screams of agony.

The return fire stopped.

Bolan swapped magazines in the Desert Eagles. He counted to ten before sticking his head up a fraction and ducking back down again. He drew no fire. Rising to his feet, a .44 Magnum cannon in each hand, he surveyed the devastated lobby of the TBT building.

He was alone with the dead.

His plan, such as it was, hinged on blitzing the enemy, taking the initiative with audacity and the willingness to confront Trofimov's people with overwhelming deadly force. He vaulted the front desk again, his combat boots crunching on empty brass casings.

The nearest of the dead men still clutched a Kalashnikov. Bolan holstered one of the Desert Eagles and shoved the second in his waistband. He picked up the AK and liberated several loaded banana magazines from the man's waistband. He put the magazines in his war bag and checked the assault rifle's magazine. Replacing it, he drew back the bolt just far enough to verify that a round was chambered.

All right.

The elevator doors opened. Bolan crouched and, with the Kalashnikov at waist level, held the trigger down and sprayed the interior. The SCAR personnel inside fell on top of each other as they spilled out, their weapons falling from their hands.

Bolan spotted a combat knife on the belt of one of the dead men at his feet. He drew the blade and used it to jam open the doors of the elevator, wedging the blade between the door seam and its electric eye. The door made a grinding noise, metal on metal, as it tried and failed to close against the foot of sharpened steel jamming the works. Satisfied, Bolan left it and checked the single stairwell leading up.

He eased the fire door open. The layout of the TBT building was similar to that of Gareth Twain's offices in New Orleans, but this building was larger and, judging from the furnishings, much more expensive. The materials used in its construction, from the marble tiles to the brass railings on the auxiliary stairs, were expensive and well-maintained.

There were no enemy gunners in the stairwell, at least not from the ground floor to the first landing. Each landing had, from what Bolan could tell, a double door setup, which was apparently used for fire containment. The next set of stairs, and the next landing, was only accessible after breaching the second set of doors. That worked for him in that he would know if an enemy presented himself, but it made it harder to blitz his way from bottom to top in his search for Trofimov.

The Russian would occupy the high ground; of that much Bolan was certain. It was a natural impulse among his type. He'd be counting on the small army of SCAR personnel and, presumably, Chinese operatives mixed in with those forces to form a barrier between himself and whomever might come calling to take him down.

Holding the Kalashnikov at the ready, Bolan eased open the first of the double fire doors leading to the next floor. Then he planted a booted foot against the second and kicked the door open.

Gunfire ripped through the hallway beyond. Bolan triggered a burst to suppress the enemy, charging forward and cutting left to take cover behind the corner. The floor was divided into what he assumed were offices, with a perimeter corridor segmented by one hallway leading from front to back, from the elevators to some larger space at the other end. The layout was inherently dangerous for him; there were any number of places the enemy could hide.

He wasn't concerned with covering the stairwell. It was inevitable that some of the mercenaries would break discipline and flee. Such behavior was fairly typical when a serious firefight came down. While they were criminals, and he would take down any that got in his way, the individual fighters weren't the target. The target was Trofimov, and he wouldn't risk himself out in the open. He would stay buttoned up in whatever hole he maintained here, trusting his gunmen to take out any threats directed at him.

When they failed, he would be trapped.

The SCAR computer system had already been breached. With the financial data Bolan had helped acquire at SCFI, there would be no hiding any records of disbursements to Trofimov's employees. Every transaction, every person on whom Trofimov, Twain and SCAR had files, would be exposed, in time. Bolan imagined that the cyberteam at the Farm was even now going through that data. Standard operating procedure would be to run the identities of the mercenaries and any other personnel involved with Trofimov and SCAR, run automated background checks on them and arrange for arrests through the myriad local law-enforcement agencies in whose jurisdiction the affected employees lived.

A clean sweep.

The cleanup was inevitable. It would happen regardless. Any of the gunners who escaped Bolan's final push for justice here would be rounded up later.

The Executioner was, in other words, free to do what he did, to charge the battlements and make sure a vile predator was stopped in his tracks.

Bolan moved quickly down the perimeter corridor. The doors to the outer offices were glass, and he saw movement through one of them. The man beyond was a SCAR gunner with an M-16. The soldier shot him in the head, shattering the glass of the closed door.

Two shooters ducked out of offices farther up the hallway. Their subgun rounds stitched the walls to either side of the soldier, converging on his location. Bolan dropped to one knee and fired back, triggering short, measured bursts. The gunners toppled, one dead before he hit the floor, the other screaming. He had moved at the critical moment, taking the bullets through his knees as Bolan's rounds cut his legs out from under him.

The Executioner stood and crept down the hallway. The wounded man was fighting through the pain and bringing up his weapon, an Uzi. Bolan snapped the AK to his shoulder and put a round through the man's head.

Rounding the corner, Bolan checked the next offices. They were empty. At the far end of the hall, he found a dead woman.

It wasn't a mercenary, and it wasn't someone he'd shot. She looked like a civilian. She'd been very pretty.

"It is Trofimov's secretary," someone said behind him.

The Executioner whirled, leveling the Kalashnikov. The gaunt Asian man who stepped from the nearest open office was smoking a cigarette. He held a Makarov pistol, casually, as if the weapon were a toy.

"Drop the weapon," Bolan ordered him.

"I do not think that would be wise," the man said. His accent was light, his English fluent. He looked at Bolan, then down at the woman. A blood trail led from her body to the office from which the Asian had just emerged.

"Did you shoot her?" Bolan asked.

"I did not," the man said. He stood a little straighter and said, "My name is Mak Wei. I am a representative of the People's Republic of China. I assume you are a representative of your own government."

"You assume correctly."

"I thought as much." He indicated the woman. "It happened only moments ago. When it became clear the building was under attack. He has only just received word that his facility in Jacksonville was lost. I am afraid the strain was too much for him."

"Drop your weapon," Bolan ordered again.

Mak regarded him coolly. "Please," he said. "Let us not engage in fictions. I can no more surrender than you can. But I would have a reasonable word with you, before we conclude this."

Bolan eyed him. The barrel of the Kalashnikov never moved; it was pointed at Mak Wei's head.

"My government," Mak said, "thought this Trofimov represented an asset we could use. His goals were our goals, up to a point, and his motivations, while complicated, did not seem likely to impede us in using him for our purposes."

"Didn't work out for you?"

"No," Mak admitted. "It seems he is more unstable than we at first thought. I saw signs of it, of course, but I took action too late. I have, what is the expression? 'Hitched my cart to the wrong horse.'"

"Something like that," Bolan said.

Mak looked at him curiously, then past him. "Are you, indeed, alone?"

Bolan said nothing.

"Amazing." Mak shook his head. "Very well, I will make certain assumptions. If you would correct me when I am wrong, I would appreciate it, but if you must remain silent, I understand."

"Go on."

"Among those who work in my profession," Mak said, "it is rumored that there are certain elements within the United States government, or allied with it, who operate much as you do. Guerrilla units, of a type. Men and women who appear from the shadows, kill the enemies of the United States and disappear as quickly as they arrive. Among them, there are reports of one man, in particular, who keeps recurring. Reports of a counterterrorist agent, if we shall call him that, who answers to your description. Tall. Perhaps ninety kilograms. An expert in small arms and the tactics of personal warfare. A man who has personally intervened in multiple operations sponsored with at least the tacit approval of my government."

"Why tell me this?" Bolan said.

"Because I believe you are that man," Mak said. "If that is so, I am telling you nothing you do not already know. My admissions will mean little beyond these walls. We both know that. My country will disavow any knowledge of me and my activities. They will provide records that prove I have left the country in disgrace, or perhaps faked my death, as so many of my men have had arranged for them. It does not matter. We both know the truth. We know it because, well, you are he. You are the warrior who has faced my country's most covert operatives, besting them time and again. I wasn't sure until now, but I suspected it as soon as I heard the first reports of interference with these schemes master-minded by Trofimov and Twain. It was all too...close to the mark, I believe is the expression."

"Do you expect me to confirm it?"

"No," Mak said. "But your reaction tells me already that it was you." He took a long drag from his cigarette and looked down at it. His Makarov had drifted off target and was pointing at the floor. "A man, near the end of his life, comes to understand a great many things."

"I don't have to kill you," Bolan said. "You could surrender."

"I suspected you might say that." Mak nodded. "I suppose I thought, in presenting myself to you, that I might have the courage to take you up on your offer. But I cannot. My family in China would suffer greatly were I to cooperate."

"I can't just let you go."

"It would not matter if you did," Mak said. "If I return to China in defeat, the successor to a long line of failed operatives returning from the United States with disgrace their only prize, I would be killed anyway. If, however, I die fighting to the last, attempting to salvage the operation in some vain, impossible way, then at least my family may be spared any reprisals."

"I'm not going to do it for you," Bolan said.

Mak looked at him. "No," he said. "I do not suppose you would. Do not worry. I will make it easy for you." He finished his cigarette, savoring the smoke as he blew it out his mouth and inhaled it through his nose again. Finally he exhaled what remained. "It is amazing to me," he said, "how precious things become, when they are the last things."

"Put the gun down," Bolan ordered him. "Get on your knees, hands behind your head."

"I am not quite finished," Mak said. "American, believe me when I tell you that, as much as I wish for my country to dominate yours, as loyal as I have been to my government, I have not lost my sense of personal honor. Watching Trofimov come apart before my eyes was a very informative experience. Had I everything to do over again, I believe I would do it differently. But now—" he stood straighter, smoothing his dark suit with his free hand "—my course is chosen, and the way is clear, however distasteful it may be."

"Don't," Bolan warned.

Mak ignored him. "You have killed the last of the SCAR men on this floor," he said. "Were you to take the stairs to the next levels beyond this one—" he nodded upward "—you would find no shortage of men with automatic weapons, just waiting to kill you. Trofimov, however, believes in leaving himself an out. This office—" he nodded back the way he'd come, in the direction from which the dying woman had apparently crawled "—connects to a private lift. That lift emerges in a large anteroom that occupies half of the floor space on the uppermost floor of the building. Trofimov himself is secured within."

"Why are you telling me this?"

"Please." Mak held up his free hand. "Allow me to finish. My men, a select team of warriors and all that remain of my forces here in the United States, are waiting outside Trofimov's office, in that anteroom. They have removed all furniture from the room. It is completely barren, a killing field containing only men and their weapons. They will be expecting you from the stairs, if indeed you were to make it past all the other men arrayed against you. You will have perhaps a moment once you clear the elevator, a moment in which to take them by surprise. I cannot guarantee that, however."

"Do you expect me to believe you?"

"I hope you do," Mak said, "for I would not dishonor my last moments by telling lies. Ultimately you will do as you will, and I can change nothing. Based on your actions to this time, I am not worried that you will succeed. We are enemies, American, but I must admit, you have my grudging admiration. With a squad of men such as you, I could bring the West to its knees, and exalt the People's Republic to its rightful place."

"You aren't making any sense," Bolan said.

"I am making perfect sense, American." Mak smiled. "Is it really so hard to believe that you have earned the respect of an enemy? At the same time, my allies have proved *not* to be worthy of that respect. I go now to my death, American. I do so willingly. I hope my men kill you. They are the best my nation could provide, and they are fierce. The fact that you are still alive, however, tells me that you are fierce, as well."

"Don't do it," Bolan warned again.

"Goodbye, American," Mak said. "I hope you will be joining me soon."

The Makarov came up, and it was no halfhearted attempt. Mak's shot came very close to putting Bolan down forever. The 9 mm round burned the air by Bolan's left ear as the soldier sidestepped and triggered a burst from the Kalashnikov. An expert marksman and sniper, Bolan couldn't miss, especially at this range. Mak hit the corridor wall and slid down it, blood spreading across his chest.

"I…think…" Mak said. He never finished his sentence. Bolan looked down at him, his eyes open in death, a strangely serene look on his face.

"Whatever you were thinking," Bolan told him, "it doesn't matter now." He offered a silent salute to this strange foe, who had proved honorable at the last, and moved cautiously into the office Mak had pointed out.

The blood trail led to a panel in the wall that stood ajar. Closed, it was obviously designed to blend in with paneling on the wall, but the seam was broken. Removing his combat flashlight from his pocket, Bolan illuminated the space, holding the Kalashnikov with one hand only.

There was a small switch set in the wall, and the floor was a metal grid clearly connected to hydraulics of some kind.

Bolan stood within the lift and hit the switch.

CHAPTER TWENTY-THREE

When the lift door opened, Bolan found himself standing behind a crowd of armed men. They were all Asian, presumably Chinese, and they held a variety of weapons. Many had guns; others held knives and even clubs. Bolan was at a loss to explain that, unless these special forces operatives expected the fight to get up-close and bloody. It wasn't, he reflected, an unreasonable expectation.

At the sound of the lift doors, the men turned almost in unison.

Bolan pulled back the trigger of the Kalashnikov.

The weapon's muzzle-blast lit up the darkened room, whose windows had been partially blacked out. As Bolan fired into their midst, he did the only thing he could do, given the complete lack of cover. He moved straight into the crowd of fighters, using their bodies to shield him. He managed to fire out the magazine of the Kalashnikov before they swamped him.

The crush of bodies wasn't unexpected, but this was the most difficult part of Bolan's play. If he let them take him to the ground, or smother him completely, he would be helpless. They could kick him to death or simply put a gun to his head, and that would be the end of his War Everlasting.

Bolan slammed the wooden stock of the Kalashnikov into one of the approaching fighters. He lashed out with a kick, breaking another's knee. He threw an elbow into the face of one, then another. He smashed his fist into the throat of yet another. Reaching into his pocket, he snapped open the switchblade he'd taken from the late Gareth Twain, and he drew the Boker Applegate combat knife from its sheath in his waistband.

The Chinese operatives were still on top of him, grunting in their attempts to grab and hold him, strangely silent. He felt a truncheon across his back and did his best to roll with the blow; a kick slammed into his ribs; someone tried to stab him in the stomach. He was able to arch his back and avoid the knife, then bring his own large blade up and slash the attacker. With the Boker and the switchblade whirling like the teeth of a threshing machine, Bolan began carving his way out of the mass of enemy bodies. There were screams, and then the gunfire started. The enemy operatives had started shooting without regard for their comrades' safety, as it became clear that the demon in their midst was rapidly scything through them like the grim reaper.

Bolan grabbed one of the operatives and wrapped an arm around his throat, twisting and turning, making the man roll with him. The unfortunate operative absorbed several rounds fired by his fellows, and Bolan backed up toward the double doors the Chinese were protecting. If Mak Wei had been honest, Trofimov would be beyond that portal.

An expandable baton sang through the air, just missing Bolan's face. He dropped the dead man he'd been using as a shield, firing a savage kick that snapped the shin of the man with the baton. Then Bolan's Desert Eagles were in his fists, and he was jacking back the hammers as the triangular muzzles covered the enemy.

Bullets punched holes in the wall behind him, ricocheting when they found the metal of the reinforced doors. A bouncing round singed Bolan's leg, but did no serious damage. He ignored the sting as he started pulling the triggers of his pistols, hurling .44-caliber death at the foreign agents who sought to kill him.

He felt the blow to his legs too late, as one of the Chinese threw himself at Bolan's lower body. The soldier toppled, and several of the operatives scrambled to hold him down. Rolling and twisting, bucking like a wild animal, Bolan was able to throw off the one trying to grab his arms. He fired the Desert Eagles again and again at close range, almost blowing the men off him as the bullets slammed into them. Another man grabbed him in a bear hug and Bolan fought blindly, slamming his elbow up and back, feeling the operative's nose give. Deafening gunfire sounded all around. Bolan was shooting; the operatives were shooting. Muzzle-blasts burned him through his blacksuit. His war bag was ripped free from his shoulder. Without realizing he was doing it, he grabbed the edge of the canvas bag, holding fast to keep it from being lost in the fray. A knife blade found his thigh and dug in deep, but he fought the pain.

One of the Chinese got an arm around Bolan's throat and began to squeeze. He felt himself being dragged down. As the air was cut off, his vision began to go black. He saw floating shapes. Several Chinese were still up and functional, and they were closing in, hammering away at him with their fists and their feet, animal rage having supplanted professional detachment. They were going to beat him to death while their comrade strangled him.

A last, desperate thought came to Bolan as the rushing in his ears became almost overwhelming.

His hand crabbed its way into the war bag, and his fist closed around the butt of the Beretta 93-R.

His first triggered blast was a 3-round burst that took the man directly in front of him. The 9 mm Parabellum rounds ripped through the man's stomach. He grabbed at his abdomen, shock registering on his face, then fell.

Bolan flicked the Beretta's selector to single-shot and began to pull the trigger.

His rounds found their mark, again and again. The men holding him jerked and roared and howled and died, falling on top of him or to the side as he shot them at point-blank range. Finally, with the last of his strength, Bolan reached up and back, grateful for the custom suppressor installed on the Beretta. The muzzle of the machine pistol was only inches from his ear as he triggered the weapon, shooting backward, catching his would-be strangler under the chin and blowing off the top of his head.

The pressure on his neck was suddenly gone.

Bolan forced himself to roll free, crawling out of the pile of corpses in which he had managed to bury himself.

He drew in first one ragged breath, then another. Holding the Beretta tightly, he waited, lying prone in the middle of the group of dead men, waiting to see if another enemy would present himself. When there were no more threats, he struggled to his knees.

The wound in his thigh screamed as he put his weight on it. Grunting, Bolan dragged his canvas war bag out from under the dead. The shoulder strap had been cut by something sharp, most likely the blade of the very knife that had stabbed him. He took his first-aid kit from the bag.

Sitting heavily on a reasonably clean section of floor in the middle of the slaughter, Bolan ripped open his pant leg. He cleaned the wound with a tube of alcohol from the kit, then sealed it with "liquid skin" and bandaged it. The knife had been very sharp. The wound was deep, but not ragged. It hurt like hell but wouldn't stop him.

He examined the Beretta 93-R. It held only two more rounds, and he had burned through the rest of his spare magazines. The war bag did have several more magazines for the Desert Eagles, however. He placed the 93-R in the bag, silently thanking the trusty weapon for once again saving his life. Then he loaded the Desert Eagles, thrust them both in his waistband front and back and walked stiffly to the double doors.

He tried them, but the scarred, bullet-dented doors were locked.

His phone began to vibrate in the pocket of his blacksuit.

"Striker," he said, answering it.

"Striker, it's Hal," Brognola said on the other end. "What's your status?"

"Hello, Hal," Bolan said. He was feeling a little light-headed from blood loss, but knew that would stabilize in a moment. He dug an energy bar from the pocket of his blacksuit, tore it open and bit off a piece. It was the best way to counteract the effects of the wound in his leg.

"The calls have made their way back to me," Brognola said. "I'm looking at a relayed, live satellite feed from the news trucks on-site."

"News trucks? Where?"

"Right outside your door," Brognola said. "The local police have the building surrounded, and there are several federal agencies on their way to you, including a very, very pissed off detachment from the FBI."

"What do they know?"

"They know what I've told them," Brognola said. "That the building is occupied by an agent of the Justice Department, detailed to take into custody one Yuri Trofimov, who is wanted for complicity in the death of FBI Agent Jennifer Delaney."

"Thanks, Hal," Bolan said. He knew the big Fed had spun the story in precisely the way that would afford Bolan the most support on-scene.

"What's your status?" Brognola repeated.

"Wounded, but functional," Bolan said. "At the moment I'm outside what I believe to be the private office of Yuri Trofimov. He's got himself barricaded in there. I'm going to knock on the door."

"And if he doesn't let you in?"

"I'm going to knock real hard."

"Understood," Brognola said. "What do you need from me?"

"Just what you're doing," Bolan said. "There are armed men still in the building," he said. "Quite a few of them. Let the locals know. If they send a detachment of SWAT into the building, it's going to get really bloody. I would recommend tear-gassing the intermediate floors and keeping the perimeter closed tight. Flush the remaining SCAR personnel into the open and take them down when they're feeling a bit more ready to cooperate."

"I will pass that along," Brognola promised. "Can you handle Trofimov?"

"You know I can."

"I talked with the Man before I called you," Brognola said. "I've apprised him of the situation to date, and of the evidence we've managed to accumulate in support of our troops. We have damned Trofimov conclusively. But there's a problem."

"Which is?"

"The scope of the conspiracy," Brognola said. He paused. "Are you all right? You're breathing hard."

"Yeah, I'm as well as can be considering I had about five inches of steel in my leg a little while ago. You were saying?"

"You've done your job well," Brognola said, "and along the way you've managed to uncover enough of Trofimov's master plan to bring down portions of our government, if word of this gets out."

"You're worried about public reaction."

"Yes," Brognola said. "And so is the Man. Between Heller and everything Trofimov managed to do, or was planning to do... If this becomes public knowledge, it will shake the public's faith in almost every aspect of our military and government operations, to some degree."

"I understand, Hal," Bolan said wearily. "It certainly won't be the first time we've had to sweep something under the rug for the common good. What do you need from me?"

"Trofimov is officially wanted for trial," Brognola said.

"Officially," Bolan repeated. "Which means that un-officially, it might be a little more convenient if he didn't get there?"

"I didn't say that," Brognola said, "and neither did the Man."

"No," Bolan said, "and I'm no assassin. I'm going to bring him in if I can. I'll kill him if I can't. Either way, he meets justice."

"I know, Striker," Brognola said. "I'd be disappointed if you said anything different."

"Then what are you trying to tell me?"

"We've made arrangements to deal with Heller and all those who may have been working with him, once we conclude our investigation," Brognola said. "Trofimov, if you do bring him in, will be joining Heller and company. Just make sure he doesn't talk to the media."

"I think that can be arranged," Bolan said. "I wasn't planning on calling a press conference." Brognola actually laughed at that, as Bolan paraphrased himself. "If he doesn't survive? He's a public figure."

"If he doesn't survive," Brognola said, "we'll write it off to a tragic accident. The entire downtown area is aware that something is happening in the TBT building. You don't exactly work discreetly."

"Guilty," Bolan said.

"It will be leaked to the press that TBT was housing certain flammable chemicals used in, let's say, developing film."

"Everything's digital these days, Hal."

"We'll come up with something plausible. But what will be significant is that a fire, a very tragic, very public fire, raged through the TBT building, taking with it the life of the face of TBT News. Actually, that's probably the easier way for Trofimov, given that we'll have to spin the massacre video as the act of a deranged, ratings-hungry nut."

"I feel real sorry about that."

"I'm sure you do," Brognola said.

The distant echo of gunfire reached Bolan's ears. It was coming from the floors below.

"I'm hearing gunfire, Hal."

"That would be the SWAT team," Brognola said.

"Don't worry. I sent a text message from my terminal, and Barb passed on your warning. I guess they decided to be proactive."

"What about the rest of what's left of Twain's organization?"

"Being rounded up as we speak," Brognola said. "There were plenty of virtual paper trails to trace, and I'm going to owe Aaron and his people a lot of overtime pay. But the mess is very nearly swept up."

"Good," Bolan said. "Then it looks like I've just got one loose end left." He flexed his knees a bit, making sure he felt steady on his wounded leg. His fingers brushed the butts of the Desert Eagles in his waistband.

"Striker?"

"Yeah, Hal?"

"Call me when it's over. I'd appreciate knowing how it turns out."

"One way or another," Bolan told him, "you know it can end only one way. Trofimov is over. Striker out."

"Good luck, Striker."

Bolan closed the phone and put it away.

He went to the damaged war bag and removed the last of his C-4 charges. Planting the C-4 and a detonator, he activated the delay timer and moved down the wall, pressing himself against it.

The charge blew. Bolan shook off the ringing in his ears, his hand on the butt of the forward Desert Eagle.

"Come in," Yuri Trofimov called from inside. "I've been expecting you."

Bolan stood at the door to the office. Yuri Trofimov sat behind his desk with his back to a large window.

The soldier stepped cautiously into the room.

The blow to the head staggered him.

He fell forward, rolling and coming up on one knee.

The person who had struck him was a very large Chinese man, apparently one of Mak Wei's people held in reserve by the anxious Trofimov. A second Chinese operative, nearly as big as the first, stood beside him. They tackled Bolan, one of them immediately punching the soldier in the thigh, over the bandage. Starbursts of pain blossomed in Bolan's vision as the first operative punched him in the face with a closed fist. The two special forces men began to kick and punch him furiously, overwhelming him.

He fought the blackness for as long as he could, but in the end, it overwhelmed him.

CHAPTER TWENTY-FOUR

Bolan woke slowly. His eyes opened, and he focused on the man seated at the desk in front of him. Trofimov offered him a smile. Somewhere, in the distance, Bolan could hear voices speaking through bullhorns.

"Do you hear that?" Trofimov said. "That is the police. They are downstairs. The last of my Chinese helpers are down there, keeping them at bay. I do not think they will last very long. But I thought we should be uninterrupted for as long as it takes to make you die, screaming in pain."

Bolan could see his weapons on the desk in front of Trofimov. Both guns were there, as were a few other items from the pockets of his blacksuit. Trofimov held a knife that wasn't one of Bolan's. It looked expensive and very sharp. There was a small stand sitting empty on the desktop. The blade was apparently a letter opener.

"This is Chinese," Trofimov said. "It was a gift from my friend Mak Wei. Have you met Mak Wei? As he is nowhere to be found, I imagine you have."

Bolan said nothing. He assessed his situation. He was strapped to a chair. The bonds securing him were phone cords, apparently ripped from the expensive-looking office phone on Trofimov's desk. His wrists and his ankles were tied. He worked his wrists, slowly, and there was a slight amount of give. Okay, he could work with that. The trick was to survive, to keep Trofimov talking.

"You realize," Bolan said, "that you sent those men to their deaths."

"What do I care?" Trofimov said.

"True," Bolan said. "What do you care about anything?"

"I care deeply," Trofimov said, indignant. "I have always cared. That is why I have worked so hard."

"Worked so hard at what?" Bolan asked. "To be a terrorist? A murderer?" He was playing a dangerous game, the Executioner knew. The trick was to give Trofimov just enough reason to talk, without pushing him to actual violence. There was no telling what the man might do if he became enraged enough, and that would end the whole game then and there. But Bolan had a great deal of experience with Trofimov's type. Egomaniacs like Yuri Trofimov, deep down, wanted to talk. They wanted the people they believed they had beaten to know it, to understand it. They derived a great deal of satisfaction from that. Bolan saw no reason to deny Trofimov that satisfaction if it gave him the time he needed. Now he was going to have to put to the test what he had told Delaney. He was going to have to see if he really could get into Trofimov's mind. His life depended on it.

Trofimov sat back in his chair. He put his feet up on the desk. Playing with the dagger, he looked at Bolan almost cheerfully.

"I am going to carve you up," he said. "I would like to know your name first, however. It seems only right."

"Matt Cooper," Bolan said. "Justice Department."

Trofimov examined the identification wallet on the desk in front of him. It was Bolan's and had evidently been taken from the soldier's pocket when he was searched while unconscious. "That is what it says here." Trofimov nodded. "What does the Justice Department want with me?"

"Isn't it obvious?" Bolan asked. "You're wanted for conspiracy to commit murder, and for treason, including crimes against the United States military and its personnel."

"Crimes against the military?" Trofimov said. "Do not make me laugh. The United States military is the greatest single source of evil in the world today! Why, in fighting the U.S. military, in hurting it, I strike a blow for true freedom, for everyone your imperialist nation has bullied and invaded over the years. All those civilians you bomb and slaughter, all those nations you believe you can tell how to run their affairs. I have helped them all, in fighting the military! History will remember me as a hero!"

"History will remember you as a fraud," Bolan said, dancing closer to the metaphorical fire.

"A fraud? You speak nonsense."

"Do I?" Bolan said. "Why did you shoot your secretary?"

"It is of no consequence," Trofimov said, looking unsettled.

"No?" Bolan pushed. "Were you a little upset about something, perhaps? Decided to lash out at the closest target?"

Trofimov leaped up, bringing the blade of the Chinese knife close to Bolan's eyes. "I will lash out against you, perhaps, Matt Cooper," he stormed.

"You could do that," Bolan said. "Then again, you might stop and ask yourself what I found when I knocked over your Vault."

"What are you talking about?"

"You remember the Vault, Yuri," Bolan said. "You know, where you were keeping all your money? What else was there?"

"You… What…"

"We found your little television studio, Yuri," Bolan said. "We found the clever little set you erected. We know you created the massacre video."

"It does not matter now," Trofimov said, backing up and sitting on the edge of the desk. "The damage is done. The entire world believes your people are capable of committing such crimes."

"But we didn't commit them, Yuri."

"Didn't you?" Trofimov seemed to warm to the subject a bit, which also seemed to calm him. "Tell me, Matt Cooper, just how many high-profile massacres have your soldiers committed through the years? We both know they have. There did not exist any conveniently taped massacres for me to show the world, no, so yes, I created one—but I did not make anything that could not have existed! Why do you think the world was so ready to believe it, Cooper? Why do you think the enemies of your nation swallowed the news so readily?"

"They wanted to believe it," Bolan said. "The enemies of the West need to believe it is evil. It justifies and rationalizes their hatred."

"They believed it because it has happened before!" Trofimov said gleefully. "Is that not truly the way of it? Do you think it would really be so hard to compile a long list of people and nations you and your miserable military have wronged, have hurt, have killed? You invade at whim! You make everyone else do as you say, and you do it because secretly you wish to control the world!"

"What do you think your friends the Chinese want to do?" Bolan countered. He could feel the phone cord around his right wrist giving way.

"The Chinese," Trofimov scoffed. "I am using them to get what I need. Of course they wish to benefit from harm to the United States. They and many others like them! They are simply the ones in position to render the most help and support to me. They have the deepest pockets!"

"You're a wealthy man, Trofimov," Bolan said. "You could have used your wealth to help people. You could have done some good in the world. Instead you used your fortune to finance your hatred."

"I did what I had to do."

"You murdered men and women whose only crime was serving in a military you hate," Bolan said. "And you murdered, or tried to murder, their families, and others whose only misdeed was to attend the funerals of those service people."

"It was easy, too." Trofimov was gloating. "How wretched is your nation, that there exists within it people who are only too happy to hurt it? American citizens, Cooper, who were willing to work with me to kill other Americans, because they, too, know their country to be evil!"

"This nation isn't evil," Bolan said evenly. It was time to make his move. The phone cord around his wrist was as loose as it was going to get.

"Of course it is," Trofimov said. "And I am going to prove it. You, or whoever you work for, you and all your soldiers, may have interfered with my operation," he went on, "but I can rebuild. I have offshore accounts. I have resources I have not tapped. I can find a way. My dream will not end."

"Your dream," Bolan said, "is a nightmare. And I'm not going to let you walk out of here."

"You?" Trofimov turned and faced him, holding up the knife. "What makes you think you have any choice in the matter?"

"You!" An electronically amplified voice sounded from the anteroom outside the office. "You, inside the office. Come out with your hands up. This is the Orlando Police Department. You are under arrest."

"Well," Bolan said, "looks like you're out of time."

"It is you who is out of time," Trofimov said. He went to his desk and opened the center drawer. He was chuckling now. He withdrew from the desk a belt harness connected to a small metal box with an antenna built into it. There was a second, smaller box connected to a wrist strap. Trofimov strapped the small box around his right wrist and shrugged into the harness. The metal box sat in the center of his chest, the antenna jutting prominently from it.

"This is your last warning," the officer with the bullhorn said from outside.

"So very trite," Trofimov said. "Soon, I will be giving *him* orders," he promised. He flicked a switch on the side of the box. "Do you recognize this?" he asked.

"It looks like one of your transmitters," Bolan said. "I destroyed the factory that produces them."

"Oh, very good." Trofimov nodded. "Yes, you are right. This is one of the clever devices that idiot Winston designed for me."

"I met him," Bolan said. "It didn't go well for him."

"Stop interrupting me," Trofimov said testily.

"Now, you wait here. I must go speak with the police."

Bolan watched Trofimov go. As soon as the Russian was out of sight, he began working his wrists back and forth more quickly.

From the hallway, Trofimov was easily audible. He spoke to the police. "I am Yuri Trofimov," he said. "I have a message for you, Orlando Police Department. This device strapped to my chest is a bomb. It is controlled by a wireless transmission generated by this device on my wrist. You should know that the wrist unit monitors my pulse, and if my heartbeat ends, the bomb will detonate. You cannot jam the transmission of the signal, for it is specially modulated to prevent this. And even if you could jam it by attempting to isolate it, you have no way of knowing what it is, for it only transmits in the event of my death and the bomb's detonation."

Bolan managed to get his wrist free. Keep talking, he thought. Tell them all about it, Yuri.

"There is enough plastic explosive built into this box," Trofimov said, "to destroy this entire floor. But there is more. Built into my desk itself is a much, much larger bomb. It is connected to a very powerful neurotoxin. There is enough neurotoxin in the canister under my desk to kill everyone for a ten-block radius, should the bomb and the top floor of this building explode."

Bolan's eyes narrowed at that. He got both wrists free, then quickly untied his ankles. Moving behind Trofimov's desk, he got down on his knees and looked underneath.

There was a metal canister, all right, marked with a biohazard label. There were Cyrillic characters stenciled across it. Bolan knew the language well enough to know what he was looking at. Cold War–era nerve gas, possibly brought by Trofimov when he emigrated, or perhaps simply purchased from the black market back home when Trofimov had the money to do so.

So Trofimov did have some tricks up his sleeve.

Trofimov had stopped talking. Bolan got up from behind the desk and hurried to the side of the doors, pressing himself against the wall.

"That will keep them at bay for a while," Trofimov said happily, walking back in. "Cooper, I am going to enjoy torturing—"

He stopped when he realized his prisoner was no longer tied to the chair. To late, he turned.

Bolan's fist smashed into his face.

Trofimov toppled backward, his nose broken and streaming blood. He had dropped the knife, which stuck point-first into the floor. It quivered slightly. Trofimov made no effort to rise.

"Well," Trofimov said, "you are free, but that changes nothing. If you kill me, the bomb will detonate."

"And if I don't kill you, but I don't let you go, you'll detonate the bomb yourself just to make us all pay," Bolan said. It was a gamble, and it paid off. He watched the fleeting expression cross Trofimov's eyes.

"Yes," Trofimov said. "Yes, you have it exactly. Do as I say, or everyone pays."

"You're lying," Bolan said. "You never considered suicide, did you, Yuri?" he said, amping up the arrogance in his voice. "Poor, scared little Yuri, who just wants to live."

"Fool," Trofimov said. This time, he wasn't lying, and that was clear in his manner. "I do not have a detonator switch, no," he said. He pulled a small .25-caliber pistol from his pocket and put it to his temple. "But I will die before I go to prison. If I take my life, the bomb explodes, and many people will die. You may not care about your own life, but I am willing to bet you care about those innocent people of whom you speak so convincingly."

"I do," Bolan said. "That's true. And I'm going to make sure you can't ever hurt anyone again."

"Shut up!" Trofimov demanded. He started to get to his feet.

"Oh, no," Bolan said, taking a step forward. "Stay on the ground, Trofimov, or I'll put you down and keep you down again."

Trofimov wisely did not move. "I could use the gun."

"But you don't want to. You like living too much."

Trofimov had nothing to say to that. Eventually he said simply, "You cannot hold me forever."

"I don't have to," Bolan said easily. "I just have to wait until the police get tired of waiting. Then they'll come in, and the stalemate will be broken."

"That is unnecessary," Trofimov said, his tone conciliatory. "Come, Cooper, we can come to an agreement. I have money. I have a great deal of money."

"Not anymore," Bolan said. "SCFI has been thoroughly cracked. Your Vault has been seized."

"As I always knew was possible," Trofimov said. "Do you honestly think I did not plan for that eventuality? Any idiot knows he cannot foresee every calamity. I did not keep all my eggs in one basket. I have many foreign accounts. I own entire foreign banks. Your simpering, foolish countrymen have made me a wealthy man, Cooper."

The sound of weapons cocking surprised both men. The SWAT team had converged in the doorway. The men outside were pointing automatic weapons at them.

"Stand down, Officers," Bolan ordered. "This man is

wearing a dead man's trigger. He wasn't bluffing. Kill him, and you kill a lot of innocent people."

"Don't worry, Agent Cooper," one of the officers said. Obviously, Brognola had made good on his promise and gotten through to those in charge. "We won't. Your instructions, sir?"

"Stop talking to him!" Trofimov said. "I am in control here!"

"Just wait him out," Bolan said. "If one of your people have a beanbag gun or a taser, have that brought forward. Take him down and we'll bundle him off to a nice, deep, dark hole in the ground, some nice maximum-security prison somewhere, for the rest of his natural life."

Trofimov went pale. It was as if the possibility that such a fate might indeed be his, that he could spend the rest of his days locked away, had never truly occurred to him. Now, staring at the guns of the SWAT team and the big man looming in front of him, he seemed to decide that he really did prefer death to capture. His shoulders slumped.

"You…you have won," Trofimov said. The little pistol at his temple did not move, however. "You have beaten me."

"You were beaten before you began," Bolan said. "Your kind always is."

"Spare me your philosophy," Trofimov said. "I am in no mood. Understand this, Cooper. I have done more than any who tried before me, including Mak Wei and his incompetent commandos. But I am not alone. There are others like me. There were others before me. Your nation cannot stop us. You are breeding us. Whenever you invade a country that does not comply with your wishes, whenever your United Nations sticks its nose into the affairs of people who are simply doing what they must, whenever your inspectors and your 'peace-keepers' and your military push your might and rattle your sabers around the world, you are creating more of me. You will never stop the Yuri Trofimovs of the world. There will always be more of me. They will not always have my wealth, my power. But they will eventually swamp you. They will eventually defeat you. They will eventually make you pay. What I do now, I do for them."

"Wait," Bolan said. He could sense Trofimov readying himself for the final act. He began to inch closer, hopefully imperceptibly. The range was wrong. He just needed to get a little closer.

"Yes, Cooper?" Trofimov suddenly sounded very tired. That was bad. He was resigned to his fate. He would pull the trigger at any moment.

"Sir," one of the officers behind him said. "Agent Cooper, sir, the building is on fire. The fire department is on scene, but they're saying they're not sure if they can contain it."

"Let it burn," Trofimov whispered. "Let it burn. Nothing matters now."

"Isn't this the empire you created, Yuri?" Bolan asked him. He just needed enough time to close the gap. He prayed his luck would hold. "Would you see it burn to the ground so easily, so readily? Does it really mean so little to you?"

"What would you know of creating, of building?" Trofimov snarled, indignant. "You kill for a living. That is all you are. You are like Twain. You will never be more."

"I wish you understood the difference," Bolan told him.

"Enough. I will die now." He gestured with the gun.

"Wait," Bolan said. He took another step closer. "Trofimov, listen to me. The United States, the West, the free world…it doesn't breed people like you. People like you need only hate to sustain them, to fertilize them. You generate yourselves. Your hatred is a product of your own failures, your own desires, your own thwarted wishes. There may always be more of you, Trofimov, but it isn't because we create them. There are always more of you for the same reason there are always cockroaches. There will always be vermin in the world, Trofimov."

"How *dare* you talk to me like that," Trofimov muttered, his finger tightening on the trigger.

Bolan took one more critical step closer. "There will always be vermin, Trofimov, and there will always be exterminators. That's what I am. I'm not a hero. Heroes are those who die for their country, who sacrifice. I haven't made that sacrifice, Yuri. I've simply taken out the trash, time and time again. I've stamped out the fires. I've removed the garbage. And over and over again, I've exterminated the vermin. That's you, Yuri. You're a roach. There will always be more roaches. There will always be infestations. And they'll always be rooted out."

"You talk and you talk and you talk!" Trofimov said. He shoved the pistol against his head, harder. "With a single bullet, I will end you!"

"But, Yuri," Bolan said, creeping closer, the range almost right, "you and I both know you fear what lies on the other side. You fear the oblivion of death. You fear what will happen when that bullet makes its way into your brain. That's why you won't do it. That's why you're hesitating even now. That's why you have this elaborate plan already in place, Yuri. You want to live. But you don't care how many people, how many men, women and children you endanger. You're scum, Trofimov. You're the lowest form of life. You're the roach, Yuri, and I'm going to crush you under my boot."

"To hell with you!" Trofimov shrieked.

Bolan struck. As he lunged, he grabbed the knife from where it stuck in the floor. In a single, fluid movement, he brought the razor-sharp blade up and around, slicing through the flexible wireless antenna jutting from Trofimov's chest unit. The arc of the movement carried the blade up and around and over, straight into Trofimov's neck. His scream turned into a gurgle, and then a wet death rattle, as the knife lodged in his artery and through his throat channeled his life-blood onto the floor of his office.

"Holy crap!" one of the officers breathed.

Yuri Trofimov slumped to his knees, blood pouring from his neck. Finally he collapsed on himself. He fell sideways, and his face landed in the pool spreading around him. In the reflection of the overhead lights, he seemed almost to be staring at himself.

Bolan stood over him. The transmitter antenna was neatly severed. It was a gamble, but it was the only play he'd had. From the look on Trofimov's face, the stricken expression he could read in the dying man's eyes, Bolan could tell his gamble had paid off.

Trofimov tried to say something. The knife was still stuck in his throat. The only sound that came out was a horrible wet rasp. Bolan shook his head.

"Don't try to talk. There won't be any doctor for you, Trofimov. It's too late for that. A woman died like that today, you know. She died knowing that it was too late." He watched the light fade from Trofimov's eyes. "The difference between you," Bolan said, "is that she died knowing she'd done the right thing. She died a hero. You, you're just dying. And even though you're surrounded by people, you're dying alone."

Trofimov tried one last time to speak. Finally he breathed his last, his eyes glazing over in the finality of death.

"Jesus," one of the cops said, coming over to stand next to Bolan and look down at the body. "You don't think that was a little harsh?"

"No," Bolan told him, looking him in the eye. "I don't."

EPILOGUE

Hal Brognola entered the interrogation room, deep in the bowels of a federal building just outside of Washington, D.C. The exact location of the facility was classified, as was its actual purpose. Only a handful of people who weren't held there knew that it was there. As head of the Sensitive Operations Group, Brognola was one of those privileged few.

The metal table in the center of the room was dented and scarred. The room was brightly lit by a bank of buzzing fluorescents set within the ceiling. There were no windows. A full-length mirror dominated one wall. The room was devoid of all furniture except for the table and a pair of metal folding chairs. One of these was occupied. Brognola pulled the other one out and sat across the table from the prisoner.

Dressed in an orange jumpsuit, Congressman David Heller sat with his wrists manacled. His ankles were chained, as well, connected by a short tether that allowed him to walk—albeit slowly and uncomfortably.

"I am an American citizen," Heller said indignantly. "I have rights! I demand to know where I am. I demand to know what charges have been made against me. I demand to have access to my lawyer! You can't keep me here."

"Congressman, and I use the term loosely," Brognola said, his tone dripping with scorn, "I suggest you shut up." Something in the man's voice made Heller be quiet. He sat staring at his visitor. Removing the small digital video player from his jacket, Brognola placed it on the table in front of the congressman. He pressed a button on the face of the little device.

The video playback on the small, full-color screen depicted a news report. The report wasn't on TBT, the widely known cable news network, it was on a competing network, which had long fought TBT for ratings.

Brognola turned up the sound on the digital video player.

"…confirmation today that the widely circulated video purporting to show American servicemen engaged in a massacre in Afghanistan is a hoax," the blond anchorwoman said, her expression a carefully composed mask of somber concern. "The Pentagon today released a statement indicating that it had been made fully aware of the findings of an internal investigation, as well as a report by its oversight committee…"

"Look," Heller interrupted, "this has nothing to do with me! I am—"

Brognola shot him a look and the Congressman was silent again. The woman in the video clip was still talking.

"…an address by the President tonight, in which the White House intends to speak plainly about the attempt to vilify the American military and undermine the war effort. Sources within the Pentagon indicate that an independent investigation into the source of the hoax may result in charges of, quote, 'high treason' for those involved…"

Brognola reached out and switched off the player. "I," he said, "am Hal Brognola of the Justice Department. I've requested this interview with you, Congressman Heller, because I'd like to impress on you just how grave the allegations against you are."

"Look, look," Heller said, "I can explain all that. It's not my fault. This is all a big misunderstanding. I know about that video, I do, but I wasn't in any way involved in it."

"Congressman Heller," Brognola said, "are you aware that for some weeks you have been the target of an investigation by the National Security Agency?"

Heller blanched. Obviously he hadn't been.

"There must…must be a mistake…" he stammered.

"I assure you, Congressman, there is no mistake," Brognola said. "You are a traitor to your country, Mr. Heller." This time, the big Fed deliberately left off Heller's title. "We have direct evidence that you have conspired with elements within the Chinese government to take direct and harmful action against United States military interests. You have aided and abetted in the commission of a series of high crimes, been at least complicit in the murder of American citizens and provided material assistance to the commission of, or conspiracy to commit, acts of terrorism both on United States soil and abroad. You are aware, are you not, that the late Yuri Trofimov has been implicated in the massacre video hoax?"

"I…"

"A real tragedy, that high-rise fire," Brognola said. "Trofimov is lucky to have died in a freak accident, before he could face a high-profile trial. Seems he must have been so desperate for ratings he was willing to fake evidence and manufacture a scandal."

Heller blinked.

"That's right," Brognola said. "You know as well as I do the true extent of Trofimov's activities, but they're being covered up, for the good of the nation. The world will remember him as a crank who tried to fake a news story, and not as one of the worst terrorists ever to conspire against American interests. Now, where do you suppose that leaves you?"

"Well, I…"

"Let me supply it for you," Brognola said. "In short, sir, you are well and truly fucked."

Heller looked up at the harsh words. "You can't talk to me like that."

"I can," Brognola said. "I have. Mr. Heller, you are going to go away for a very long time."

"I want my lawyer," Heller said.

"I don't think you understand," Brognola said. "I thought I was making the situation very clear. I will try again. Do you have any idea the sort of damage that could be done to this nation if it came to light that a highly placed government official was complicit in acts of terrorism and murder, much less an active participant in and accessory to them?"

"But I wasn't—"

"Spare me the act," Brognola said. "I've seen the evidence against you. I know what you've done. There may be people in the world you can fool with your wide-eyed histrionics, but I am not one of them. You, Mr. Heller, are very shortly going to disappear into the deepest, darkest hole available to the United States government."

"What do you mean?" There was real fear in Heller's voice.

"You've heard of Guantanamo Bay, of course," Brognola said. "And I know you're aware of the supposed 'secret prisons' operated by the Central Intelligence Agency throughout the world. You sponsored a resolution condemning them, didn't you?"

"I don't recall."

"Of course not," Brognola said. "No matter. Mr. Heller, there are certain people so bad, so dangerous, people who represent so imminent a threat to the United States, that they cannot be allowed to see the light of day. Now, the United States government is not composed of murderous barbarians, despite what you may have heard on certain cable news channels. If this were some banana republic, and if I represented the sort of people that, say, TBT believes people the U.S. government and its military, why, I would just draw a pistol from within my jacket and put a bullet in your head."

Heller flinched. Obviously he feared that exactly that would be his fate.

"Relax, Mr. Heller," Brognola said. "I have no intention of killing you. I am, however, going to make you disappear."

"What do you mean?"

"In a few minutes," Brognola said, "you're going to be transferred. You will be taken to a prison facility known to only a handful of people within the United States government, including the President himself. There, you will spend the rest of your natural life with other traitors, terrorists and murderers—people who share a quality in common. Like you, all of them are important enough that we cannot have the public exposed to news of the full extent of their crimes. If ever the American people knew just how far you were willing to go, simply for money, they might well lose all hope in the government. Corrupt as it often is, it's the only government we have, Mr. Heller. And it is my pleasure to see to it that a treasonous piece of filth such as yourself never again threatens it."

"No!" Heller shouted. He tried to rise, but the chains on his waist and around his ankles stopped him from becoming fully upright. He landed heavily in his chair again. "Please! I'll cut a deal! Anything!"

"There are no deals," Brognola said. "There is only justice." He rose and walked out. Heller was still shrieking and wailing as the door closed behind Brognola. Without missing a beat, the big Fed opened the door adjacent to the interrogation room. There, he found Ambassador Wu Lok sitting in front of the two-way mirror, watching in rapt horror as Heller put his face in his hands and wept like a child.

Brognola closed the door behind him and sat opposite Lok. The ambassador wasn't bound. He had with him a small suitcase, which had been brought to him from the Chinese Embassy.

"You heard?" Brognola asked.

"I did," Wu said grimly.

"I want there to be no misunderstanding here, Wu," Brognola said. "We're fully aware of what your government has tried to do. And we know it's not the first time."

"You can prove nothing."

"I can prove a lot of things," Brognola snapped, "and we're well past the point at which you've got any leverage with me, so drop the attitude."

Wu looked humbled. He bowed his head slightly. "As you say."

"Now," Brognola said, "I know, for example, that there's an off-the-books Type 052 Luhu-class destroyer sitting in international waters just beyond our reach. And I know it's not the only craft of its kind."

Wu looked surprised, then alarmed that he had given away too much through his reaction.

"Yes," Brognola said, "you should be worried. We're completely aware of most of what you do, you know," he said, only partly bluffing. "We know that you extend the hand of friendship only to hold a knife behind your back. We know you're working against us. Trade between our peoples is an important thing, Wu, but don't think we won't sacrifice it if we have to. Everyone will suffer if we do, but we won't let your government continue to attack us from the shadows."

"You intend to do what, exactly?"

"Well, we sure as hell can't try you," Brognola said. "The world doesn't need that sort of polarizing event right now. No one will benefit from the publicity. You brought us close enough to the brink that time your people seized that radar plane and its crew, a few years back."

"Tell me what you require of me," Wu said simply.

"Take whatever boat you've got waiting to your destroyer," Brognola said. "Go home. Tell your handlers in Beijing that if they want an open war, all they've got to do is keep working against us as they've been doing. Tell them that with every sleeper cell and covert, plausibly deniable operation they conduct on American soil, or against American interests abroad, the world edges closer and closer to a war between our nations. Make sure they understand that no one—*no one*—will benefit if that happens."

"I am no one's servant," Wu said indignantly.

"No?" Brognola said. "Then you can join Heller in a prison so secret, a place where you'll be buried so deep, that you'll die never again seeing daylight or another human face. Do you really want that?"

"You know I do not," Wu said.

"Then do as I tell you," Brognola said. "Get on your ship, go back to China and don't ever come back here." The big Fed stood, smoothed his suit and opened the door. He turned back to give Wu one last, hard look. "We'll be watching you, Wu," he warned. "And we won't ever forget."

The Executioner

Don Pendleton's ®

DEATH RUN

A dangerous sport masks a deadly threat....

For a group of fundamentalist extremists, stealing a shipment of weapons-grade plutonium from Pakistan was almost too easy. Now they have everything they need to construct a terrifying weapon on U.S. soil. They believe their plans are virtually undetectable—but Mack Bolan is on their trail!

GOLD EAGLE ®

Available in May wherever books are sold.

TAKE 'EM FREE
2 action-packed novels plus a mystery bonus
NO RISK
NO OBLIGATION TO BUY

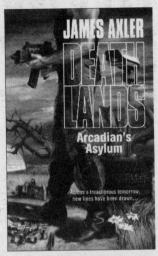